SCARY STUFF

SHARON FIFFER

SCARY STUFF

MINOTAUR BOOKS ✖ NEW YORK

SCARY STUFF. Copyright © 2009 by Sharon Fiffer. All rights reserved. Printed in the United States of America. For information, address St. Martin's Press, 175 Fifth Avenue, New York, N.Y. 10010.

www.minotaurbooks.com

Library of Congress Cataloging-in-Publication Data

Fiffer, Sharon Sloan, 1951–
  Scary stuff / Sharon Fiffer. —1st ed.
    p. cm.
  ISBN 978-0-312-38778-5
  1. Wheel, Jane (Fictitious character)—Fiction. 2. Women detectives—Illinois—Chicago—Fiction. 3. Antique dealers—Fiction.
4. California—Fiction. I. Title.
  PS3606.I37S33 2009
  813'.6—dc22

                                      2009012740

First Edition: October 2009

10 9 8 7 6 5 4 3 2 1

To Steve, Kate, Nora, and Rob ... for getting
me through the scary stuff

Acknowledgments

Writers seldom ask innocent or random questions. I have an indulgent circle of friends and family who answer the strangest queries from me as well as share their stories and advise me on medicine, mystery, murder, collectibles, life, spelling, and comma usage. I would like to thank a few of those people by name: Dr. Dennis and Judy Groothuis, Walter and Rosie Chruscinski, Jane Baker and the entire crew of New Trier Sales, Steve Fiffer, Susan Phillips, Laura Brown, Catherine Rooney, Keiler Sensenbrenner, Gail Hochman, Kelley Ragland, Matt Martz, Ragnhild Hagen, and all librarians everywhere.

SCARY
STUFF

1

Jane Wheel, gripping the arms of the uncomfortable seat, closed her eyes. The woman in the seat directly in front of her had a lot of blond hair piled up on top of her head secured by purple butterfly clips. Violet cubes and stars dangled from her ears. Jane did not want all of those twenty-first-century plastic accessories to be her last earthly image.

She imagined her best friend, Tim, in the seat next to her furiously whispering, *Your plane is going down and you want to tell a stranger that a cherry-red Bakelite barrette would be more flattering?* No. She would not let imaginary Tim distract her from the terror of this dropping, lurching plane. He should be here, hysterical and panicky, beside her. When he had insincerely offered to go with her to visit her brother, why had she not pretended to believe that he really did want to go? Jane and Tim had an enduring friendship based on real, true, honest dishonesty. They faked stuff all the time. Why had she chosen that moment to tell him she appreciated the offer, but knew he'd love a little more time in L.A. while she went to see Michael and his family?

"No," she whispered out loud. Inhale and exhale. Think about good things. Any normal person would conjure their loved ones—son, husband, parents. Jane rejected that thought. Too painful. If she pictured Nick's grin, Charley's hands, Don's wink, Nellie's grimace, she would be too overcome to remember any survival techniques that might be required.

Jane Wheel, girl detective, could review her cases. Ha! Jane Wheel, accidental private eye, finder of dead bodies, spotter of antique forgeries, champion of the innocent . . . wait, was that Detective Oh's voice in her ear? *Mrs. Wheel, are you not equally a friend of the guilty?*

Jane hardly expected her messy life to flash before her eyes. She doubted the whole life-flashing cliché. It couldn't be true, and yet how in the world had it become a cliché? Whose life was simple enough, straightforward enough, coherent enough, to form itself into a slide show and flash before his or her eyes?

Nonsense. Life was a crooked path, a roller coaster, a corn maze, a garage sale of the cast-off and formerly beloved. It was a stew of desire and joy and disappointment and confusion. It could no more flash before one's eyes than . . .

The plane then leveled as planes, more often than not, do, finding its way into a welcoming and amenable altitude, and the debate raging in Jane's panicky head—all about the right way to panic—ceased.

"Ladies and gentlemen, we are about to begin our descent . . . attendants, please ready . . ."

Jane's life, after adamantly refusing to flash before her eyes, stretched out once again before her. The sheer terror of being inside a small prop jet being dribbled like a basketball by thermal currents gave way to the everyday annoyance of passengers ignoring the pilot's admonitions, unfastening seat belts, and rummaging around for their carry-on baggage. When the woman seated in front of her began the sideways wriggling half-stand that signaled her desire to get out first, one of her hair clips fell and landed in Jane's lap. Since the woman had already made it into the aisle, Jane didn't bother to call out her loss. Instead, Jane, the magpie, slipped the purple clip into her pocket, bestowing upon it the cachet of a good-luck charm, which meant she would have a difficult time ever ridding herself of it, always remembering how it somehow kept a plane aloft on a breezy California day.

Pulling down her own beat-up leather carry-on, Jane found herself smiling at her seatmate, a young man in a USC sweatshirt who had slept through the turbulence. She was happy to be alive in this cramped little plane and delighted that she wouldn't have to hug her seat cushion or breathe normally into a mask or slide down some plastic tube into darkness. Jane simply had to deplane, retrieve one other bag with gifts for her niece and nephew, and walk out into the oppressive desert heat where she would spend two days with her little brother, Michael, whom she hadn't seen in two years.

Family. Memories. Old wounds. Bitter arguments. Unexpected joys. Unrealistic expectations. Inevitable disappointments. Perhaps this trip was slightly similar to sliding down a chute into the unknown. Scary stuff.

"Aunt Jane, this is the most special one. Don't you think so?"

Jane's niece bent her head down close to the table where a gold and red stamp lay under a glass dome magnifier, a hefty vintage paperweight that Jane had found at the Pasadena flea market and gift wrapped for her niece.

"If you say so, Q, it must be," Jane said, "but I admit it, I am out of my depth."

Jane collected Bakelite, buttons, sewing tools, measuring tapes, yardsticks, cigar boxes, flower frogs, anything with letters and numbers, kitchenalia, Catholica, old spice jars, maps, ephemera, wedding photos, crocheted potholders, autograph books, high school yearbooks, old fabric, scissors, knitting needles, vintage office supplies, wooden boxes ... among other things. When Jane was faced with a row of coins in a glass case or an array of colorful stamps, paper-hinged or never-been-glued, however, she was befuddled. Collections that were somehow meant to be collections eluded her. She seemed to feel only the pull of the used and worn; the "mib" (mint-in-box), or "uncirculated," designation was one she respected, but did not covet.

"They are beautiful, though," Jane said, moving the magnifier over the row of tiny works of art Q had laid out for her inspection. "Miniature paintings ... or when all together like this ... a paper quilt?"

Q, whose given name "Susan," after a beloved maternal grandmother, had been shortened to "Suzie" by a former nanny, then further trampled on as "Suzie Q" by a nursery school teacher, and been thrown out with the bathwater and shortened permanently to Q. It suited her. She twisted her long open face into a question mark as soon as she opened her eyes in the morning.

"If you like collecting stuff so much, why don't you have stamps?"

"I have marbles," Jane said, mentally reviewing the old Mason jars on the shelf above her kitchen window, "and tons of jacks and red rubber balls."

"What does that have to ...?" Michael began to ask, folding up the newspaper he had been reading.

"Yeah?" said Q, understanding the mysterious connection her

aunt was making even if her father did not. "See, you like little stuff . . . stuff with colors, so why not stamps?"

"I don't know really. I resist collections that need to be fussed over, maybe?" Jane asked.

"Nope. You send me letters and pictures all the time of your stuff and it's all neat and tidy and lined up and stacked and arranged and all that. You fuss, Aunt Jane."

"Stamps can be valuable, right?" Jane asked.

Q nodded so hard that her blond ponytail bobbed up and down.

"That's it, then. I never collect anything that I actually might make money on," said Jane. "I only accept poor stuff, old throwaways and castoffs," Jane said, picking up a stamp hinge, licking it, and sticking it to her niece's forehead.

"No you don't. Why—"

Michael stopped Q's grilling by reminding her she had to change her clothes before they took Aunt Jane out to dinner. Jane picked up the stamp album and the envelopes of loose stamps and replaced them in the drawer of the large square coffee table, eyeing the table carefully. She liked it. It was a large solid square with a roomy drawer to stash whatever needed stashing. But she was aware, even as she admired the piece of furniture, that she didn't love it. She never intended to apply a test to every object that fell into her path, but it often happened anyway. *Like it, but don't love it,* said that inner voice—the one that made itself heard most frequently at shopping malls or in the homes of people who bought retail. Jane could like new things, but without any backstory—the faint coffee-cup ring branded into the oak of her used desk, for example—a piece of furniture was just a piece of furniture. No drama, no romance, no—

"Baseball cards?" Jane asked, reaching for a cardboard shirt box in the back of the drawer.

"Yeah, I didn't know where to keep them once the baby was born and I lost my home office. Not that I'm complaining—a nursery is a much better use of the space since I never get any work done when I'm home," said Michael, laughing and picking up all of nine-month-old Jamey's toys at once by gathering corners of a pale green blanket and holding it hobo style, an elephant rattle still making a faint rain-on-the-roof sound as the bundle swung from Michael's hand.

"But how do you have them at all?" Jane asked. "Didn't Nellie whisk them away in the night? I mean, how did you manage to hold on to your baseball cards?"

Jane looked straight at adult Michael, holding his own son's toys, but only saw little brother Michael—ten years old—sprawled out on the floor sorting his cards, much like Q had been studying her stamps. Jane remembered their mother Nellie's complaints about his stuff scattered all over the place.

"If I find those damn baseball cards on the floor, Michael, they're going straight into the garbage," Nellie would say. "Mooning over these damn collections is the ruination of getting you to do any work around here."

Nellie must have thrown out Michael's baseball cards. Every mother threw away her son's baseball cards. It was the rule. It was the very thing, the unforgivable act, that made sons leave the homes of their mothers! Lamenting all the things your parents did to you was part of generic adulthood—but the specific crime committed by parents was what they made their kids throw away. Hopes, dreams, self-esteem were all important enough; but what Jane preferred to focus on were the moth-eaten stuffed animals, fractured dolls, scribbled coloring books—the possessions of their offspring that they didn't value enough to save. Jane, until recently, had thought Nellie threw out everything, swept away Jane's and Michael's child-hoods with a few brisk arcs of her wicked broom, but Jane had been wrong. She had discovered her mother's secret closet of memories—never mind that those souvenirs weren't the ones that Jane had really wanted. The whole incident had made Jane rethink what childhood memories amounted to anyway—do they belong to the child or the parent? Both, of course, but whose are the truest? Jane longed for her first rock collection, but Nellie thought her little plaid wool coat and hat from toddlerdom was the relic worth pack-ing into mothballs.

"I don't understand how you could have those cards, Michael, when she threw everything away that I cared about."

Michael laughed and put his hand on top of his sister's head. Six years younger, six inches taller, he was the poster boy of the suc-cessful junior partner. Of anything.

"C'mon, Jane, you know why," Michael said, half whispering.

"Why?"

"She liked me best," Michael said. "Now go get ready. We like to get out the door as soon as the babysitter gets here. Big night for Q being included and baby brother staying home. Monica is really good about this stuff, figuring out how to make Q the big deal, even while everyone is making such a fuss over Jamey all the time."

Jane dressed quickly in a light cashmere skirt and short-sleeved sweater, the only matching outfit she had brought to Michael and Monica's house. She had traveled light to Los Angeles from Chi-cago, and even lighter from L.A. to Palm Springs, leaving most of the contents of a large suitcase with Tim Lowry to send home. He was shipping back several boxes of flotsam and jetsam he had picked up at the flea markets and shops in and around Los Angeles for his own business in Illinois. As picker and dealer, Jane and Tim had had a productive trip. Maybe their adventures would not make it to the big screen any time soon, maybe their lives would not be turned into a movie script as they had been falsely promised, but they had found vintage treasures. Oh yes, and they had successfully caught a murderer. Lured out to L.A. by a producer who showed interest in turning Jane's recent PI adventure into a movie, Jane discovered that although Hollywood had its charms, she was far from ready for her close-up. Jane hadn't wanted that so-called fame and fortune anyway—the satisfaction of settling into her new career, as former police detective Bruce Oh's partner, now with another case solved so far away from home, too—was justification enough for her West Coast trip.

And now she was reconnecting with family; her brother, Michael, and his lovely wife, Monica, their precocious daughter, Q, and perfectly adorable baby boy, Jamey, whom she was meeting for the first time. Talk about the perfect cliché! Michael was a successful lawyer at a large commercial real estate firm, whose business, according to Michael, was surviving the economic downturn surprisingly well. Monica worked part-time as an art therapist, and the children, although spaced slightly farther apart than they had planned, according to Monica, were smart, sweet, perfect—practically ordered from a catalog.

Jane brushed her lashes lightly with mascara and dug around in her purse for a lipstick. Looking in the mirror, she made a face, exaggerating a frown. She didn't want to be the jealous older sister. She herself had a handsome husband and a darling son. They just might be catalog worthy themselves! She had a career. Two careers! She wasn't just a picker; she wasn't just a detective. She was Jane

Wheel, PPI—Picker and Private Investigator. She had a great adult life, too, damn it. Okay, so Charley, a geology professor, traveled a lot, sometimes seeming to prefer spending weeks at a dig site out of the country to making his way through the maze of boxes and bags of stuff Jane "picked" from estate sales, rummage and flea markets to resell to dealers. And sometimes Nick, a clever and smart middle-schooler, seemed to prefer Charley's digs, discovering dinosaur bones, to Jane's treasure hunts for Bakelite buttons and McCoy flowerpots. And didn't Jane choose to live in Evanston? Close to Chicago and close to Kankakee where her best friend, Tim, lived, where she and Michael had grown up, children of Don and Nellie, owners of the EZ Way Inn? So not only was Jane enmeshed in her own satisfying—in its own way—family life, but she was also close to Don and Nellie, practically a phone call away.

Oh, damn it all, Jane thought, trying to coax her frown into a relaxed pout so she could apply lipstick. *Not only does Michael have his life figured out, he figured out how to get away from Kankakee, away from the EZ Way Inn, away from Nellie. And, somehow, he even managed to keep his baseball cards.*

Q, almost ten years old, was thrilled to be going out to dinner with her parents and mysterious Aunt Jane. She had other aunts . . . her mother had two sisters and both of them lived in California, so Q saw them regularly. They were friendly and they gave her lovely clothes on her birthday, or the newest toys and games, and Q was always properly grateful. But it was Aunt Jane who sent her the packages wrapped up in brown paper that thrilled her. Sometimes the packages didn't even arrive on or near a birthday. Aunt Jane would write a note on the back of an old postcard with a picture of a place like Paris or London or Amsterdam or Budapest that Q already wanted to visit someday. Aunt Jane would write, "Shall we visit the Tower of London together? Love, A. J." and Q would tape the cards up above her bed, imagining a trip with her aunt that would zigzag all over the world. One of Q's favorite presents from Aunt Jane was an old metal globe. Stuck to its surface was a tiny gray airplane with a magnet glued to its belly. With each new postcard, Q would move the plane to the next city to which her aunt had introduced her. They were going to have fine travels together, she and Aunt Jane.

She was so different from her mom, who was tall and blond like Q. Aunt Jane was small with short dark hair that she always messed up with both hands when she talked about stuff. She got excited and danced around a lot, too. She wore lipstick, but no high heels even though she was short. Q thought this made her brave somehow. Her other aunts wore high heels and took small steps. Aunt Jane bounced when she walked and seemed like she was always ready to run off and do things. Q was going to be just like her when she grew up. Except she would be taller, and blond, of course.

"Is everybody in this state a natural blonde?" Jane asked, pulling Q's ponytail and looking around as they were seated at a table in the middle of the large dining room.

Monica laughed. "It seems that way, doesn't it? You're an exotic creature here, Jane. By the way, any seafood dish here is terrific."

Jane ordered a Grey Goose with extra olives and Michael, in a whisper, ordered Pinky on the rocks for Monica and himself.

"What's a Pinky?" Jane asked.

"Scandinavian vodka—too pretty, too precious, but once you taste it . . ." said Michael.

"He hates to order it, though," said Monica, laughing.

"True. I hear Nellie barking in my head every time I ask for it. 'Pinky? Pinky? What the hell's a pinky? We don't serve no pinkies here.'"

"A friend of mine from college came in with me once and he wasn't a drinker. Asked for blackberry brandy and Nellie looked him in the eye and said, 'No blender drinks, buddy.' Scared the hell out of him," said Jane.

"Must have made it hard for you to bring boyfriends home," said Monica, "Nellie being such a character."

"Yeah, the only way I got to stay in touch with old Blackberry Brandy was to marry him." Jane laughed. "I figured if Charley could be a good sport with Nellie from the beginning, he was the one to hang on to."

"Will you get oysters, Aunt Jane?" asked Q.

"You like oysters, Q? At ten? Man, I had to be old and drun . . . drug by the hair to try them."

"I like the shells. And once my aunt Sherry's boyfriend found a pearl in one of his oysters and he got to keep it."

The waiter arrived with Jane's Grey Goose and two pale pink cocktails for Michael and Monica. He also placed a juice concoction with a multifruit garnish hanging off the edge for Q.

Jane tried a sip of Monica's vodka and, in spite of her EZ Way Inn indoctrination against anything trendy, fussy, or pastel, she nearly swooned at the delicate hint of strawberries and clean finish of the vodka. As loyal as she was to Grey Goose, she had a feeling she might just have to step out with Pinky now and then, if she could find it in Illinois. She had a feeling this ethereal drink just might be one of those Californian mirages. Maybe she could find a bottle to bring home to Tim. He had tried to woo her away to Cîroc. Now she would tempt him with Pinky.

Jane's pleasant vodka reverie was interrupted when a group of men emerged from what appeared to be a private dining room opposite their table. They were holding unlit cigars in one hand and cocktails in the other. The waiter was explaining that he was arranging a spot in the garden where they could smoke. From the expression on his face, Jane assumed the waiter would prefer to tell them to go home and smoke up their own spaces. This party of men must have some kind of clout.

"Jane, before they go out there and poison the garden, come with me to see it. It's one of our favorite spots. You'll love it, lots of garden antiques and stuff—right up your alley," Michael said, pushing back his chair and jumping up to hold his sister's chair.

"You have lovely manners, Michael. Really, you do," said Jane. She knew where they came from, too. Despite all their complaining about Kankakee and being raised at the tavern, Jane pretending to hate it and Michael truly disliking the place, they had both learned their manners from Don and Nellie. Something about the customer always being right or respecting their elders or some old-world politeness of Don's—whatever it was, the two of them had learned to say please and thank you, to listen when people spoke to them, and to hold the door for the elders. Don had always treated Jane like a young lady, holding out her chair for her, taking her heavy book bag from her when he picked her up from school. Nellie liked pulling out her own chair, carrying her own heavy packages, so Don gave her a wide berth. But with Jane and Michael, the manners had taken hold.

Just as Jane was about to ask Michael about his last conversation with their parents, one of the cigar smokers approached them. He was listing to the right, and Jane wasn't sure whether he had had too much to drink or whether he was just physically and perhaps permanently off balance.

"I thought it was you," he said, coming up within twelve inches of Michael's face. "You crook. You cheat." He spoke low and fast. "I can't do anything about it right now, but I know a lawyer who's going to help me, and if he can't, I'll beat the—"

"Hey," said Jane, "who are you?"

At the same time, Michael shook his head. "I'm not who you think I am. Look at me."

The garden was lit by gas torches and Michael stepped closer to one, his face clearer than it had been in the twilight. "Please," said Michael, "look at me. I'm not your guy."

The stranger stepped back and stared directly at Michael, ignoring Jane, who was rocking back and forth on the balls of her feet, readying herself for a fight. Michael might be taller, but he was younger and if she had to protect him she would.

"God, I'm sorry, man. That is so weird."

"Weirder for me," said Michael. "The last time it happened, the guy said he was going to have me killed, then he looked at me in the light and said I wasn't who he thought I was."

"Nope. You haven't got his eyes, but out of the light, you look just like this other guy. Can I buy you a drink or something?"

Michael shook his head and stuck out his hand. "No hard feelings."

"What the hell was that?" said Jane, watching the man return to his buddies and light up his cigar.

"I don't honestly know, but that's the third time it's happened. Six months ago, I was in Columbus, Ohio, for a conference and a guy comes up and shoves me into a table and says he's going to re-arrange my face for breaking his wife's heart. Monica was with me . . . first time she had left the baby overnight. I had begged her to come for the weekend, just a little break for us. And this freaked her out so badly she almost flew home that night. The guy apolo-gized, said he believed me that I wasn't the guy, but that I looked just like this crook. I wanted to ask him about it, but Monica was crying, and by the time I got her calmed down, the guy was gone.

"Then about six weeks ago, I was in L.A. for a meeting, and this guy comes up to me on the street and says he's going to kill me. But then he looks me close in the eye and says, you're not Joe, are you? He believed me right away when I said I wasn't and he said he was sorry. I asked him who the hell Joe was, and he kind of laughed and said the kind of guy you don't want for a twin, and he just took off. I didn't tell Monica then and I'm not telling her tonight, so . . ."

"I won't mention this," said Jane, "but—"

"What?" asked Michael, pointing out two vintage urns over-flowing with bird-of-paradise.

"You've got to find out who Joe is."

"My wife and daughter are in there, and Monica has been out of her mind superstitious since Jamey was born. I'm not doing anything right now, except ordering a great dinner for my sister. Okay?"

Jane nodded. "Order for me. Take liberties. I love everything. I'm going to stop in the ladies' room."

"I'm so glad you finally came out here, Jane," Michael said, giv-ing her a quick hug.

Jane did go to the ladies' room. She applied fresh lipstick and ran a hand through her hair. Then she returned to the garden and approached the cigar smokers, hoping that the skirt and sweater that Tim had selected as her "dress-up" L.A. outfit was as "hot" as

Tim assured her it was. Jane knew that "hot" at her age probably translated to tepid at best, but she didn't care. She just wanted to make a favorable enough impression on the man who had threatened her brother.

"Excuse me, may I have a word?" Jane asked.

"Change your mind about the drink?" he asked, stepping away from his companions, blowing a smoke ring.

"Thanks, no," said Jane. "I just wanted to know more about this guy Joe, who people confuse with my brother. Who is this man?"

"People tell me I'm stupid to trust the Internet anyway, but I'd never been burned before, I always say. But this guy, 'Honest Joe,' sold me a bunch of phony stuff, then wouldn't return my money. No returns, no Joe. Seemed like he was selling bunches of stuff for a while, then poof. The guy disappears from the site. . . ."

Jane felt the man steaming up as he spoke of the incident.

"My brother looks like Joe? And Joe runs an Internet scam?"

"Oh yeah, but his eyes are way different, and he's different when I looked close at him. But from far away . . . I mean, I memorized what this guy looks like . . . but it would be weird out here and all."

"Why?" Jane asked, shrugging away the hand he rested on her shoulder. The lack of balance she had noticed before she now saw was directly related to drinking. He was beginning to slur his words.

"Old Joe lives in the Midwest. Sent him checks to some godforsaken little town in Illinois."

"What town?" asked Jane, holding her breath for the answer.

"Something with Can . . ."

"Kankakee?" asked Jane.

"No. What's a Kankakee?" He stepped back, tripping a little, and then he regained his balance. His friends had risen to leave. One went inside to pay the check and the others drifted toward the parking area. "Name was like some kind of candy, I think. You know, it wasn't the money. I got the money. It was the principle of the thing. People don't cheat each other that way. Maybe they do, but I've never had trouble. Not in my dealings. This guy is just a jerk, that's all."

His friend gave him a wave from the parking lot but Jane blocked his view, then put her hand on his shoulder and turned him toward her.

"What was he offering? Real estate? Property or vacation homes?" Jane racked her brain for some kind of Internet scheme that could provoke the victims to become violent. "Was it stock of some kind? Oil leases? What was it you were buying from Joe?"

He reached into his pocket and pulled out a business card and gave it to Jane. The light was dim in the garden, but Jane could make out that he was a general contractor. He put his hand over his mouth and shook his head.

"Don't tell those guys, okay?" He leaned in close enough for Jane to smell the last whiskey sour he had downed.

Jane crossed her heart and sealed her lips.

"Roseville," he whispered.

"Pottery?" asked Jane.

"Like my grandma had." He rocked back and forth on his heels and pinched out the lit end of his cigar with stubby fingers. "I'd kill for Roseville."

2

The food was as promised—California cuisine at its best. Fish barely out of the ocean, vegetables just pulled from the garden outside. Even the garnish was flawless; edible flowers and herbs meticulously tied into what was supposed to look like careless mussy-tussy bouquets. Jane slurped her oysters, sauced with a light tamari, after Q carefully checked each one for a hidden pearl. Michael poured three different wines, all heavily recommended by the sommelier, all from leading California vineyards.

Jane kept mum about the man who mistook Michael for Joe, as also promised, but she allowed herself to study Michael, to reacquaint herself with her brother's face, staring at him as often and as deeply as she could during dinner.

She and Michael shared some similarities, she knew. Their jawline followed the same genetic map, and when they smiled, they both revealed Don's strong even teeth. They were aging similarly, too, around their mouths—tiny lines that disappeared with grins—but their eyes were completely different. Jane's were such a dark brown that they often appeared black. Michael's eyes were a light gray that one would remember as blue if he wore a blue shirt like the one he had on this night. But if he had chosen an olive sweater? His dinner companions would swear that Michael's eyes were sea green.

So why had the stranger, whose name Jane knew was Ralph Mowbry from the business card he had given her, been so sure that Michael was not Joe. Just by eye color? A changeable characteristic in so many faces?

"Do you really have a tower of cigar boxes up to the ceiling, Aunt Jane? With something different in each one?" asked Q. "Daddy said you did, that you had them since you were my age."

"I do have a lot of them," said Jane. "And I keep old checks and receipts for some of my things in them. I guess a few have some shells, and there's one with some carved-bone buttons." Jane partially closed her eyes and pictured the stack of El Producto and White Owl boxes in the northwest corner of her office. Box by box, she thought about their contents, which she knew by heart. "Fourth one from the bottom has keys and key chains, fifth is Bakelite advertising mechanical pencils, six through ten hold receipts from house and rummage sales for some furniture, and—" Jane stopped and glanced at her niece who looked enraptured. Jane saw that her sister-in-law, Monica, looked, in equal measure, horrified.

"They don't reach quite to the ceiling," said Jane. Scrupulously honest, at least to a child, a blood-related child at that, Jane added, "I do have very low ceilings in my office."

"How does Charley—" Monica began to ask.

"Put up with it?" finished Jane, tearing off a bite of expertly seared tuna.

"I was going to say 'feel about it,' but I'll settle for 'put up with it,'" said Monica.

"He has a study filled with rocks and picks and books and field guides. He understands the tools of the trade, so to speak. He's got an eye for the object that tells a story, holds a key to history," said Jane. "And he travels. A lot."

"What does Nick collect?" asked Q.

"Fossils, like his dad," said Jane, "not that his dad is a fossil, you understand, and let's see, baseball cards, like your dad . . ."

Jane looked up from her perfectly browned potato quenelle just in time to see Michael wince.

"Oh no, Michael doesn't collect anything," said Monica. "He told me how your mom threw out his cards and his gloves and souvenir programs and everything else and how free and unattached he became to objects. Q is the only collector in our house and I'm hoping she'll outgrow it."

Monica, whom Jane had always believed to be genuinely kind and she knew to be flawlessly polite, had drunk one more Pinky than she usually consumed. It brought her to the brink of the kind of honesty that people were able to avoid in everyday life. It delighted Jane that she was a few Grey Gooses behind, so that instead of leaning forward and confiding, girlfriend to girlfriend, that Michael was indeed hoarding baseball cards in the back of the drawer of their coffee table, she could enjoy watching Michael squirm and accept Monica's disapproval of her own hoarding habits with amused goodwill.

"Be careful, Q. Not only did I not outgrow it, my stuff has practically outgrown me! That's why I had to go into business. If I find stuff for other people, it helps me thin out my own herd."

Q shook her head, her mouth full of *pommes frites*. "What herd?" she managed to get out.

"Okay, let's say I like crocheted potholders—"

Q shook her head again. "What's *crocheted*?"

Jane was going to have to educate this girl on her own turf—that much was clear. How could someone, even a Californian ten-year-old, not know what a hand-crocheted potholder looked like?

"Okay, sweetie, let's say I like salt and pepper shakers," Jane said, placing the restaurant's fine vintage crystal shakers with sterling silver tops in front of Q. "If I have a customer who really likes shakers, who has a giant collection, and who will pay me to find pairs of them that she doesn't already have, I have all the fun of finding them, of hunting them down, and then the collector pays me more than I paid for them. That makes it easier for me to let them go. I've collected them . . . I own the hunt . . . I just don't have the shakers on my shelf anymore."

Q shrugged. Jane thought she knew how Q took in this information. Sure, sounds reasonable enough, but if you keep the shakers, you own the hunt *and* you own the stuff. Jane knew that was the trouble. Jane hated to give up the stuff. But she was learning. Tim was teaching her to trade up; swap four or five of the most desirable white McCoy pottery vases for one small, stunning piece of Weller or Hampshire. That was the road Tim was trying to put her on. Jane looked at Q who was cheered by the arrival of dark chocolate mousse served in a candied-orange shell. It was difficult to not want the hunt, the stuff, the shakers, the McCoy, and the Weller. And the Hampshire. Jane shrugged, too, picking up a spoon. And the mousse.

After they all had tasted the airy chocolate and an apple tart served with a wedge of locally made cheddar so sharp it could break your heart and a banana-caramel bread pudding, Michael wanted to order brandies all around, but Q was sleepy. Monica was slightly flushed and seemed as if she could be persuaded to go in either direction—home to bed or out to the garden for brandy and cigars. Michael had all his wits about him, but he had polished off the last of the wine, and noting Q's fade from miniature adult into sleepy-faced child, he was ready to go. Jane had stopped after one drink, barely sipping the wines Michael had ordered and coaxed her to try, so she asked if Michael would like her to drive.

"Not a bad idea," Michael said, handing her the keys.

Q tucked her hand into Jane's as they stood and waited for Monica to stop in at the ladies' room. Late diners across the room were talking quietly, when one, a woman, squealed and rubbed her cheek. She held out her hand to her husband who said loudly, "It's just a pearl, isn't it?"

Q squeezed Jane's hand hard. Jane watched her niece bite her bottom lip.

"Next time, honey," she said. "Maybe next time it'll be us."

Monica and Q climbed into the backseat and were asleep on each other's shoulders within one minute of leaving the parking lot.

Michael gave Jane instructions, but knew his sister's excellent sense of direction and trusted her to find her way back to his house, a fairly straight shot down six miles of freeway.

"So you're not a collector anymore, Mikey?" asked Jane. "Doesn't your wife ever look in drawers?"

"Not if she thinks they're empty. C'mon . . . like you tell Charley everything."

"I'd tell him if someone threatened to kill me."

"I thought we were talking about baseball cards," said Michael. Jane waited.

"You saw how quickly the guy backed down. That Joe must have some kind of birthmark or something. When I've been confronted, all the jerks needed to do was get a good look at my face to know I wasn't the guy they wanted."

"Yup," said Jane. "You've had pretty patient guys, you know, the kinds that get up close to look at you. What if some real thug thought he spotted the crook who ripped him off and he didn't bother to come across the room. What if he had a gun?"

"This detective thing's getting to you, Janie. This isn't cops and robbers. This is real life. No one is going to shoot me because I look like an Internet huckster who sells phony signed rookie cards. Next exit, then left," Michael said, sinking down into his seat.

"Roseville," said Jane.

"What?"

"Nothing," said Jane, pulling the BMW into her brother's driveway, next to the babysitter's hatchback.

"For a minute I thought you were going all Citizen Kane on me," said Michael. "Look at my women back there," he said softly. "Aren't they something? And now I've got a son, too. I'm lucky, Janie. I've got everything in the world I want."

Jane smiled but didn't comment. Maybe it was because she used to work in advertising, maybe it was because she now made her living in two worlds, both of which were strongly influenced by need and greed, but she had never known anyone, anywhere, any time, who had everything he wanted.

After helping Michael get Q and Monica, a surprisingly heavy sleeper, into the house and up to bed, Jane made herself a cup of ginger tea. Setting her cup on the coffee table, using one of Monica's many Pottery Barn coasters, Jane carefully slid open the drawer where Q's stamp collection was stored. Jane reached behind it and pulled out the white cardboard box labeled "baseball cards." Inside were loose cards—Jane was pleased that none were rubber-banded together. She wasn't a collector of sports cards, but she had found them for several clients and true collectors despaired when they saw perfectly fine collectible cards damaged by the wear and tear of the rubber band.

"A 1951 Bowman Mantle rookie card," whispered Jane aloud. It didn't take an expert to know that this was one valuable card. Odd, though, since 1951 would have been a little early for her little brother's boyhood collection. There were other rookie cards in the box, too, some of them signed. Most of the players were names Jane recognized, Hall of Famers, legends. Some were from before Michael's time, before Jane's time, and some played long after Michael's collecting days. Her brother must have been acquiring these as an adult. Jane estimated that the box was worth several thousand dollars. These were certainly not his childhood cards. Nellie had not spared Michael's baseball collection from her ruthless purges of their childhood treasures after all. *Ha!* Jane thought. *Even if she did like you best, you had to buy back your childhood memories just like I did.*

A piece of acid-free paper separated the top layer of cards from another layer. Jane lifted a corner of the tissue, expecting to see more of the same, cards of similar value. Oddly . . . surprisingly . . . she saw exactly more of the same. One, two . . . six Bowman Mantle rookie cards. Five Hank Aarons. Five Jackie Robinsons. Four Nolan Ryans. All rookie cards. And although Jane was certainly no expert in sports memorabilia or ephemera, she was pretty sure, based on the sheer quantity of such rare and valuable cards, all mingling together in one box, most—if not all—of these cards had to be fakes.

3

When her alarm rang at 6 A.M., Jane sat up in bed, startled out of a dream where miniature baseball players chased her with bats, pelting her with orange and blue baseballs. She wasn't surprised by the dream, only by the fact she had managed to sleep at all.

After discovering her brother's secret stash of baseball cards, she had returned to the guest room, and packed for her next-day, early departure, arguing with herself over what she should do. She had poked her nosy nose into business where it didn't belong and found out something she shouldn't know. Something she didn't want to know.

Was Michael a crook? An Internet scam artist?

Of course not. He was a lawyer working for a real estate firm and making a magnificent salary. He and his family were more than comfortable, living in a lovely home just outside of Palm Springs. He didn't need to nickel-and-dime his way through an Internet baseball card forgery racket. The whole idea was ridiculous.

Then again, Mantle rookie cards might be worth a few thousand dollars. Not exactly nickels and dimes. Monica had expensive taste and could only work part-time since the baby was born. And maybe the new baby had put a strain on their budget. Maybe Michael had lost money in the stock market. Hadn't everyone? How could a real estate firm still be making money? Maybe he was a gambler and had debts . . . they weren't that far from Las Vegas . . . maybe he had fallen into a bad habit . . . losing their life savings at the blackjack table. It was this line of thinking and questioning that had kept Jane up most of the night. There was no answering to accompany the questioning. She had no idea what, if anything, she should do about the cards. After all, maybe this was partly her fault. She had been a lousy sister, avoiding a visit for years.

Jane had to be honest. Hadn't she resented Michael moving so far away? She had envied his easy relationship with Don and Nellie—birthday cards and bouquets, a holiday visit every five years or so, the occasional swing through Kankakee when he was in the Midwest on business. Michael had absented himself from the day-to-day of Don and Nellie and the EZ Way Inn, and Jane was jealous that he didn't get the daily calls, the nags, the judgments, the worries, the criticisms, the . . . oh hell, how had she managed to make it Michael's fault that Nellie loved to torment Jane?

And if Jane had stayed in closer touch, been a better older sister? Might she have saved Michael from this fall into fraud? Oh God, how serious was this crime? If Michael were knowingly selling forgeries . . . ? Was that a felony? Was he sending them through the mail? Did that make it a federal offense? How much time would he have to serve? Jamey wouldn't even know his father, unless Monica brought him to the prison for visits, and although Jane liked Monica well enough, she just wasn't sure enough of her grit—could she stick with a man in prison? And Q. What would happen to Q?

Jane would step up. That's all there was to it. She'd be a real aunt to her niece, take her to all the places she had promised her in postcards and funky souvenir gifts. Every stamp that Q cherished? Jane would take her to the country where it originated.

The problem, of course, with speculation of the magnitude in which Jane was engaging was that it begged hundreds of questions without answering one. And the one for which Jane needed an answer was whether or not her brother, Michael, was a crook.

"Are you meeting Tim at LAX, then flying back to Chicago together?" Michael asked, holding up the coffeepot to offer Jane a refill.

"Joe?" said Jane.

"As in 'cuppa'?" asked Michael.

"As in, are you Joe? Do you have anything to do with the Internet scam that these guys have been accusing you of?"

Michael set down the coffeepot. With a quick look through the kitchen door toward the stairs that led to the bedrooms where his wife, daughter, and baby boy still slept, he came over to the table where the breakfast he had made for his sister remained untouched.

"I am not, nor have I ever been, a character named Joe. I haven't sold anything under false pretenses on the Internet. I have not broken any laws or committed any acts of fraud," said Michael. "And that's all I am going to say about it."

"I'm sorry," said Jane. "I want to get to the bottom of this, and I have to ask, you know, because—"

"Don't tell me why you have to ask, okay?" said Michael. "It's fine. You asked, I answered. Now I have a question."

Jane nodded.

"Who asked you to get to the bottom of this?"

"Why do I need to be asked? You might not think you're in any danger, but if you've been threatened . . . not just here, last night, but in other parts of the country . . . ? Someone who looks just like you has pissed off a lot of people, Michael, and you might think it's nothing, or at the most a minor aggravation, but it's dangerous. It's dangerous for you and your family. What if you're out with Q or the baby and someone comes along who thinks you're the guy who ripped him off on the Internet? And this guy decides to stay at arm's length so he can throw a punch first and look into your chameleon eyes later? Then it won't be an amusing little story to tell over drinks—how you look like some con man.

"According to Ralph Mowbry, our contractor pal from last night, this Joe character lives in Illinois, and I am going to find him and shut him down—or at the very least, get his picture off the Internet, so you are not mistaken for your evil twin. Who's my client? You're my client, Michael, whether you hire me or not."

"Am I supposed to sign a contract?" Michael asked.

"What's a contract for?" asked Q as she came in the door. "Can I go to the airport with you?"

Jane prepared herself for an unpleasant flight to LAX, but this time, the small plane afforded a fairly smooth ride. Her thoughts remained unsettled, though, offering a bumpy ride of another sort. She had looked into her brother's eyes at the breakfast table and believed what he told her, but something about that box of too-good-to-be-true baseball cards was much too good to be true. Q had come along on the ride to the airport, preventing any further discussion of the matter, so that's what she was left with— an honest-eyed declaration from Michael that he had nothing to do with con man Joe.

Jane and Tim had not planned to meet at LAX; they were flying back to Chicago separately. Since their arrivals in Chicago were only thirty-five minutes apart, they would meet in baggage claim at O'Hare and take a Northshore taxi back to Jane's house in Evanston. Even though Jane hated flying, especially alone, especially on such a long flight, she was grateful to have the time to think through a plan of action. Michael might not have signed a client contract, but he had agreed she should—if she so desperately wanted to—pursue the identity mix-up, as he preferred to call it, and Q was her witness.

Jane was a list-maker. She didn't know if it was the way all professional detectives worked . . . she had only been semipro for a few months . . . but Detective Oh always nodded when she took out the small notebook she used for her pickers "want" list, and went through the facts established or questions raised while working on a case. She would have to admit to Oh that she hadn't made it to her licensing exam last month when she returned to their office . . . of course, if she was already busily working on this new case . . . perhaps he would forget to ask about it.

1. Call Ralph Mowbry to find address of the phony Roseville dealer—where he sent his check.
2. E-mail Michael for a complete description of those who had confronted him—all details—location, description, what they said . . .
3. On which Internet auction site did Mowbry shop? eBay? What are the other auction sites?
4. Check price on a 1951 Bowman Mantle rookie card.

Jane knew there should be more on this list, but as the plane flew over the Grand Canyon, her lack of sleep caught up with her and she closed her eyes. Before drifting into one of those quasi-naps that airplane travel allowed, she thought about her brother's eyes. Why was everyone so quick to believe they had been mistaken when they got in his face?

The gods of travel were on the side of Jane Wheel this Thursday morning. She had planned on her plane being delayed or Tim's flight being late, so she had carried two paperbacks and three small notebooks in her giant purse. The only thing for which she was unprepared was a calm, tanned Tim Lowry standing next to the baggage carousel sipping a latte from the coffee kiosk.

Tim was good-looking in such an old movie-star way. Retro handsome was how Jane thought of him. A Cary Grant or a young William Holden. Light on his feet somehow. He had been Jane's best friend since first grade and, since he had lost his own partner a few years back, and no one had come along yet to replace him, Tim was devoted to Jane. More precisely, devoted to Jane as well as devoted to improving Jane.

"Stretch your face a little, sweetie, you have sleepy cheeks," Tim said, draping one arm around her for a quick hug, holding his latte high and away with his other.

"How does somebody not get those lines?" said Jane, rubbing the side of her face.

"The good news is they still go away. In a few years, we'll look in the mirror and think we slept funny, then realize the joke's on us for good. I saw some magnificent Botox usage in L.A., though, after you left." Tim spotted Jane's case and grabbed it as he continued the conversation, just as if he and Jane had not been separated for three days.

"I'm so glad to see you," said Jane, hugging him again.

"It's only been seventy-two hours," said Tim.

"I thought you might stay there. I thought I might get here and find some uniformed airline personnel with a letter on a silver tray announcing your decision to take up permanent residence in Los Angeles," said Jane. "I was a little worried. You were so happy there. . . ."

"I'm happy everywhere. That's cute, though, that you were worried and that you thought I could produce a miracle like that. Can you imagine airline personnel actually on duty in baggage claim? You are one cockeyed optimist."

At Jane's house, Tim disappeared into the guest room, *his* room as he referred to it. Jane did have to admit that no other guest had ever spent the night in the fourth bedroom, a fact that actually seemed pathetic when she allowed herself to think about it.

No phone messages to review since she had forwarded the house phone to her cell. Who would have called anyway? Detective Oh had been in California with her. Tim was there, too. Charley and Nick were in South America and called weekly on her cell. Jane stared at the phone and the vintage leather address book that sat next to it on the forties wooden phone table with attached seat.

"I have got to get some new friends," she said aloud, then realized she was staring at a blinking light. "Whoa, maybe I've got one."

She had turned her cell off before boarding the plane in Palm Springs and reversed the forwarding. It always surprised her when pushing buttons, answering prompts, and clicking any kind of mouse, pound sign, or highlighted text actually gave her the information, performed the task, or got her where she wanted to go.

"Yeah? Where are you? Aren't you in California? Don't you get home today? Call me. It's your mother. Nellie. Oh all right, Don, I know it. But what if somebody checks the calls before they get to her? You don't know how they work, either, for God's sake, I—" Next, a click, then dial tone.

Right. Jane had accounted for Oh, Tim, Charley, and Nick, but, momentarily, she had forgotten her best phone-a-friend buddy. Her mother. Nellie. As her mother herself had so eloquently described herself.

Jane would call Nellie back, of course. After coffee, after some unpacking, after dinner, after a Grey Goose, after two . . . at the least, after a hearty debriefing with Tim.

"So I went to this sort of seminar with my friend Bill," said Tim. "He's into this kind of spiritual stuff and this workshop was being given by a psychologist who promised a kind of self-awareness, self-discovery, self-empowerment . . ."

"Is this going to end with you handing me the latest self-help book by Belinda St. Germain?" asked Jane.

"Close. Actually, though, part of this lecture I really liked. It was about living life through family groups. He said, in order to find peace and happiness and success and all that, you had to be aware that you always needed the same family members with you during each stage of your life."

"Right, well, Nellie's always right here in my pocket. . . ." said Jane, patting her cell phone.

"No. It's more like archetypal family members. You always need an elder and a child and a feminine companion and a masculine companion and a spirit brother and a spirit sister and a teacher . . . I don't know, there's a few more, too, and when you lose someone, you're adrift until you replace him or her . . . and some people stay adrift . . . and that's when things go haywire. They drink or eat too much or whatever, trying to fill that empty slot. . . ."

Tim got up and poured them both more coffee. "Like addictions to gambling and stuff, they're just ways of filling up that emptiness when your family circle isn't in order."

"This sounds a little New Agey for you, Tim," said Jane.

"Yeah," said Tim. "But there was something about this guy, what he was saying. It makes sense, you know, that balance thing. You just need these certain figures, you know, in order . . ."

Tim continued to explain the spirit-family concept, but Jane drifted in and out. On the one hand, she could see how one needed to balance out the self with these "others." Jane herself could point to those who balanced her life—Charley was a great partner, Nick the questioning child. And she could even see, with Nick off with Charley, how Q filled in and made the scenario complete. And Tim was the friend—all-purpose—and who could ask for a better teacher figure than Detective Oh? And her dad, Don, made a good elder. Nellie . . . just how did Nellie fit into the spirit family tree? Jane could not shake the image of a real tree, with her mother perched on a high branch like a vulture, waiting to swoop down and feast on Jane's entrails . . . that is, shortcomings. Too harsh, Jane knew, but the image felt too accurate to shake. So what was Michael in her spirit family tree?

Jane loved her brother—she knew that. But if Tim's latest mumbo jumbo had any merit, and let's face it, the mumbo jumbo almost always did, even if it eventually went one "mum" and one "jum" too far, in order for Michael to have a real place in her life, she had to choose him as part of her family. Had she? She barely visited, barely knew him. Maybe he needed her, and without her, he had fallen out of synch with his spirit family and filled in all those slots with bogus Hall of Fame baseball cards?

"Blood isn't enough," said Tim. "You choose your family in this life and they change all the time."

"Except for you and me," said Jane.

"Yes," said Tim. "Except for you and me."

"You are always my spirit friend," said Jane at the same time Tim said, "I am always your spirit god."

Tim suggested they check the classifieds to see if there were any house sales over the weekend that made it worth his while to stay over. Jane had finished unpacking and was rummaging in her purse for Ralph Mowbry's business card. He'd had nearly twenty-four hours to sober up. Maybe he could give her names and addresses so she could move forward in her search for Michael's twin.

"*Pioneer Press* doesn't get here until late, dinnertime," Jane said. "With the mail."

"I've already got the classifieds up, sweetie, looks like a good weekend around these parts," said Tim, calling to her from the sunporch where Jane kept her desk, her computer, her files . . . among so many other essentials

Jane, holding Mowbry's card in her hand, paused in the doorway. As much as the room screamed at her to be organized, to be decluttered, to be "groomed" in some way, the space never failed to make her smile, to welcome her with some kind of secret handshake. Yes, she did have pillars of cigar boxes that reached to the low ceiling as she had confessed to Q, but she also had an old oak desk that held surprisingly organized files of receipts and client "want" lists and descriptions of annual rummage sales, complete with her notes on where to park and maps of labyrinthine church basements that led to the "treasure rooms."

Jane moved the overflowing box of old gas station road maps

that she had fished out of someone's basement just before the whole California debacle and sat down next to Tim.

"I always forget that you can check online. Isn't that weird? I guess I love the rush of getting the paper and turning to the classifieds, tearing out the page and circling and highlighting..."

"Yeah, but if you check in the morning, you can sometimes do some early alley picking... I like to think of it as a prequel to a good sale," said Tim.

"I thought your days of shopping in the 'big store' were over, Mr. Quality Dealer, Mr. Time to Trade Up," said Jane.

"L.A. sent me back to my roots," said Tim, clicking the mouse next to the sales that interested him. "Stuff was so overculled... and overpriced. It made me feel nostalgic for the old days, you know? Of course, you know, you're still living them," Tim said, electronically flipping to the next page.

"Does this mean you're staying for the weekend?"

"I'll stay tomorrow, anyway. We could shop and then I could cook up some food for you for the week. When do Charley and Nick get back?"

Jane looked at the wall calendar pinned to a giant oak-framed classroom bulletin board. "A week from next Sunday. They've been gone for three weeks. This is the longest I've ever been separated from Nick. I feel like he'll have actually grown and changed and—"

"Yeah," Tim said, "look at this one. *Three generations worth of stuff! Collectors, crafters, hobbyists—wear your grubbies and come prepared to dig.* That's what I'm talking about. Back to our roots!"

Jane waited until Tim had printed up their sale list and gone off to inventory the kitchen before making her call. Although filled with the most charming collectibles—Bakelite-handled utensils, jolly print tablecloths, and collectible dishes from Deco to Depression to Homer

Laughlin and Russell Wright, Jane's kitchen, even when she wasn't just returning from a trip, often lacked food. When she heard Tim opening and closing cupboards, swearing and lamenting, she dialed the phone.

"Mr. Mowbry, this is Jane Wheel, we met last night at Eden? The restaurant, where you mistook my brother for 'Joe'?"

Ralph Mowbry was between meetings, or so he said, but he found the address to which he had sent his check to Honest Joe. No last name—the check had been made out to Honest Joe, Inc.

"Herscher, Illinois?" Jane said, unable to stop herself from laughing.

"Yeah, I thought it was Hershey, I guess, like the candy. Funny, huh?"

"It's just that it happens to be a town I—" Jane hesitated to say that it was a town just outside of Kankakee, a town she knew well since childhood, since it probably wouldn't be smart to place Michael anywhere near a location Mowbry had for "Joe."

"May I also ask how you knew you were mistaken about my brother? You got close to him, then realized that he wasn't Joe."

"Yeah, it was the eyes, Old Honest Joe has him some crazy eyes . . . listen, I'm being called in for this conference, so I've got to go. Sorry again about last night."

Mowbry hung up.

Jane ignored Tim's questions from the kitchen about the age of her condiments and the expiration dates on boxes of couscous and Googled *Honest Joe*.

247,000 hits.

Honest Joe's Used Cars and Honest Joe's Pawn Shop were in the family of what she might be looking for, but sifting through all the references to politicians, Web sites, blogs, and Myspace pages seemed inefficient at best. Jane typed in *Honest Joe's auction sites.*

77,800 hits.

Jane typed in *Online auction sites.*

3,000,000 hits.

Jane typed in *Herscher, Illinois.*

1,553 pop.

Finding Honest Joe, who might be one of the 1,553 who lived in and just outside the village of Herscher, on foot seemed a lot more promising than letting her fingers do the walking. Might as well score a few more points with her spirit brother, too.

"Hey, Timmy, how about after the sales this weekend, I give you a ride back to Kankakee?"

4

For dinner, since neither of them had the energy or will to visit the grocery store, Tim invented—with assistance from Jane—a new dish that they dubbed *chisotto*—a chili-and-cumin-laced black bean soup, using some withered-but-forgiving carrots, celery, garlic, and onions, a bag of black beans, a can of diced tomatoes with Arborio rice stirred in slowly at the end, risotto fashion. Jane's contribution was shredded cheese she found in the back of the refrigerator and a dollop of spicy salsa topping each serving.

"This is one of the better 'animals in the jungle' dinners to come out of this kitchen," said Jane. "With fresh cilantro, this would be fit for company."

"I wish you wouldn't use your 'you find it, you kill it, you eat it—animals in the jungle' method of feeding your family to describe my expertise at the stove."

"Pantry supper?" asked Jane.

"That makes me want to strangle you with my calico apron strings."

After they finished, Jane let Tim map out their route for Friday-morning sales. She called and left a message for Charley on his cell phone—even though she knew he wouldn't get the message until Sunday, when he came into an area that had any kind of service.

"I'm home. Tim's here with me until Saturday or Sunday, then I'll go to Kankakee with him and visit, then back here, I guess, counting the days until you and Nick get back." Jane grimaced at her own words. If she had known how to erase the message and start over, she would have. And no one could have been more surprised than Jane herself, when she heard her voice break, saying she missed them, she loved them, and wished them "such a good night."

Jane was so used to their being apart during her travels and Charley's fieldwork, she thought she was immune to any kind of sentimental longings. She and Charley had worked out their deal long ago—they would have much more to offer each other if they pursued individual lives as well as their married family life. It had been the only kind of agreement that would have allowed Jane to overcome her fear of marriage, family, husband, child, one house, one street, in sickness and health, for better or worse, one life forever and ever. And although it had been mostly Jane's deal at the beginning, Charley had come around, Jane knew, to her way of thinking. He was happy with his globe-trotting freedom; he was grateful that his fieldwork and fascination with relics much older than the ones Jane dragged through the door were understood and appreciated.

Jane shrugged off her embarrassing lapse. When she was busy, this wash of emotion never rolled over her. She needed a giant day-long rummage sale or an estate sale at an old Chicago bungalow. Or, she admitted to herself, a case to solve. Jane had learned that nothing took her mind off her own troubles like mucking about in someone else's messy life. And hadn't brother Michael handed her a lovely gift-wrapped problem? So she could start out with the mistaken identity, find Honest Joe, and maybe find a nice little case of fraud and who knows what else? What was it Oh had told her when he was still with the police department? "Nothing like a murder to put one's own small life in perspective."

Jane planned to spend Thursday night wrapping some packages to mail out to Muriel, a dealer in Ohio for whom she found the occasional relish dish, silver spoon, general odd and end. It drove Tim crazy that Jane still worked for Muriel, since he had offered her a partnership in his own house-sale business and shop and wanted her talents used exclusively for the benefit of his own customers.

"Muriel took a chance on me when I was just starting out. She gave me tools and taught me how to tell the difference between bone and ivory. She—"

"I'll give you a hammer and a cat's-paw so you can tear walls apart and yank on nails at a demo sale, too, honey, if that's all it takes," said Tim, removing his laptop from a padded leather case. "I mean, if you're going to be wrapping up stuff and sending it, and not sending it to me, you should be selling online yourself. Why should you be the middleman?"

"Show me," said Jane.

Tim flipped open his Macbook, signed in to his eBay account, and showed Jane the list of items he had up for sale. She was shocked to see that some of the items he had purchased last weekend at a California flea market were already photographed, described, and sported bids.

"How did you do it all so fast?"

"It takes a digital camera and fingers to type with," said Tim, clicking rapidly from item to item, checking the bids and the bidding history.

"No, I mean—" Jane stopped. What she meant was, how did Tim know he would be able to part with those items? He had just bought the cool transistor radios, one red and white, one a perfect turquoise gem; Jane had watched him bargain for them along with a box of radio knobs and dials. Didn't he want to put them on a shelf somewhere, get to know them first? See if he might want them for his own collection?

"Honey, I know what you're thinking, but I don't collect transistor radios. I don't collect any electronics, so what's the big deal?"

"How do you know?" asked Jane. She looked around her office. So many of the items that were gathered here were not necessarily objects that she knew she collected. Not until she found one or two. Take the pins for example. Industrial pins—big giant safety pins hung from old square nails pounded into the bottom slat of a primitive wall cupboard. She found her first pin at the Chelsea flea market in New York City. She didn't know what made her pick it up out of a pile of trinkets on someone's card table, but when the seller asked for fifty cents, it seemed more than reasonable. It seemed handy and functional and clean lined and well designed and . . . in some way impossible to describe . . . it seemed beautiful to her. She found a few more at rummage sales, in thrift stores. That first pin, though, the one that winked at her in the sun on a beautiful Saturday morning in Manhattan, that pin had started her search for locker pins, laundry pins—anything that looked remotely like an oversized safety pin and all the better if it had a number or letter on it. Why did she love them? She had no idea. But how would she have developed the relationship with them if she hadn't brought the first one home, allowed it to get comfortable.

And that, she supposed would be Tim's whole point if she recited this story to him. All the more reason to slap up the photos on eBay ASAP and commit to selling your lucky finds rather than adopting them.

"Tim, can you look up auctions by seller?" Jane rarely dipped into the tempting waters of eBay. She knew how dangerous it could be. Once, in an antique mall, in eBay's early days, a chatty shopper next to her in line at the checkout described the phenomenon to Jane. "You know how sometimes you just have to go to an antique mall because it's a Tuesday afternoon and there aren't any house sales or rummage sales or garage sales or flea markets or auctions or anything? Well, with eBay, you're covered any day of the week at three A.M."

So dangerous.

"Natch." Tim clicked over to advanced search and asked for the name she wanted him to check out.

"Honest Joe."

"Original. Nope. Nothing listed for sale by Honest Joe."

"Do you use any other auction sites?" asked Jane.

"I've dabbled," said Tim.

"Will you look at others you know of for Honest Joe while I check in with Bruce Oh and"—Jane sighed—"Nellie. I owe Nellie a call."

"Yeah?"

"Hello, Mom," said Jane. Her mother's phone manner never failed to astonish and appall her.

"It's about time."

"For what? I got in this afternoon and just—"

"How's the baby?" asked Nellie. "I know, Don, I'll tell her, give her a chance to answer, for God's sake.

"How's the baby?" Nellie repeated.

"Jamey is great, very cute, active, brilliant, all the things one could want in a baby," said Jane, "and Q is magnificent. She's smart and funny—I can't believe how big she is already—"

"What's the surprise for? If you don't go out and visit your brother and his family more than once every five years, do you expect kids not to grow?"

"When was the last time you visited, Mom? I forget," said Jane.

"That's different," said Nellie.

"Right," said Jane, "you have all those surgeries to perform, all those rockets to launch."

"We got a business. Leave a tavern for a few days and a bartender will rob you blind. Close a tavern, and your guys'll find a new place and get comfortable. Besides," Nellie yelled, answering a challenge that Jane had not even voiced, "we don't have that much business anyway. Think these idiots will believe we're coming back? If we close for a day, we're done. They get in a habit, these guys, and as long as we got a few crawling in here every day, we got to keep 'em coming."

"Don and Nellie's version of 'keep the customer satisfied'?" said Jane.

Jane's dad picked up the extension. "Hi, honey."

"Hang up, Don, it makes it hard to hear when you're in there with the TV on."

"How were Michael and Monica doing? And the kids?" asked Don.

"Good, Dad, they send their love."

"That Q sends me letters, writes them all by herself. She's quite a girl," said Don.

"Hey, I was getting to all this," said Nellie.

"We should go out there and spend a little time with them," Don started to say.

"Oh yeah," Nellie cut him off, "and who's going to keep the place open?"

"Carl, maybe, could—"

"Oh jeez, Carl. He's got more aches and pains . . . you think he could load the coolers? Write the orders? I wouldn't trust Carl—"

"Mom? Dad?"

"How about Carl at night and Johnny during the day? The two of them—"

"Want the place to burn down? Remember when Johnny emptied the ashtrays into the wastebasket without checking to see if there were cigarettes still burning?"

"How about—?"

Jane hung up. It would be several minutes before her parents realized she was no longer participating in the conversation. The phone call had served its purpose. They knew she was home. She knew they were still alive.

"Oh." Bruce Oh answered the phone in his customary style to which Jane would never grow accustomed.

"Oh. I mean, hello. I expected the machine. I thought you would still be in California."

"We arrived home an hour ago. What did you plan to tell the machine, Mrs. Wheel?"

"Let's see. That I'm home and that I have a case to work on—just a little case, really—my brother's been mistaken for someone who seems to be cheating people on the Internet and I thought maybe I could find him, maybe we—"

"And politely ask him to stop looking like your brother or ask him to stop cheating people?"

"I really haven't planned very far ahead," said Jane. Oh always asked honest, direct, if sometimes puzzling, questions, but Jane thought that these queries were a wee bit sarcastic. They sounded more like Tim than Oh.

"Is anything wrong?" she asked.

"Mrs. Wheel, when were you going to tell me that you did not show up for your licensing exam last month? Because, you see, if you continue to avoid taking that exam, you will only be able to make these polite inquiries and not really conduct yourself as a professional. If that is your wish, to be my assistant, I understand. I would, however, as I told you before, like to offer you a partnership."

Jane had meant to tell Oh about missing the exam.

"I'm sorry." The reason she missed it, the amazing sale that she attended that day instead, the multilayered excuses for not telling him she had chosen the sale over the exam—all of that melted away. She could have explained it, in a carefully punctuated run-on sentence left on his answering machine, but not while talking to the man himself. Bruce Oh was a man whom she didn't fully understand, but she knew that he was someone to whom she could neither lie nor ply with excuses. His success as an investigator could be attributed to intelligence, deductive reasoning, instinct, but Jane knew that the real reason he succeeded was because he asked the right questions, the ones to which you had to give honest answers.

"Lawyers often say, Mrs. Wheel, that you should never ask a witness on the stand a question to which you do not already know the answer," Oh had told her when they first met. "In my business, I feel it is essential to ask the question to which someone cannot help but answer truthfully. Even if it seems somewhat unrelated to the case at hand. Once you get a person in the habit of telling the truth . . . they often continue in spite of themselves."

"Detective Oh, I do wish to take the exam. Apparently I didn't want to do it more than I wanted to attend the sale that was happening at the same time. I should have told you immediately. I serve two masters . . ." Jane said.

"At least two, Mrs. Wheel, but I hope I am not one of them. I am sorry for acting in any way that made you feel obliged to apologize to me. I received a notice from the exam board that I just this past few minutes opened, that's all, and I was surprised. But you are a PPI . . . as you have reminded me. The sale was part of your professional life, too. We will put this aside and you can tell me more about your brother and his twin."

Jane told Oh what had happened at the restaurant, and repeated her conversation with Ralph Mowbry.

"And this Herscher, Illinois, is near your childhood home in Kankakee?"

"Just west. Even though the address was a post office box, I can't imagine that it would be hard to find this guy Joe. I mean, it's a small town, he has to use the post office all the time for payments and mailing out packages, and apparently, he looks just like Michael."

"And your brother has asked you to do this for him?"

Jane tried to remember the exact words of her conversation with Michael.

"He didn't ask me not to," she said.

"Definite progress, Mrs. Wheel. Although the path from being asked *not to do* something to being asked *to do* something is not always a direct path, it is, nonetheless, a path. This sounds very much like the beginning of a real case."

"Hey, Janie," Tim shouted from the kitchen, "I think I found Honest Joe."

Jane promised to keep Detective Oh in the loop and hung up. She wanted to find Honest Joe, sure, but in some ways, she hoped that Tim hadn't beaten her to it—without even leaving the house. Now that she was on a bona fide path, according to Oh, she wanted to be able to actually tread on it a bit. If Tim had just a hit a few keys on the computer ... what kind of mystery adventure would that be?

"Boom's On-Line Auction?" asked Jane.

"Who knew? I can't even remember the route I took to find this site, I just kept clicking on links from auction to auction. Boom's had a seller listing for Honest Joe," said Tim.

"What's he got for sale?" Jane pulled out an old piano stool from the corner, gave it a twist to bring it up to the right height, and cozied up next to Tim, settled in at the kitchen table.

"*Had* a listing for Honest Joe. Nothing current. I searched by past auctions and he ran three or four that closed a few weeks ago for, let's see ... marbles, old marbles, clay, glass, yeah, okay, he sold those. Some pottery ..."

"Roseville?" asked Jane, recalling Mowbry's passion for the stuff.

"Nope," said Tim, "unmarked. A lot of restaurant ware ... some creamers and sugar bowls, look at these flips ... hey, Bakelite ..."

"Where?"

"No picture here, this one's too old. But listen to the description:

I don't know for sure how to test Bakelite, but my sister said this stuff smells right—whatever that means. I found this at a sale in an old Woolworth's box and "junk jewelry from grandma" was written on the cover. Remember, I sell old stuff that's used. I don't guarantee anything, I just do my best to tell you what I see. No returns—just bid what you want or sit on yer *[sic]* hands, but no complaining to me later. Here's five bracelets, all kind of mustardy-colored, four of them are one inch wide and the other one's about an inch and a half. They're thick and just slip on. There's also some red dangly earrings and a necklace with the red and yellow beads.

"The bidding started at one dollar and it sold, after a five-day auction, for forty-three dollars?" said Tim. "A sucker born every minute."

"Why? That Woolworth box? That's where Bakelite came from, dime-store jewelry, that's a—"

"Honey, that's a ploy. Old 'aw shucks, I'm just old Honest Joe' knows what he's doing. No guarantees, no returns, he just drops enough hints to make you think you see something that you don't see at all. The pictures aren't posted anymore, but there are pictures of the restaurant plates and they're just enough out of focus to make you wonder. He gives you a song and dance about being a country-boy scavenger, but come on, he's on the Internet and he knew enough to say *Bakelite* so this would come up on a keyword search—even though he doesn't guarantee it to be Bakelite or old—just says it's labeled *junk*."

"Which is enough for some people . . ." said Jane.

"Yeah . . . some people," said Tim, punching her arm.

Tim took Jane on a little mouse tour of the site, pointing out that there was no reliable feedback system as there was on eBay. Honest Joe's location was the Midwest, but there was no easy way to e-mail him unless you were a registered Boom user. Jane wasn't ready to feed her own e-mail address into the gaping maw of Boom quite yet.

"What about pictures? Is there a picture of Honest Joe? Why would someone put a picture up anyway?"

"No, all of his merchandise pictures are down and there's no current auction running. But look at this," said Tim. He showed her a current auction, this time for a wire egg basket. The site had a kind of inset with a seller's panel with a space for a picture. This seller was a very reliable-looking middle-aged woman with graying hair and wire-framed eyeglasses. "Doesn't Maude look trustworthy?"

"I guess," said Jane. Knowing how many times in her haste to get to a lot of sales in one morning she had overpaid sweet little old ladies for boxes of dishes, all cracked below the first layer of plates, and stacks of books that allegedly had never been stored in a damp basement, she didn't really want to commit to trusting someone on appearance alone. "I guess just the fact that she's willing to put her picture up . . ."

"Exactly," said Tim. "That's the trick here. Seeing a nice old face like that? You think maybe it is a basket from the thirties, the one her mama collected eggs in, instead of a piece of 'vintage-inspired' junk she bought at T.J. Maxx last weekend. But I'd bet my own antique wireware collection that it cost somebody a couple bucks new at a dollar store and she got it for a quarter at a garage sale. Put up a photo and tell a story and 'Maude' will sell that stupid thing for over twenty dollars, plus shipping and handling for which she's charging ten dollars! Maude's probably some old grizzled picker . . . more like you. Look, the bid's already at fourteen something."

Jane looked closer at the woman's picture. She could see, faintly, two diagonal marks on the bottom corners of the photo. Photo corners. This picture had been taken out of a photo album. Jane supposed someone could remove a picture of herself from a family album to use as an auction ID, but if you were already digitally photographing your merchandise . . . and this egg basket was a digital image . . . why would you scan in an old picture like that? You'd do it to create a persona. You might find a picture of a stranger, one who presented the right image. You'd do it to look reliable, just to make someone who wanted to see a vintage wire basket instead of a cheap imitation, who wanted to believe the description, trust enough to see his fantasy.

"These people aren't vintage dealers, they're creative writers," said Jane.

"They're crooks," said Tim.

"Honest Joe—" said Jane.

"Is a crook," finished Tim.

"—stole my brother's face," said Jane.

5

Tim had only found two sales that were must-sees—he had five or so backups just in case they didn't fully sate themselves at the ones he had earmarked as winners. While drinking her 5 A.M. coffee, Jane read the classifieds he had pulled out and agreed with his choices. Both sales claimed that the owners were moving into retirement villages and they had to downsize. Listings included cupboards full of dishes, closets full of clothes, and one of them claimed a library of four thousand books stored in a dry basement.

The plan was to drive to the sales together, stop back at Jane's house, drop off any of Jane's large purchases, then leave for Kankakee. Jane had planned on driving the two of them, forgetting that Tim had left his Mustang in Jane's garage while they were in California. Instead of driving together, they would convoy—for about two minutes—until Tim took off, speeding on his merry way, returning to his own house and successful estate sale business, T & T Sales, in Kankakee. Jane, arriving at least thirty minutes behind Tim, would drive directly to her parents' less than thriving business, the EZ Way Inn.

Since both of the sales required entry numbers, which wouldn't be given out until 8:30 for their 9 A.M. and 10 A.M. openings, Jane offered to go by both addresses at 5:30 A.M. to sign up on the list that one of the regular pickers, dozing in his car, would be keeping. There was always a picker who got there first, clipboard or old note-pad in hand, making sure that the first twenty or so early birds signed up in order of arrival for numbers. Jane signed herself and Tim up as numbers 7 and 8 at the first house and 10 and 11 at the second, where the sale would open an hour later. Perfect. Since the person who handed out numbers and was in charge of guarding the door usually admitted around twenty or thirty at a time, depending on house size, Jane and Tim would be into both houses, if they moved fast enough at the first one, in the first wave of shoppers.

Jane didn't mind doing the early round of signing up while Tim slept in. She wanted to make a stop to visit her dog, Rita, who had been staying with Miles, an Evanston police officer. Jane had met Miles when she worked for Bruce Oh when he, too, was still with the department. A single woman in her thirties, Miles moon-lighted as a dog trainer and it was she who had convinced Jane to adopt Rita when the shepherd mix had shown up at Jane's house a few years earlier.

"I'm not really a dog person," Jane had protested, all the while rubbing Rita's ears and looking into her brown eyes.

"Who is until they actually own a dog?" asked Miles. "Be-sides, Rita picked you. If she could, she'd take care of you, so you have sort of an obligation, don't you?"

Nothing convinced Jane of an obligation faster than to have it suggested that it might be an obligation. She was just guilt-ridden enough to take on all comers when it came to the needy, the broken-down, and in Rita's case, the sad-eyed, hungry, and homeless. Be-sides, it's a lot easier to take on the responsibility of a pet if one is given the open offer of free and unlimited dog-sitting. Miles had a tiny house with a huge yard, fitted out with a kennel, a dog run, and space for training and play. Her dream was to work exclusively with the police canine corps, but so far, no positions had opened. She did, however, use her many opportunities with Rita to practice her training skills.

"Watch this," she said to Jane. "Rita. Dinner."

Rita, miraculously, Jane thought, picked up a bag and shook it out over three small dishes. Miles had put the puppy chow into a reinforced oilcloth bag with a Velcro flap sewn onto the bottom that Rita somehow managed to open and close. Some kibble didn't make it into the dishes, but for the most part, a meal for the three puppies that Miles had recently decided to keep for herself out of her Lab's litter was served. The most amazing part of this exercise, to Jane's mind, was not the manipulation of the flap on the bag, but the fact that Rita didn't eat any of the food herself—not what was in the dishes nor what had spilled between them.

"I was going to apologize for leaving her another few days, but now I'm excited. When I come back to pick her up she'll be able to do the ironing."

While they played with the dogs out in the yard, Jane told Miles about her brother's mistaken identity, her plan to go to Herscher and find the dishonest Internet dealer.

"So you park in front of the post office and wait for a guy who may or may not look like your brother to show up?" Miles asked.

"I haven't worked out my plan exactly," said Jane, who had indeed originally planned to park in front of the post office and wait for a guy who looked like Michael to show up.

"Then?" asked Miles, throwing an orange squeaking pumpkin for Rita to catch in midair.

Jane realized at that moment why she loved having Bruce Oh

as her mentor. He asked her questions, but they were so mysterious and open-ended that she didn't mind being confused. And the confusion often led her directly to where she was supposed to be. Or so it seemed. And if Oh's questions did not lead her in a straight line to a solution? Well, after all, the questions themselves were fairly circular in nature. But these direct queries from Miles? Jane found herself giving circular answers.

"If I see the guy, I guess I will approach him and ask him in a nonthreatening—"

"Look, I know Detective Oh is training you and he's the best, and I would never want to intrude, but if this guy is ripping people off and selling fake merchandise, or damaged goods or whatever he's doing to make his customers so mad that they actually approach your brother in a public place and threaten to knock his block off, this guy—"

"Honest Joe?" Jane offered.

"Yeah, Honest Joe. This guy, despite the fact that he looks like your brother, might be dangerous. Or at the least, not want to be approached."

"It does make sense," said Jane, "that if my brother is mistaken for the guy, that the guy himself might have been approached and be a little wary . . ."

"Wary, yeah, he might be wary," said Miles.

"So I'll approach with all due caution and . . ." Jane hesitated. "I guess I'll just figure it out when I get there."

Perhaps that is why, because of that nondecisive answer, Jane found herself, six hours later—after two semi-interesting house sales where she bought very little if you don't count out individually the five bags of old mystery books with names like *The Old White Hag* and *The Golf House Murder*, having no idea whether or not she'd ever read them, but knowing she'd love to see them lined up on her bookshelf; and where Tim grumbled the whole time about people's poor taste and what design on the cheap was doing to furniture construction in general, not to mention any kind of middle-class appreciation for craftsmanship, and where she found an old desk which she did not want, but whose drawers had not been emptied, and for a very few dollars she filled a bag with all of the drawer detritus, which included some very cool old office supplies, an excellent paper punch, and four wooden advertising rulers—driving to Kankakee, Illinois, with Rita, her large panting shepherd mix, sitting in the backseat of her car.

Even thinking that sentence silently made Jane catch her breath.

Miles had carefully packed up Rita's toys, rawhide bones, and a few dozen plastic bags, all the while fielding protests from Jane, who, at first, thought Miles didn't understand that Jane had not come to pick her dog up, but to visit before making one more trip.

"I won't be more than a few days and unless you really—"

"I would keep Rita here forever, except for two things: She's your dog and wants to be your dog, and secondly, you need her."

"No, no I don't," said Jane, "I'll be staying at my parents' and—"

"Jane. You need to have Rita with you. If you are going to approach anyone and ask any questions, you will be so much safer if Rita is by your side. Or if she's growling through an open car window while you stop this guy on the sidewalk to ask him a few questions. And by the way, I wouldn't launch into anything right away, I'd just ask for directions or something so you can size him up, look into his eyes," said Miles.

"That's excellent advice, since I really need to look into Joe's eyes and see why everyone knows Michael is Michael once they get up close," said Jane, "but as far as Rita—"

"You need her," said Miles, slipping the handle of the leash she had just attached to Rita's collar into Jane's hand.

Jane shrugged. She loved Rita, she really did, but she still didn't believe she was a dog person. "Does she really growl if you leave her alone in the car?"

"If you tell her to," said Miles.

Jane had packed light for her trip to Kankakee. A few changes of clothes, a box of old advertising ashtrays, mostly for whiskey and beer, to add to Don's collection, and an old HAPPY HALLOWEEN crepe-paper streamer/sign, that Jane thought Nellie might be willing to hang up over the dining room of the tavern. Nellie didn't care to admit it, but she liked holiday decorating at the tavern—not at home, but at the EZ Way Inn, where it gave the dark interior a spark of festivity. Or maybe it just suited Nellie's dark sense of humor since the tavern remained a kind of seasonless cave for most of its customers.

Just as she was getting ready to lock up, Jane went back into her office and picked up her laptop. In case she didn't find Honest Joe, she wanted to continue to check for his auction listings. Maybe she'd actually have to win the bid on one of his items to see what made people so angry. Since Rita was going to be accompanying her, Jane remembered to throw in a bag of dog food, some rubber toys, and her dog's water and food dishes, both sturdy hand-painted crockery bowls, one monogrammed rather formally with the name *Crooky* and the other with a hand-painted *Luna*.

Jane had picked them up over the years as part of her collection of personalized pet dishes. She said when she picked up her first, *Scratchy*, that it was her love of letters and initials and monograms that inspired her to buy dog bowls at garage and rummage sales, usually for fifty cents or less. Once she had them lined up on a shelf in her garage, she had half thought that maybe she would begin acquiring pets and naming them after the dishes. *Buttons, Polo, Boopsie, Melville, Dogfred . . .* Then Rita wandered into her life, and Jane had immediately called her Rita after "Lovely Rita, Meter Maid," the Beatles song that had been playing in her head that morning. On her great wall of dog dishes, there was no Rita, so when she realized that the dog was now her dog, she chose her two favorite dishes and let them suffice. Rita never seemed to mind eating and drinking out of Luna's and Crooky's old bowls. And using these two made her feel a little more hopeful about this collection, one of her more naïvely sadder accumulations. Jane had been so startled when she heard Nick refer to the twenty or so dishes lined on the shelf as "Mom's wall of dead dogs" that she asked Charley if he thought Nick was an unduly morose adolescent. Her husband had barely looked up from the papers he was grading.

"Just realistic. Why do you think people got rid of the dishes?" asked Charley.

Jane had opened her mouth to answer, but nothing came out. Why had she never thought of that?

"I mean it's not like the dogs graduate from high school and go off to college, then the parents downsize, I mean—"

"I get it, Charley," said Jane finding her voice. "I just never thought it out."

Now, driving down Interstate 57, with Rita, Jane realized that having a dog in the car gave her permission to talk out loud. Perhaps this is why people became dog people—it allowed them to become slightly less dependent on the voices inside their heads.

"Rita, you should know that Nellie isn't really an animal lover, so things might be a little tense. Stick close to me, nod your head, and try to pick a seat next to Don so you don't get swatted every time a stray hair falls off your head. Yeah, shedding . . . try not to do that, okay?"

Jane sat up straighter and searched the rearview mirror. Rita, eyes wide and staring, mouth slightly open—in disbelief or apprehension, Jane did not know—was listening to every word.

"A companion who lets me finish a sentence, doesn't point out my mistakes, and growls on command," said Jane. "Maybe I am a dog person, Rita."

She took the second exit for Kankakee. It was not the one closest to her parents' tavern, but the route took her through downtown Kankakee, past the courthouse and post office, past the buildings and stores she remembered from her childhood. She and Tim lamented the changes in their town; they often chanted the names of the places in which their mothers had shopped and got their hair done and where they met their own school friends for movies and sodas on Saturday afternoons. The Fair Store, Jack and Jill's, Matt's Toy and Hobby, Carolyn's Candy Store, Thom McCan, Kresgee's, Alden's, Lecour's, Bon Marche, Samuel's, Roger's, the Record Bar, I.C. Drugs, the Kankakee Book Store, the Paramount, the Luna, the Majestic. It was a litany of loss.

On an impulse, Jane turned off Court Street and drove down Schuyler toward the river. When she got to the bridge, she turned again, planning a drive around Cobb Park and a glimpse at the old houses, the dream palaces of her childhood, one of which Tim was in the process of rehabbing for his own. When she and Michael were young, they had lived within walking distance of this park. She remembered holding Michael's hand, crossing Emory Street, to get to the playground.

Here it was; autumn, all gold and orange and crunchy, in Cobb Park, Kankakee, Illinois. Did it get any better than this? Jane parked, snapped the leash onto Rita's collar—perhaps a bit more clumsily than Miles would have, but she got the job done. She grabbed a few plastic bags, jammed them in the pocket of her jacket, and explained to Rita that it might be better to take care of any business here since the EZ Way Inn stood in the middle of a large gravel parking lot with no grassy nooks and crannies for either comfort or privacy.

Jane strolled around the perimeter of the park with Rita and ached with that awful sentimental flu that she came down with every fall, every trip to Kankakee. Was it her imagination or was it always October when she visited? She stepped on something and it was just large enough to nearly unbalance her. When she looked down, she saw a buckeye underfoot. She saw another and another . . . thousands carpeted the grass.

Of course. This was the buckeye tree where she and Michael, bringing those old state-hospital-made baskets from Nellie's pantry, gathered buckeyes, popping the shiny brown horse chestnuts out of their soft spiny shells. Oh, the satisfaction! And when you got a double? Or one that came out albino white, then turned brown as you held it in your hand? They would gather a basketful, then Jane would count and sort and shine them up in front of the television that night. Don would always select one to put in his pocket as a lucky piece.

Rita sat as Jane bent over, scooping up the buckeyes. Why were there so many? Didn't children come and collect them anymore? Jane wiggled her cell phone out of her jeans pocket and scrolled and clicked.

"Hey!"

"Michael, you'll never guess where I am!"

"Two twenty-one B Baker Street?"

"Cobb Park, right under the buckeye tree!"

"Wow! Are there any good ones left?"

Jane smiled and crouched down next to Rita. "So many, Michael. I'm filling my pockets. I'm on my way to Mom and Dad's, but I just stopped here . . ."

"Yeah. Send me one, okay?"

"Thanks so much for a great visit, Michael. I won't let that much time go by, okay, I'm sorry if I haven't—"

"Honey, everybody gets busy. Life. Q misses you. She told me that 'you get her,'" said Michael, laughing. "I told her she's ten and not old enough to be misunderstood yet, but she seems precocious. Just like you."

"I better go. I'm on the trail of Honest Joe. You be careful, okay?"

"Do what you want, but I didn't say I'd pay you, right?"

Jane clicked off and put the phone away.

The Kankakee River sparkled, the leaves glistened, the air was crystal clear, warm with only the slightest whiff of the coming winter. Jane could feel her brother's hand in hers, could feel the weight of the baskets that they carried home. She stuffed her pockets with buckeyes and stood up.

"My brother is not a crook," she told Rita. Jane knew now, in this magical childhood spot, that it was true. Whatever those baseball cards meant, whatever they were doing snuggled up to Q's stamp collection, they had nothing to do with the whole Honest Joe mess. "Right?" Jane asked her dog, who was showing remarkable composure as squirrels ran here and there, gathering, sorting, hoarding, and providing the stalwart Rita with nonstop temptation.

* * *

Even though Jane had brought Rita along for protection, she decided to leave her in the car when she parked in front of Edna's Diner on Herscher's main street. She had originally planned to stop at the EZ Way Inn and head to Herscher on Saturday morning, but fired up by a conversation with Michael and possessing the good luck of a fresh buckeye in her pocket, she decided she could spare an hour to ask questions in Herscher before she herself was grilled by Nellie in Kankakee.

There was only one customer at Edna's lunch counter and the tables were empty. The waitress was trying to hustle the man, tapping her foot, snapping her gum, and gesturing toward the clock on the wall.

"We close at two today, same as always, Bill. Finish that coffee and giddyap," she said. Looking at Jane she added, "Cook's gone. No more orders."

"Just wanted to ask a question. Do I keep heading east on seventeen to get to Kankakee?" asked Jane.

They both nodded and Bill added, "There's back roads, too, but that's the quickest."

Jane nodded and thanked them. She then took out her cell phone and scrolled through her pictures, stopping on the one she had taken of Michael at the airport before she left. It wasn't a great shot, but it was clearly his face.

"Hey, do either of you recognize this guy? I think he lives here or used to live here . . . ?"

The waitress shook her head, and while old Bill leaned in for a closer look, she took the opportunity to steal his cup and saucer.

"Looks like Jim," he said.

"Jim who?"

"Jim Speller. Looks like him. Can't say it's him, but it looks like him," said Bill. "That's my daughter, I got to go."

A truck had pulled up next to Jane's car and honked. The woman driving waved and smiled at Bill.

"Do you know where I might find him?"

"He lived there all his life," he said, pointing to a dark gray frame house with a mansard roof across the street. It was a hard house to miss. Every window was plastered with black cats, grinning jack-o'-lanterns, and witches. Cobwebs were strung on either side of the broad porch and a life-sized—or death-sized, to be more accurate—mummy sat on a wooden folding chair next to the front door.

"That Halloween house?" Jane asked.

"Haunted house, that's right," said Bill.

Jane watched Bill climb into the truck. She thanked the waitress who came out of the kitchen, jacket on, key in hand. They walked out together.

"Know anything about the people who live in that house?" asked Jane.

"I guess they like Halloween," she said. "I'm not from here, but one of my customers said they always fixed it up every year, but she was surprised that Ada did it up this year. Edna heard her and said the only thing that would surprise her is if Ada didn't fix it up. They argued back and forth about Ada for a while."

"Why?" asked Jane.

"I don't know. 'Cause she's so old, I guess."

Jane didn't have much of a story ready for Ada or Jim, if that was who Honest Joe really was, but she was here in Herscher and the information had come so easily, she had to take advantage of the opportunity. Wouldn't Detective Oh tell her that she should just approach and ask questions that made someone want to tell her the truth? And didn't she want to clear this mess up?

The porch stairs creaked with her every step, and if the house hadn't been so obviously rickety, she might have thought it was a recording of spooky sounds, part of the elaborate holiday décor. There was a doorbell, but an old rag had been hung over it. She lifted the heavy brass knocker shaped like an owl. She could hear the sound echo in the house. She knocked three times. Jane thought a curtain fluttered at the window and she straightened her shoulders, trying to not look like anyone dangerous or selling something. No one answered. She felt something rub her ankle, making her skin prickle, and she looked down to see a cat rubbing against her shoe. Not a black cat, but a large tiger-striped male. She felt her eyes well up and itch just looking at the animal. Why did cats always sneak up on those who were the most allergic to them?

Time to go and take Route 17 east to Kankakee, to the EZ Way Inn. She'd return tomorrow as originally planned. Hurrying to get off the porch, Jane stuck her hand into the cobwebs and shivered. They felt like the real thing.

6

"Where the hell is that dog going to sleep?"

"Hi, Mom," said Jane, bending to kiss Nellie's cheek. Jane knew that people got smaller as they got older. Nellie had started out small, though, and Jane had a disturbing image of one day arriving at the EZ Way Inn, and tiny old fist-shaking Nellie would hop into her pocket.

"Janie!" Don, who had started out big, was holding steady. He bear-hugged Jane, and despite his claims of arthritis and aging, she felt as if he just might lift her off the ground.

"Welcome back! Got some pictures of Q and the baby?" Don asked. "And what about the movie? Are they going to make that movie about you?"

Jane was not much of a photographer. She caught the occasional Nessen-designed lamp on her cell phone camera to send to Tim and she had remembered to get a photo of Michael's face, but those recognizable images were the exception, not the rule. Even when she remembered to bring the higher quality camera that Tim insisted she carry, she usually forgot to use it. Luckily, she had a DVD of photos from Monica that she could show her parents. After a slide show on the new laptop Oh had insisted she should have, she'd make the prints Don wanted so he could pin them up on the EZ Way Inn bulletin board, next to the sign-up sheet for the bowling league and the final results of last summer's Wednesday golf league.

"Pictures back at the house. I have to show them to you on my computer," said Jane. "And no movie, I'm afraid. Free trip to California, but no Hollywood movie deal."

"I told you so," said Nellie. "Just like them trips to Florida where they make you go get your picture taken looking at apartment buildings. They fly you down there, but then lock you up with salesmen in the middle of nowhere."

"Not exactly like that," said Jane, "since I was—"

"Yeah, I know. Aggie and Willy went on one of those things, said they never even got to see the ocean."

"This was—"

"Did you see the ocean?" asked Nellie.

"No, but—"

"Yup. You want soup? I saved you a piece of coconut cream pie."

Jane sat at the almost empty bar. She didn't know the two men finishing bottles across from her. A group of six women drank coffee at a table in the dining area next to the barroom.

"Isn't it late for them to be at lunch?" asked Jane, checking the large old jewelry-store clock hanging over the door. Almost four. Since the Roper Stove factory had closed across the street, Jane wasn't even sure where these women had come from. These days, Nellie served lunch sporadically, made soup when she felt the urge, and ordered a pie or two from the local bakery when the spirit moved her. Jane noticed today that Nellie was wearing an apron and still washing bowls and plates. It almost looked like the old days—

postlunchtime rush—after they had served hundreds of hamburgers, Polish sausage sandwiches, and bowls of soup in a thirty-minute time span.

"Don't you know those girls?" asked Nellie. "That's Christine and Zarita and Joyce. That there's Swanette and I don't know the other two names, but they all used to come in every day. They loved my vegetable soup."

"Those *girls* are about eighty years old," whispered Jane. "They've been retired for decades. Are they ghosts?"

"Funny," said Nellie. "You'll be old someday, smarty. They're having a birthday party for Christine and they wanted to have a reunion here. Called me and asked if I'd make vegetable soup and get some pie. They're having a really nice time, too."

"You remember the girls, don't you, Janie?" asked her dad.

Jane did remember the office girls, as they had always been called. When she was around Q's age, she had begun working summers at the tavern, helping cook and serve and wash dishes in the heyday of serving the Roper boys, as they had always been called. The office girls had always left her a tip. Jane rushed to serve them and clear their dishes, and under the coffee cups and saucers she had always found dimes and quarters. Since no one ever tipped at the EZ Way Inn, this was an event, and Jane always offered the money first to Nellie who would shake her head and refuse it.

"They left it for you. I don't get a tip when you're not here. It's yours," said Nellie. "Put it in your bank at home."

Jane watched the women for a moment, talking and laughing, probably telling stories of their days working for the vice presidents and sales directors and whoever else held the white-collar jobs across the street. She had to say hello.

In that short walk from the bar to the table, Jane felt herself grow younger and younger, until she was, once again, a shy ten-year-old. She didn't want to interrupt what appeared to be an intimate and happy party, but she had to greet these women who had been the career women of her childhood. They had dressed smartly and worn their hair in the latest styles. Even Nellie had been respectful, deferential, and that was such a rarity that Jane had put them on an even higher pedestal.

"Miss Munsterman?" asked Jane. "I don't know if you remember me, but—"

"Janie, oh my, Janie!"

"Look at Jane!"

They fussed over her and made her feel even more like a child, which was far more enjoyable than Jane would have imagined. Christine, who had always been the ranking member of the group, serving as secretary to the factory president, took Jane's hand in hers. "You know, dear, I was feeling pretty young until I saw you all grown-up."

The girls laughed and demanded to know about her life and Nick, whose picture they had already noted on Don's bulletin board. Jane filled them in on both husband and son. Zarita then asked about her career. Don had bragged to them about her successes in business up in Chicago.

"I worked in advertising as a creative director. It was great fun, but . . ." Jane hesitated. A feeling of gratitude for these women who had been such unknowing role models washed over her. She didn't want them to know how disillusioned she had become in the business world, how she had one day been valuable and cherished and the next, downsized and out, how it had never been quite what she had expected.

"And now, I have followed my love of antiquing and foraging

for valuables and I'm a picker," Jane said. Six absolutely blank faces stared up at her. "I find treasures for people."

"Like on *Antiques Roadshow?*" asked one of the women Jane had not known before.

"Sort of," said Jane.

"She finds junk for people who'll pay a lot of money for it," said Nellie, bringing over a large paper plate covered in aluminum foil. It was the rest of the pie, Christine's favorite, for her to take home. "And she solves murders."

Now those blank faces brightened.

"You sell the stuff of people who are murdered?" asked Zarita.

"No," said Jane. "I ... well, actually, I guess I ... it's two careers. I am a picker and I also work as a private investigator."

"Here's her card," said Don, coming over. He had asked Jane the last time she was home if he could have a few, just in case, and Jane was shocked to see him whip out her JANE WHEEL, PPI card and lay it on the table.

"It's like meeting Sherlock Holmes," said one of the girls.

"More like Watson," said Jane.

"More like Sanford and Son," said Nellie.

"No," said Christine. "Like Jessica on *Murder, She Wrote.*"

Swanette had been quiet the whole time Jane had been standing there. Jane remembered almost nothing about her. She had never talked to her, but her name, Swanette, had stuck with Jane. Now she pushed back her chair to get a better look at Jane.

"You always were a collector. I used to bring you interesting rocks I'd find on the farm."

Now Jane remembered. Swanette was the youngest of the group, a secretary at Roper Monday through Friday, but on the weekends, she helped her husband on the farm they owned. She remembered Don saying he heard she could drive a tractor like a man . . . whatever that meant.

"I remember. I actually still have part of that rock collection."

"Sure you do. That's what you acquisitive collectors do," Swanette said. "I was just telling the girls. I'm moving into a retirement apartment, and I don't have any family to take my things. And my late mother-in-law's things . . . I have to find a place for those . . . I've got so many things to get rid of . . ."

Jane picked up her card and wrote Tim's number on the back.

"If you want to have a sale, he's your guy," Jane said.

"I want you."

Jane smiled. "I've never done a sale by myself. I wouldn't . . ."

"Here's the deal. You come out to the farm tomorrow morning and look over my things. Give me an idea of what they're worth, what you think I should do. Then if you think this Tim is the man for the job, I'll give him a chance. I'll write down the directions."

"I hate to turn this down, because it's right up my alley, but I'm here on business already. I have to—"

"The farm is just west of here, in Herscher, and it'll only take you twenty minutes to get there. Here." She handed Jane a napkin with carefully printed directions.

"Is nine A.M. okay?" asked Jane.

After the girls left, Don patted Jane on the back and told her what a good daughter she was.

"Yes, I am, but what in particular am I being good about today?"

"Swanette's had a hard time of it. Her husband was a sonofa . . . a bad guy. Drank a lot, left her with all the work. Swanette was a beauty . . . and a brainy woman, too. Always doing the crossword puzzles and using the big vocabulary. Her husband was a brute. Moved his mother into the house and Swanette had to take care of her, too. Then he died, and she was left with the mother who was an invalid. And that niece of hers lived with her for about five years, too. Christine stopped in here last month for a cup of coffee on her way back from Swanette's after the mother-in-law finally died and she said you could hardly make it through the house."

"My specialty," said Jane. She began clearing the plates from the table. "Where's Mom?"

"Out playing with your dog," said Don.

"Yeah, right," said Jane, walking over to the window. But her father was not joking. Nellie had taken out one of Rita's rubber toys from the backseat and was throwing it high and wide. Rita was jumping and catching it, wiggling with delight while in the air.

"Sometimes I think everything I remember from my childhood is wrong," said Jane to Don, returning to the table for the last of the dishes. "And sometimes not," she said. Under each plate was a quarter.

After Jane helped Nellie finish cleaning the kitchen, Jane pried Don out from behind the bar and persuaded them both to leave the EZ Way Inn in the capable, if shaky, hands of their elderly bartender, Carl.

Back at the house, Jane sat Don down at the kitchen table in front of her laptop. She inserted the photo CD Monica had given her. With a click of what seemed to Don a magical button, a slide show of Q and Jamey began. Q laughing, Q bent over her stamp collection, Q holding her brother on her lap, hardly able to fit her thin little arms around him, Jamey sleeping, Jamey awake, Jamey in the stroller, Jamey and Q lying on a blanket. After it had cycled through three times, Jane asked Don if he knew which of the photos he'd like her to print.

"All of them," he said

Nellie, pretending not to have time to sit down and look at any pictures, no matter who they were, had found one excuse after another to stand behind Don, pausing long enough to glimpse each photo at least twice.

"Print up one of them on the blanket," said Nellie. "I sent them that blanket."

Jane selected the shot and put it up on the screen.

"This one?"

"Yup. I bought that quilt at the church sale last spring and sent it to them for the baby."

"They must like it," said Jane. She could see that the quilt in question had beautiful appliqués of fruits and vegetables. Jamey appeared to be drooling over a ripe tomato.

"Yeah?" said Nellie. "Enough to get grass stains on it."

Monica might not have intended to pay her this compliment, but by photographing the children on Nellie's gift, she had elevated the humble handmade blanket to iconic status. Nellie talked tough, but was, for Nellie, tickled pink.

Nellie was, for Nellie, also showing signs of becoming a loving caregiver. Not to Don, who was told repeatedly he had not been firm enough with Carl the bartender about keeping the rinse tanks clean; nor to Jane, who was roundly scolded for allowing Nick to miss so much school—with permission or without—and for repeatedly letting Charley leave the country. No, Nellie's warm beating heart, so long encased in permafrost, was being thawed by none other than Lovely Rita.

Like Miles, Nellie seemed to communicate naturally with the

dog. Jane watched her mother raise a hand, lower it, palm down, or beckon with a crooked finger and Rita, seemingly, did everything that Nellie desired.

"Does Mom know what she's commanding the dog to do, or is she just adjusting what she says to what Rita is doing?" Jane asked her father.

"The old chicken and the egg," said Don, not looking up from reading the *Kankakee Daily Journal*.

Jane wasn't sure if this really was the old chicken and the egg question, but it was a puzzle. Since Jane and Michael had never really had a pet—too hairy, too smelly, too dirty were just a few of the excuses—Jane had never seen this dog-whispering side of Nellie. Michael had once brought home a free puppy from a friend's house. After two days of untrained puppy in Nellie's immaculate house, the puppy had disappeared.

"It wanted more space. It wanted to live on a farm," Nellie had told them.

Even at a young age, Jane suspected this farm for puppies was a euphemism for something terrible, but two days later, Fuzzy Neilsen, a long-time EZ Way Inn customer who did live on a farm, told Jane that the puppy had adjusted very well to country life.

"Happy as a pig in sh . . . slop," said Fuzzy.

Now, witnessing Nellie carry on some sort of a conversation with Rita—and it did seem to be two-way, since Nellie was doing a lot of emphatic nodding as if Rita were filling her in on many secrets of the canine universe, many of which Nellie seemed to approve, Jane thought that just maybe, the puppy really *had* requested a transfer to the farm and Nellie had obliged.

Jane planned to leave early in the morning to drive out to Herscher. She would meet Swanette at her house, do a quick inventory of her stuff, and bring along a better picture of Michael that she could, if necessary, show around town. Edna's Diner would have more customers . . . perhaps even Edna herself would recognize the photo. She might not even have to ask random passersby questions if someone at the haunted house opened the door to her. Jane was ahead of schedule. If all went smoothly, she could set Swanette up with a T & T Sale, meet Honest Joe and have a stern talk with him, eat Saturday-night supper with her parents and Tim at Pink's Café, and be back in Evanston on Sunday to receive her weekly call from Charley and Nick.

How lovely when things just fall into place!

7

Nellie didn't go into the EZ Way Inn on weekends. She might have agreed thirty years ago to help her husband out in the business, even though she barely approved of taverns, but she put her small square foot down firmly when it came to weekends. Saturdays and Sundays belonged to her to do with as she saw fit. Housework, laundry, yard work, shopping, church were her usual choices. Nellie explained all of this to Rita who sat at respectful attention, watching her as she moved back and forth in her kitchen.

Jane had slept surprisingly late—Saturdays were usually predawn wake-up calls for house sales—and when she awoke in her childhood bedroom, she felt oddly well rested. Rested and . . . what was this other feeling? Starving. She was ravenous. Something smelled delicious. She grabbed the robe hanging on the door, one of Nellie's terry-cloth rejects that she left for Jane to use when she visited, and noted that Rita had already deserted her post at the foot of the bed.

When she got to the kitchen door, Jane not only smelled the bacon but also heard the delicious sizzle. Nellie, already dressed for the day in slacks and a gray sweatshirt, was flipping pancakes and nodding at Rita, who sat watching every move.

"That's right, I could tell this is what you liked," said Nellie, pausing as she collected the food to transfer it to the table.

"I'll help," said Jane, grabbing the pitcher of warmed maple syrup. She wanted to pretend her mother was talking to her, but she could see that Nellie had directed the remark to the dog.

Nellie put two pancakes on a plate, crumbled two pieces of bacon over the top, and set it on the floor for Rita, who waited. Nellie nodded and said, "It's okay, you can start," and Rita, Jane was almost certain, smiled before falling to her food.

"I don't usually give her table food," said Jane. That was a lie, since she always gave Rita anything she thought she might like—and she was still so surprised that she had a dog that she often forgot to buy actual dog food.

Nellie didn't dignify Jane's remark with any indication that she heard it.

"Another one?" Nellie asked.

Jane nodded. Nellie had already put three pancakes on her plate. Four seemed about right. Jane had forgotten how much she had loved weekend breakfasts. Nellie always cooked, and it was all new and just for them, not leftovers from the tavern.

During the week, before school and work, Nellie never had time to make a hot meal, so Jane and Michael were on their own. Powdered-sugar doughnuts, the kind that came in a package and made you cough if you inhaled, and even cookies and coffee were acceptable before-school nourishment. A glass of milk or juice might be encouraged but never required. There was just no time to worry about the basic food groups or a mid-morning drop in blood sugar. But on the weekend, when there was no EZ Way Inn calling, Nellie sectioned grapefruit with surgical precision, stirred up lemon-blueberry muffins, fried bacon expertly, and poached, fried, and scrambled eggs to everyone's taste. Some mornings, she slowly fried potatoes in butter until they were brown and crispy on the outside, soft and salty on the inside.

Jane watched a pat of butter melt over her pancakes and marveled at how much one meal could bring back an entire childhood. Marcel Proust had his cookie and it might have been a damn fine one, but Jane Wheel preferred Nellie's pancakes.

Although she and Charley and Nick normally eschewed red meat, Jane helped herself to three slices of bacon and, chewing carelessly and talking with her mouth full, asked her mother, "What's the occasion? I didn't think you and Dad made big Saturday breakfasts anymore."

"Dad never made them. I did," said Nellie. "I just thought you two might be hungry, that's all."

"Where is Dad?"

"He's at the tavern. He always opens up on Saturday mornings. I meant you and the dog."

Jane ignored Rita's elevation to being her equal.

"Do you have a picture of Michael, Mom," asked Jane, "as an adult? From the last few years or so?"

"You've got all the pictures on your computer," said Nellie.

"No. I don't want one with him and the kids. Just Michael."

Nellie rose and crossed to a small shelf over the sink where a few old cookbooks rested. Since Jane had never seen Nellie consult a recipe, she assumed these had been handed down from Nellie's mother or had been gifts from someone and that Nellie had decided to use them as decorative kitchen artifacts.

Cracking open an ancient copy of *The Joy of Cooking,* Jane

watched her mother remove a photograph of her brother. It was fairly recent. Michael wore a suit and smiled in a loose, easy manner at the photographer.

"Your dad took this when Michael stopped here on his way home from a business meeting last year," said Nellie.

"You keep it in a cookbook?"

"Why not?" asked Nellie. "I keep you in here, too." Nellie flipped to desserts and took out a picture of Jane and Nick in front of a papier-mâché volcano Nick had built for the school science fair two years earlier.

"I got my mother and father, too," said Nellie, removing a fragile snapshot from the casserole section. Two young people looked straight at the camera with serious expressions. All business, each held a baby, bundled up against what Jane assumed was an autumn chill since the trees were nearly leafless.

"Is that you and Aunt Veronica?" asked Jane.

"Nope. Look at how young Ma and Pa were. I think Ma wrote on the back. It's faded. Nineteen thirty-something . . . thirty or maybe thirty-nine . . . that's a three, right? I'm old, but I'm not that old."

"Can I take this?" Jane asked, holding up the picture of Michael. "Just for today. I'll bring it back."

"What for?"

Jane knew better than to talk to her mother about any of this—Michael, Michael's evil twin, Internet scams—because none of it would make sense to Nellie, and all of it would cause worry and angst that might manifest in several unpleasant displays.

Then again, Jane could see no convenient lie or plausible excuse.

"Someone who looks like Michael has been cheating people over the Internet and whoever-he-is apparently lives in Herscher."

Bruce Oh had advised Jane to acknowledge her own action . . . to stop minimizing her own involvement . . . to own her new profession.

"You might have stumbled across your first body, Mrs. Wheel, but ever since, it seems the mysteries have sought you out. You might try to stop seeing yourself as the accidental detective," Oh had told her.

"I've traced him to Herscher," Jane said to her mother, correcting herself. "I thought after meeting with Swanette, I might show this photograph around town to see if I could find him."

"Then what?" asked Nellie.

"Ask him to stop?" said Jane, realizing full well that she wasn't exactly sure what, if any, crime Michael's twin had committed.

"Okay," said Nellie.

"Okay?" asked Jane.

"Okay," said Nellie. "Sounds like you got a full day ahead." Nellie bent down to get Rita's plate. She cleared the rest and ran a sink full of soapy dishwater. "You liked that, didn't you?"

Jane caught herself before she answered. Her mother was talking to Rita.

An hour later when Jane was showered and dressed and ready to meet Swanette, she couldn't find her mother in the house.

The kitchen was unoccupied, clean and shiny as a domestic museum, as though no one had ever cooked a meal there. Jane walked through, grabbing her bag, figuring she'd find Nellie and Rita out in the yard.

Close. Nellie was sitting in the front seat of Jane's car talking to Rita who was sitting in the rear. Although the windows were closed, Jane could see her mother's lips moving. She was conversing again with Rita.

"Mom?" said Jane, opening her door.

"I'm going."

"Not a good idea. I have to work with Swanette—"

"I can help. Swanette knows me better than you and she'll trust me to tell her what's what. She's got so much damn junk. Christine told me, you can't even move in her house."

"But I have other work to do while I'm in Herscher. I told you," said Jane.

"Yeah," said Nellie. "I can help with that, too."

Jane slid into the driver's seat. She knew already it would take a crowbar to remove Nellie from her car. There was no use arriving late to her meeting with Swanette. She had a twenty-minute car ride to convince Nellie to wait at Swanette's while she visited the haunted house to see if old Bill's old Jim was old Joe. Old Honest Joe.

"What the hell is that?" asked Nellie, when a loud ringing started as Jane backed out of the driveway.

"Hello," said Jane, trying to cradle her cell phone while straightening the steering wheel. "Hang on, Tim, until I'm on the street. . . ." Jane placed the phone on the seat next to her.

"Hello," said Nellie, picking up the phone. "What do you want, Lowry? Why're you calling when she's driving?"

"Mom! Give it!"

"Yeah? What kind of business?" asked Nellie.

"Mom. Push the button that says speaker. Put him on speaker."

Nellie turned away from her and waved her hand. "Can't read anything that small. No, not you. Yeah, we're going there now. Then we've got some detective work to do. Yeah, we'll be just fine." Nellie turned back to Jane. "How do you hang this thing up?"

"Give it to me."

"Never mind, I got it. End, right?"

Jane had a toolbox in the trunk of her car. Maybe she did have a crowbar with her, and if she did, maybe she could use it on Nellie. She wanted her out of the car. Now.

"Swanette called Tim last night," said Nellie. "You gave her the card, so she decided she'd talk to him. He's coming out, too, but a little later. Had a meeting this morning."

So much for things falling into place in an uncomplicated fashion.

Jane drove for fifteen minutes, straight west out of Kankakee, toward Herscher. Jane didn't speak, Nellie murmured a few consoling words to Rita, concerning, Jane surmised, her driving.

"Look, I got to tell you something," said Nellie.

"Talking to me or the dog?" asked Jane.

Jane glanced down at the directions Swanette had given her and clicked on her turn signal.

"This is something you should know. I had to come with you today," said Nellie.

"So you could save Rita when the airbags deployed?"

Jane looked straight ahead at the road, then to the odometer. She had to go 3.6 miles then prepare to turn in at Swanette's farm. Country driving always made her nervous. All of these look-alike county roads, numbered or lettered, and no one around to answer any questions about directions. No landmarks, unless you consider the livestock, and one couldn't very well turn at the two cows or go straight past the trotting horse. Jane much preferred the anonymity of a city street to the isolation of the country road. Having Nellie sitting next to her, clucking and chuckling every time she hit a rut, only made her more anxious.

"If you don't want to know, then I guess I don't have to tell you," said Nellie, unfastening her seat belt as Jane turned off the county road into a long driveway.

Swanette's farm, at least the farmhouse, was not that large. A compact two-story white frame structure with a glassed-in porch, or Florida room, as Jane had heard them called, attached. There was a pole barn around the back, and a few sheds, maybe an old chicken coop. Unlike so many farms, Jane saw no tractors or equipment parked under the trees. A beater station wagon, up on blocks, and a small hatchback were parked in front of the barn.

Swanette was out the door to greet them before they even got completely out of the car. She hugged Nellie, which caught her so much by surprise that Nellie hugged her back. Although Jane saw no reason to admit it, she knew it was probably for the best that her mother had come with her.

"I called your friend," said Swanette. "I decided I'd be taking advantage by asking you to do all the work for free. I'm going to pay you and pay him, too."

"No need to worry about—" Jane stopped talking as she stepped into Swanette's living room.

"What in the world happened here?" said Nellie.

Jane tried to shush Nellie, but the woman would not be shushed.

"How long have you been living this way, Swanette? Are you crazy?"

"Mom!"

"Let's see, Lee died almost fifteen years ago and my mother-in-law passed away last spring. My niece lived in the back bedroom for about six years back in the seventies–eighties, so I would say the house has been as you see it for . . . well . . . way too long."

Swanette was dressed in a pair of navy blue slacks and a maroon turtleneck sweater. Jane noticed a stylish matching jacket was draped carefully over the back of a kitchen chair. Her short gray hair was professionally cut. Her hands, Jane noticed, were manicured, her nails polished with a tasteful deep pink. How did this well-groomed, sane-looking woman live in this—even to Jane's stuff-loving eyes— insane asylum of a house?

Every surface—and there were plenty of surfaces—was covered. Tables, bookcases, end tables, and coffee tables were pushed up next to each other to display collections of porcelain, thimbles, salt and pepper shakers, plates, souvenir snow globes . . . everything Jane had ever seen on a flea market table of mixed smalls was represented here in multiples. The windows were streaked with heavy clinging dust, so that despite the sun shining, barely any light entered the room. There were several lamps, most of which Jane thought were from the forties and fifties, many with fraying cloth-covered cords, none switched on.

Built-in bookcases on either side of the fireplace were filled with magazines and newspapers. Jane could see that there were photo albums and postcard albums stacked on the shelves in between fifty-year-old issues of *Life* and *Look*.

"I would love to have a photograph of your faces," said Swanette. "I told you there was a lot of stuff. Didn't you believe me?"

"Of course I believed you, but—" Jane began to say. Nellie cut her off.

"But we didn't think you were crazy! Swanette, you could have died in a fire from all this junk. Could have just exploded, all the dust and garbage—"

"Oh no," said Swanette, beginning to laugh. "I don't live here. I mean I haven't been living here for the past several years."

Swanette explained that her mother-in-law, who had never really cared for Swanette, grew more and more eccentric after her son died. Since she didn't trust Swanette and she needed almost round-the-clock care, Swanette had hired full-time help and kept watch over her mother-in-law from the outside.

"Where the hell you been?" asked Nellie.

"I took an apartment near the high school. I was doing some substitute teaching, so it was convenient. I came here on weekends to work in the garden, and when I was allowed, I poked my head in. I knew it was a disaster, but she was just hanging on and all this junk made her as content as she could be. Tell you the truth, I kept putting off doing anything with the house, thinking she was going to be dying any minute, but spite and malice are powerful medicines. She was a woman who lived on hate. She had her nurse Carla hire a guy from town to come out here and move stuff around—from the basement to the coop to the shed and back to the living room. She had a truckload of stuff she moved here with—probably some good old antiques if we can find them. Never threw anything from her mother or her aunts away, had stuff packed up and stored all over the farm. I just didn't have it in me to fight her on this stuff. She thought her name was on the deed with mine and Lee's—his dad left him the place and insisted that her name be left on some of the papers that described the acreage. It wasn't really a legal thing, but Lee always told her she was a part of the farm. She had no equity in the property, but she believed her name was on the deed and we never really tried to make her understand that she had no legal claim. She acted like she bought it with us or something, but I never took a thin dime from the old battle-ax.

"I've been trying to call the handyman who worked for her, but he didn't answer his phone this morning. I think he had the keys to the sheds—Mother Flanders had him put padlocks on the doors. I'm just going to put an ax through them if I can't find the keys."

"She let a nurse and a handyman into the house, but not you?" asked Jane.

"Yup," said Swanette. "She said as long as she paid them, she could make them do what she wanted, but since I had just married Lee, married my way into my connection, she didn't trust me. She told me I thought I was better than them because I had a college degree and used big words, worked in an office. She was certifiably crazy, and it didn't help that on top of crazy, she was mean as spit."

"Yeah," said Nellie, "but you can understand it, right? If you hire somebody, you pay them and they do the job, fine. And if you don't like them or the job they do, you fire them. Family you're just stuck with."

"Sweet sentiments," said Jane.

Nellie was already stacking up newspapers, shaking them and blowing the dust away. "Any law against burning trash out here?"

"No," said Swanette and Jane at the same time, although with considerable differences in emphasis.

Swanette shook her head. "I burned trash all the time."

"No," repeated Jane. "We'll sell those newspapers and magazines. Leave them, Mom."

"They're filthy dirty," said Nellie.

"We'll wipe them down a bit, shake them out, but they're really in great shape. No rips, no yellowing. I don't smell any mold or mildew in here. I think the books and paper stuff will be good. Mom, you can wash dishes and glassware, but don't throw anything away unless it's garbage. Not by your definition, but by mine."

"You don't have a definition of garbage! You don't throw anything away."

"Old food. You can throw away old food."

Nellie headed for the kitchen, grabbing a large plastic bag from off the counter. She stood in front of the stove and began to sweep all the spices in their grease-filmed tins and bottles into the bag.

"No," yelled Jane. "Those old tins are vintage. Just old food. Smelly moldy stuff, scraps—that's garbage. Everything else can be cleaned—but just a little—and sold. Tim will think he's died and gone to heaven when he sees the graphics on that bottle of celery seeds."

Swanette tried a number on her cell phone, then shook her head. "I don't know where that guy is. He always came out here to check the property on Saturday mornings."

Jane had planned on taking the photo of Michael and heading into Edna's Diner after a brief walk-through at Swanette's house. The stacks of books, magazines, and file boxes with newspaper-wrapped china bulging out the cardboard sides made any kind of walk-through, brief or detailed, almost impossible. Although Nellie's energy and scrubbing techniques would be helpful, she couldn't be left unsupervised or half of the good junk would disappear.

"When did Tim say he would be here?" asked Jane.

Nellie looked at one of the six kitchen clocks hanging on the wall and shook her head—whether at the number of ticking clocks or the passage of time in general, Jane couldn't be sure.

"In a half hour or so," Nellie said. "Why did she need so many damn clocks?"

"She liked backup," said Swanette. "She always said that no one could trust one of anything, including husbands. Lee's father was her second husband and I'm not sure she ever put any faith in him. She liked setting people up against each other. She'd tell her nurse to watch the handyman, said she didn't trust him, thought he was taking her stuff and selling it off. Then she'd tell the handy-man that the nurse was stealing from her. Each one of them told me about the other. God knows what she told them about me."

Jane wandered around, opening cupboards and closet doors, as Swanette described the old lady. Jane tried to tune out the parts of the description that sounded like her. After all, Jane had explained multiples in her own collections by saying how much she liked backup. None of this boded well for her golden years.

When Tim drove up twenty minutes later, he found Nellie at the sink up to her elbows in soapy water washing out crusty blue canning jars, with stacks of filthy pink and green Depression glass plates and cups waiting their turn. Jane and Swanette were in the back bedroom used for several years by Swanette's niece. Jane was on the floor dragging out boxes of teen movie magazines and comic books from under the bed. Spotting a silver bit of jewelry in a box, Jane fished out a charm bracelet.

"Man, woman, birth, death," said Tim in a low ponderous voice, then added, dragging out each syllable, "in-fin-i-ty."

Jane shook her head.

"You don't remember Ben Casey on TV?" asked Tim, holding the bracelet up to her face.

"Sounds familiar, but—"

"This is a good TV collectible—show was on in the sixties—and it opened with the old mentor doctor drawing these medical symbols on the board. The charm bracelet was a hot item."

"You're my age, Timmy, how do you know so much or remember so much?"

"Research, honey. You keep digging up the stuff, I'll write the history on the price tags."

Jane left Tim with a stack of *Teen* magazines to page through and told Swanette she would be back in an hour. She wanted to visit the "haunted house" and, if no one answered the door, still have enough time to ask questions at the diner before the lunch crowd left. Jane wanted to follow Miles's advice and bring Rita along, but assumed she'd have to pry the dog away from her mother. Since Rita's bacon breakfast, she hadn't strayed two feet away from Nellie. Walking back through the house into the kitchen, Jane whistled but saw neither the dog nor her mother. There were, however, stacks of glistening green and sparkling pink glassware drying on the now wiped and cleaned kitchen counter.

After only an hour, Nellie had made a substantial dent in the filth and clutter.

"I wonder what would happen if I locked her in the chicken coop with all those boxes," Jane said aloud, wondering if that were indeed where her mother had gone.

No such luck. Just as she had been earlier in the morning, Nellie sat in the front seat of Jane's car, chattering away to Rita in the back.

"No," said Jane. "Not this time."

"Just drive," said Nellie. "I'm going to tell you a secret."

Jane tried to remember if Nellie had ever uttered these words to her before. No. She was sure that Nellie had never volunteered any information, personal or otherwise, let alone given up any secrets. Nellie's relationships with both Jane and Michael . . . and probably with Don, as well . . . had at their core a firm belief that information was given on a need-to-know basis.

When Jane had asked the typical childhood questions of her mother—How did you meet Dad? What was it like when you went to school? Et cetera—Nellie had refused to participate. Her answers ranged from "I don't remember" to "What's the difference? Who cares?" Michael always said their mother missed her calling. She should have been with the CIA.

Now Double O Nellie was offering to tell her a secret?

Jane drove.

"Well, when I was— What the hell?" Nellie began rummaging through Jane's purse to locate the loudly ringing cell phone.

"Forget it, don't answer it," said Jane. "Keep telling me—"

"Yeah?" said Nellie, pushing several buttons and assuming that one of them would allow her to answer the phone.

"Mom, I'll get the message later. Please don't answer my phone, I—"

"Yeah, it's me. She's here, but she's driving. Yeah. Yeah. No. Yeah. Okay. Yeah. Wait a minute." Nellie turned to Jane. "What time do you think we'll be home?"

"Why ask me? Seems to me like you're running the show," said Jane.

"Dinner. Yeah. Bye."

Jane parked in front of Edna's Diner. The haunted house across the street, in the October light of midday, looked just as dark and forbidding as it did yesterday in the late afternoon. The enormous oak trees that hung over the roof isolated the house from any sunlight, from any connection to neighboring structures. Set back on the lot, on a mostly commercial street, it stood teetering on its foundation, defiant. Just try to tear me down, it seemed to say, I was here before you and I'll outlast you all.

"It was your dad," said Nellie.

"What's the secret?" asked Jane.

"I'll tell you later," said Nellie, opening her car door and getting out before Jane could slam down on the childproof locks and hold her mother captive until she talked.

"Rita, I swear, if you shift your allegiance to that woman . . ." Jane began, opening the car door for the dog. The house was forbidding enough that she thought it might be a good idea for Rita to come with them and sit at attention at the door.

Nellie was batting down the cobwebs on the front porch by the time Jane caught up with her. Jane lifted the knocker.

"I already knocked," said Nellie.

"Of course," said Jane.

No one answered the door. Jane thought, just as she had the day before, that she saw the curtain flutter. Jane lifted the knocker again and let it fall.

"Oh hell," said Nellie, "somebody's got to be home. Where are people who live in a house like this going to go?"

Without waiting for Jane to answer, Nellie turned the giant doorknob and the door swung open. Jane put her arm across her mother to stop her from walking in.

"You can't just walk in, Mom," said Jane.

"I know that. You think I'm an idiot?"

Jane moved her arm and Nellie walked in past her.

"Hello! Anybody here?"

"Mom!" said Jane, "Stay." Rita sat down and faced the street. "I was talking to your pal Nellie," said Jane, following her mother, ready to hog-tie her and throw her back in the car.

"I'm calling out," said Nellie. "The door was open."

Jane watched openmouthed as her mother walked straight through the dark foyer into the front parlor. Nellie stomped her feet as she walked, making twice as much noise as she needed to—Jane figured it was one more way of announcing their presence. Still no one came or answered Nellie's repeated hellos.

Jane, after scanning Swanette's place, was in high scanning

mode. This house, so haunted and forbidding from the outside, was much cleaner and cared for inside, although it was almost as full—top to bottom—of stuff. Shelves ran around the parlor molding and continued, Jane could see, into the dining room. Every inch of shelf space was filled with jack-o'-lanterns, witches, black cats, and devil heads. They were mostly papier-mâché candy containers, some, Jane guessed, nearly a hundred years old. It was the largest collection of Halloween objects that Jane had ever seen, and she was still only looking up at the shelves. When she allowed her eyes to roam, she saw that the giant mahogany dining room table was set with Halloween paper decorations, honeycomb crepe pumpkins and witches, all in fine-to-mint condition. Jane had to get a closer look.

She forgot that she had cautioned her mother not to barge into a strange house—indeed, she forgot she was in a strange house. Jane, overcome with curiosity and longing to authenticate this treasure trove, made a beeline for a paper black cat with a honeycomb body. She reached for the fragile cat just as the door from the kitchen swung open.

A woman stood still in the doorway, her head cocked as if she were listening as well as looking into the front of the house. The inside of the house was as sheltered by the oaks as the outside, and although there was a kitchen light on behind the figure, Jane stood in the dimness of the dining room, made darker by the heavy wood trim and velvet-curtained windows. At first Jane wasn't sure the woman saw her. She wore old-fashioned wire-rimmed glasses with the lenses tinted a smoky gray and seemed to be looking beyond Jane into the parlor. She was wearing a long dark skirt and a long black shawl-collared cardigan, belted around the waist. She was thin and, Jane could see, even in this low light, old. In fact, Jane wasn't sure she had ever seen an older-looking human being. Her hair hung to her waist, gray and knotted, and her hands were as gnarled as the roots of those oaks. Those hands, though, appeared strong. One held open the door and the other held a knife. It was a large, gleaming silver knife, with an evil serrated blade, pointed directly at Jane.

Jane swallowed hard and hoped that her voice would not fail. In scary dreams, she always opened and closed her mouth like a fish when confronted with evil and nothing came out. This was real, and she prayed for sound.

"The door was open, we're sorry if we scared you," Jane said, sounding hoarse, but audible, thinking even as she said it how weird it was to be apologizing in this manner, for possibly scaring the scariest-looking woman she had ever seen . . . who just happened to be holding a knife.

The woman continued to look past her, squinting behind the wire-framed glasses with tinted lenses. Loudly, too loudly for the room, she shouted, "Cousin Nellie? Is that you, Cousin Nellie?"

Jane turned to look at her mother standing a few feet behind her.

Nellie nodded and shouted back, "Yes, it's me." Nellie then looked at Jane.

"Secret's out," she said, shrugging her shoulders.

8

"We were born on Halloween," said Cousin Ada.

"That's no reason to fill up your house with this—" said Nellie, stopping when Jane kicked her under the table.

Ada, the old woman, whose knife-wielding appearance startled, to say the least, was marginally less frightening sitting across from Jane, an enormous pumpkin, with its seeds scooped out, in front of her. Jane and Nellie had interrupted her in the act of what Ada referred to as "the yearly carving."

"When we were kids, Ma and Pa carved lots of pumpkins and we put them all over the yard, lit up, and people drove from all over to see. Got to be a tradition that people in town helped and brought over their own jack-o'-lanterns and we'd have maybe hundred, two hundred maybe, all over. We got to be the haunted house. Ma made caramel apples and popcorn balls and spooky punch that had smoke coming out of the bowl and we'd have us a birthday party like no other kid in the world," said Ada, stabbing the blade into the pumpkin's middle. "You remember, don't you, Nellie?"

"Nope," said Nellie.

Jane wasn't sure if her mother was being difficult or truly didn't remember her cousin's birthday parties. Since Jane had never heard of Cousin Ada before, Jane wasn't sure how to characterize Nellie's behavior. Garden-variety rude? Daily dysfunctional? Sociopathic?

"And then you and your sister came one summer and we played in the cornfield and I got lost for so long? And Ma shook me and told me it was dangerous to go playing in the tall corn like that?"

"Nope," said Nellie.

Nellie's reluctance to hop aboard the reminiscing train didn't stop Ada. She kept naming events in which she was sure Nellie had participated.

"Stop kicking me under the table," said Nellie to Jane. "She can't hear me. She's deaf as a post. I don't think she can see very good, either."

That was not a comforting thought since she was hacking away at the pumpkin as she talked. Jane pulled her chair a little farther away.

"She recognized you, Cousin Nellie," said Jane in a whisper. "I thought you told me you didn't have any family. You always told Michael and me that we didn't have cousins."

"You don't. Except for her, maybe," said Nellie. "I think."

"You think what? That she's a cousin or that there aren't any more?"

"And you brought me your girl?" said Ada, turning toward Jane. "She's pretty, Nellie. Like you as a girl."

"Everyone says I look like my father," said Jane. "Do you live here alone, Ada?"

"Her hair's the color you had, Nellie, when you were a girl."

"May I look around at your beautiful house?" Jane asked, almost shouting and positioning herself directly in front of Ada.

"Look around, sure," said Ada, waving the knife around her

head and pointing toward the dining room. "The kids always want to see the haunted house, don't they, Nellie?"

Jane involuntarily ducked as the old woman swung the blade, then slipped out the kitchen door. Nellie could take care of herself, catching up with "Cousin Ada." Jane could hear Nellie describing Jane as a junk dealer who was working out at Swanette Flanders's farm, clearing out the house for a sale. Nellie was transparent, not so subtly advising Ada that she could use a little "clean-out sale" in this house.

While Nellie lamented the clutter at Swanette's, Jane was free to check the house for "Jim," the man Jane suspected of being the Internet "Honest Joe." The man at Edna's Cafe had not hesitated when looking at Michael's face—he said it was Jim Speller and Jim lived in this house. Was he Ada's son? Did Ada have a husband, a family tucked away behind the cobwebs?

Jane walked back to the entry hall through the dining room and front parlor. As in many old homes, that small front parlor was just a miniature of the main event on the other side of the house. A "visitor's parlor," Jane had heard it called. On the other side of the house was a large double room with fireplace and mantel, crowded with stuffed upholstered chairs, small chests and tables, every surface displaying some homage to Halloween.

This house was almost as crowded as Swanette's farmhouse, but the quality of the clutter was different. What was it? This house was dark, but not because the windows were streaked with grime, blocked out with stacks of unread papers. This house was dark by design. Heavy velvet drapes hung at almost every window, and although there were lamps, when Jane switched one on, only a small pool of light spilled out. Jane switched it off and peeked at the bulb under the shade. Twenty watts. Not enough light for even one corner of the room. The furniture was old—but Jane couldn't pinpoint the period from which it came. It wasn't ornate Victorian, nor was it simple Arts and Crafts. Handmade? Jane would have to check for tool marks, but there wasn't enough light in here now. Square and bulky, the chairs and two sofas were upholstered in still sturdy fabric. Heavy wool afghans clung to the back of each piece like matching sweaters. Jane imagined Ada and friends, wrapped and lashed into their chairs like hand-knit mummies.

There was a small room in back of the parlor. Jane stepped into it, admiring the tall oak bookcases, the broad desk and chair. It was a lovely office, undecorated. No black cats, no springy skeletons hanging from the ceiling. A desk lamp was switched on, its green glass shade glowing, illuminating a small neat pile of papers on the desk. Letters removed and unfolded, but still paper-clipped to the envelopes in which they'd arrived. Jane leaned over to read the second paragraph, the only one visible since the salutation and the first paragraph were covered by the envelope flap.

> . . . *although you specified no returns in your post and I realize I have to live with the poor deal I made, I just want you to know that I have reported you to the auction site and given your information to an auction watchdog blogging site and will do everything I can to make sure that no one is ever cheated like I was. How do you sleep nights, Honest Joe? Passing off cheap glass trinkets, plastic junk . . . machine-made quilts as hand-stitched? You have cured me of online shopping. Like my father used to say, when a deal is too good to be true, it is! My husband is ready to—*

"Trick or treat?"

Jane hadn't heard Ada come in behind her.

"I was looking for—"

"Candy?"

"Paper and a pen, actually, I need to jot down a note . . ." said Jane, relieved that she hadn't actually picked up the letter. Detective Oh always cautioned her to use her eyes and ears in place of her hands whenever possible. *No one gets caught looking at the bag, Mrs. Wheel, one gets caught holding the bag.* If Ada's eyes were as bad as they seemed, Jane would appear to have been leaning over the desk, scanning it for a simple piece of paper. And after all, Ada had encouraged her to look around, hadn't she?

Jane turned toward the voice, her newly minted, confident I-am-Jane-Wheel-PPI smile in place, but instead of Ada, she faced a much younger woman who appeared to see perfectly well what Jane had been doing.

"I'm afraid you won't find anything too practical here. No scratch pads and such. It's more of a display area," she said, gesturing toward the books in the floor-to-ceiling cases. "No one's read those books in years, yet they treasure each and every one, keep track of them, dust them every week. Look at the inkwells and those silver things. Those were for stamping in wax to seal envelopes. You ever see such things outside a museum? They like to keep things the way they were, everything in the house the way it was when they—"

The doorbell chimed, a ponderous two-note bell.

"They're starting early, those kids. It's a week before Halloween. Ada's lucky she doesn't hear them most of the time. Kids come from all over to ring that bell and run away. I mostly just ignore it."

"But what if someone—"

"No one visits Ada."

"My mother and I are here. Ada is my mother's cousin and I'm Jane—" Jane stuck out her hand, but the other woman stepped back and cut her off.

"No. Ada's got no family."

"I'm afraid you're mistaken. Are you her neighbor, or a friend?"

"I check on her. I'm a . . . I work for a few people in the area. I been stopping in to check on Ada since . . . for about a year, I guess. She never mentioned family. I haven't got one contact phone number for her."

"Well, here we are," said Jane, surprised at how suddenly proprietary she felt about Cousin Ada, whose existence had come as a total shock twenty minutes earlier.

"I got to go now. You'll find what you're looking for in the kitchen."

"What?" asked Jane. What had she said she was looking for?

"Scratch paper. Junk drawer's in the kitchen."

Jane heard the front door open and close.

"Jane," Nellie called. "Is that you at the door?"

"I'm coming," she called back. She violated the no-hands rule and turned over the envelope on the desk. It was addressed to "Honest Joe" at the same post office box number she had gotten from Mowbry. Ada seemed a little spooky all right, but certainly didn't seem like anyone who was running any kind of bait-and-switch scam on the Internet. In fact, Jane saw no computer or likely spot where one might be. Like most old homes that hadn't been renovated, Jane could count the electrical outlets she had seen on one hand. Where would someone plug in a computer? Or a printer or scanner . . . something that would enable a person to post photographs—phonied up or blurry or genuine—for an Internet auction? Jane couldn't see even one grounded outlet in this den.

Jane looked up at the oversized bookcase. A lovely dark oak

library three-step ladder with a smooth turned handrail was at the other end of the case. The books were arranged, Jane thought, by the color of their leather bindings. At least that's how it appeared in this light, almost as if the books on their shelves were a trompe l'oeil painting, with swipes of dark green, navy, and maroon with glints of gold writing on the spines against the dark wood background. Jane climbed the ladder, reached up and selected one of the books, compelled to touch it, feel its weight in her hand.

"Sir Walter Scott," she said out loud, breaking the spell that the library had momentarily cast. This collection of books, with the fine leather bindings and gold leaf, was probably quite valuable, thought Jane, replacing the book and reaching for the one next to it. She would ask Tim to do some research.

Jane almost lost her balance on the ladder when she grasped the next book and its spine collapsed between her two fingers. For a moment, Jane was afraid the binding had been turned to dust by mites and she would find that these beautiful books were crumbling into powder one by one. What she removed from the shelf, however, was not a book. It was a piece of heavy brown kraft paper, with a swipe of maroon paint on it. The sheet was cut to the size of the books, then loosely folded and stuck between two intact books, to fill in the space where a volume was missing on the shelf. A quick brush with her hand turned up three phantom jackets in the area she could reach from her perch on the ladder. Inside the makeshift book "jackets" were written in pencil BYRON, KEATS, and SHELLEY.

Back on the ground, Jane looked up and thought she spotted five or six more missing books whose places were being saved with the ghost jackets. It might be Ada's way of keeping the shelf looking perfect while she took volumes out to read, but that was unlikely.

Ada's bad eyes argued against the supposition that she might have a stack of books on her bedside table.

"Jane!" Nellie called. "Where the hell did she get to?"

Jane wondered if Nellie was at all worried that Jane had left her alone there to catch up with Cousin Ada while Jane returned to Swanette's farm. Jane enjoyed that thought for a moment—Nellie, confused and worried, a bit frightened to be alone in this haunted house with a cousin who might be harmless enough, if a bit eccentric. The enjoyment was brief. Jane entered the kitchen to find both women brandishing knives. Nellie had one arm cradling a gigantic pumpkin, and with the other hand, she plunged a butcher knife into the vegetable, carving the mouth into a toothy frown.

Ada was telling Nellie what she planned to give away for treats on Halloween—homemade taffy if Nellie would stay and help her "pull" the candy into shape—and Nellie was shaking her head violently.

"I can't stay here, Ada. Don needs me at home. And no kids are going to eat that homemade stuff. Just buy some candy bars or suckers or something. Parents nowadays take away all that homemade stuff."

"Mama always said the homemade's better," said Ada.

"Maybe, but when your ma made it those were safer times. Now people are afraid of crazy people with razor blades and rat poison," said Nellie, concentrating on sharpening one of the fangs on her pumpkin. She didn't notice that Ada looked like she was about to cry, her wrinkled face crumpling like one of the crepe-paper decorations in the dining room.

"Maybe you could make homemade candy for the children you know, who are neighbors, and give out store-bought candy on Halloween night," said Jane.

Ada looked up and, although she at first seemed hopeful, shook her head.

"Won't work," she said.

"Shouldn't we get back to Swanette's?" asked Nellie. "We got work to do, Ada, we got to go."

"You haven't said hello to Brother," said Ada.

Jane was still standing in the doorway to the kitchen. Ada was in front of her, facing her. Nellie was behind Ada and began a vigorous arm-waving, head-shaking pantomime of refusal. *NO* she mouthed to Jane. *NO.*

"I'd love to meet your brother," said Jane. "What's his name?"

"Brother James is upstairs," said Ada. "I'll take you."

Nellie was practically jumping up and down, waving her butcher knife like a sword over her head.

"No, Ada," said Nellie. "Just tell him we said hello. We got to go."

Ada started out the door where Jane let her pass in front of her and lead the way.

"We can say hello in person, just to be polite," said Jane. "Sounds like you don't get out here very much."

Nellie waved Jane away from her, shaking her head, preparing reluctantly to follow along in the parade to Brother Jim.

"Leave the knife, Mom," said Jane.

"You might be sorry," said Nellie, plunging it into the top half of her pumpkin, either as a statement of contempt or the beginning of her jack-o'-lantern's left eye.

Jane followed Ada as she slowly climbed the stairway to the second floor. No electric lights were turned on and the spare October light offered no natural illumination. Jane could feel Nellie close on her heels.

"For someone who didn't want to come up to see her cousin, you're tailgating pretty close," Jane said, turning around to look at Nellie.

Her mother looked straight ahead, keeping her eyes on Ada. Jane had spent a lifetime studying her mother, struggling to read her. Nellie was an untranslatable book. After so many years, she thought she had memorized all of the movements and expressions, even if she didn't always know what they meant, but Nellie had a look on her face now that Jane had never seen before. Part fear, part grim determination and something else. To Jane's surprise, Nellie began to chuckle. It was an evil little laugh, but Nellie did seem to be amused about something.

"What is it?" Jane asked. "What's funny?"

"You. If you think my secret was a big surprise, wait until you see Ada's," said Nellie, now openly laughing.

At the top of the stairs, Ada paused in front of a closed door, and knocked.

"Brother, I've brought Cousin Nellie and her girl."

There was no answer.

"We're coming in now, Brother."

It took Jane's eyes a moment to adjust to the darkness in the room. Expecting more of the large wooden furniture and heavy drapes, Jane was prepared for a gothic scene, complete with an invalid brother propped up in bed. She steeled herself to not recoil at even the most horrible disfigurement or strangeness, not wanting to give a startled reaction, partly out of concern for Ada's feelings, but mostly to rob Nellie of any satisfaction.

The heavy furniture, the crowding that characterized the first-floor rooms, was absent. In fact, there was no furniture except for a small round table in the center of the room. On the table was a tall gold vase with two handles. It reminded Jane of a loving cup, an old athletic trophy.

"We're here, Brother," said Ada. She stood aside and held out her hand as if presenting the trophy to Jane.

"My brother James," she said. "He's delighted that you came to see him."

Jane looked around, knowing there wasn't anyone in the room, but holding on to some hope that the situation might become clearer.

"Hello, Cousin James," said Nellie, now openly laughing. "How are you?"

"Oh Nellie," said Ada, smiling slightly herself. "You know how he is." Ada looked at Jane who shook her head. With her strong left hand, she grasped Jane's wrist.

"Dead, dear. Brother James is still dead."

9

"I wish you could see yourself," said Nellie.

Jane didn't have to look at herself in the mirror. She felt the blood drain, she felt the wash of *eau de creepy* come over her as she stood with Ada in front of what she called her brother's "cremains."

What Jane found especially odd was how matter-of-fact Ada was about the situation. Here was her mother's cousin, which made her Jane's second cousin, she assumed—she would straighten this all out with Nellie later—who was a candidate for top model in *Halloween Monthly* or *Crone's Digest*, complete with the long gray hair, ominous air, and black clothes, now completely composed and practical as she chatted about Brother James's death.

"A year ago, James felt sick," Ada explained. "I gathered the healing herbs from the yard and made him tea and my mama's broth and fed him all the cures we used growing up, but nothing took. He got weaker and weaker, and one day he told me he was going to die that evening. He had made a list for me of what I was to do, the phone number I was supposed to call. He had arranged for the man to come and take him away . . . everything. He knew how hard . . ." Ada paused here, her voice catching. "We were twins. He knew me better than anybody and we took care of each other all our lives."

Nellie, in what could only be called an awkward gesture, patted Ada on her shoulder. "You seem to be doing good, Ada."

Ada shook her head. "I was always slower than the other kids, I couldn't hear very good and Ma and Pa didn't know that for a long time. And since I didn't know it, either . . ." Ada shrugged her shoulders.

"Brother made sure nobody took advantage of me."

Ada put one bony hand on the urn.

"He still does."

Jane nodded. It was truly remarkable that Ada's faith could provide her with the confidence to carry on, even when she had seemingly never been prepared for life alone. Here was Ada, aged anywhere from 75 to 175, keeping up this house, even managing to decorate it for the holiday, fretting over whether or not she'd be able to hand out homemade candy to trick-or-treaters.

"I'm sure he watches over you, Ada," said Jane.

Ada nodded.

"He told me I'd never have to worry about a thing and he was right. With his help, everything runs smooth as silk."

Ada backed away from Brother James and ushered them out of the room.

"We have to go," said Nellie. "Ada, you understand? We have to go back to Kankakee."

Ada nodded. Back on the first floor, Jane automatically reached for a light switch. A faint light came on overhead.

"No dear, no lights necessary yet. It's hardly night," said Ada, switching off the power.

"Will you finish your pumpkin, Cousin Nellie?" asked Ada.

"Yes, finish it, Mom. I think I left my sweater in the study," said Jane. "I'll be right with you."

Jane heard Nellie protest, but the two older women walked back toward the kitchen while Jane detoured back to the study. It was time to use her hands as well as her eyes. The mail that had been neatly stacked on the desk had envelopes with it. Jane needed to jot down names and addresses. She would ask Ada, too, but she had to be cautious. A devoted sister might not want to believe her brother had anything to do with something dishonest. She would probably be right. If he had been dead for a year, how could James Speller be Honest Joe? And even if Brother James were Michael's physical twin, he was Ada's actual twin—the photographs of the two men certainly wouldn't match up in age. Michael said everyone who had approached him had mentioned the face or the eyes, but no one said anything about the photo having a man in it wearing vintage clothes—which is the only way a photo of Jim Speller and a photo of Michael would match up agewise. Jane stopped in the doorway and scanned the bookcases again. She looked for photo albums or any frames with family photos tucked among the books, but she saw none. There were no photos on the desk, either, no pictures, no trinkets . . . just one heavy glass paperweight, a carved wooden box that Jane guessed might be used for stamps although it was empty now, and an intricate silver-topped inkwell and pen. It was museumlike in its arrangement. Only the small pile of mail had given the room any sense of contemporary life. Now that it was gone, the room had turned back into a giant display case.

Now that it was gone.

Jane walked into the room, stepped around to the other side of the desk, and carefully opened the drawers one by one. Stationery that Jane assumed had belonged to the parents of Ada and

James was in the top center drawer. The side drawers held bottles of ink, a few brass clips, and some yellowed envelopes. Jane picked up a silver cigarette case. Opening it, she smelled old tobacco. JWS was engraved on the front of the case. Brother Jim was a smoker, or perhaps he was named after his father? Fine, all the trappings of the men who had used that office, who had sat in that chair eighty years ago, but where was the mail that had been there less than thirty minutes ago?

The woman who had presented herself as the caregiver must have taken it. She had pretended to leave, simply opening and closing the front door. She waited for Jane to go upstairs with Ada and Nellie, and came back into the room and got it. She could be Honest Joe herself. Jane hurried into the kitchen.

"Ada," Jane said, speaking loudly and carefully directly in front of her cousin, "I need to ask you some questions."

"Leave her alone," said Nellie, who was opening and closing cupboard doors, seemingly taking stock. "She doesn't know anything."

"Do you know who this is?" Jane held up the photograph of Michael.

Ada took it with both hands and held it in front of her face. Her smoky glasses hid her eyes, but Jane could see movement behind the lenses. It was like watching someone read a script. Memorizing the lines. Ada concentrated, looking back and forth, back and forth.

"No," she said, handing back the photograph. "I don't know that boy."

Jane slipped Michael's picture back into her bag.

"Okay, how about the woman who checks in on you? She was here a little while ago, in the study with me. Maybe she's a nurse or a neighbor?"

"No, I don't need a nurse. I feel fine."

"Is there a woman who drops in on you, comes by to say hello? She's about my height, maybe younger than I, but with dark hair, a premature gray streak in front," Jane said, thinking hard about anything that distinguished the ordinary-looking woman who had appeared behind her in the study. "She walks softly, she was wearing soft black canvas shoes, like ballet flats—"

"What the hell does that mean, 'like ballet flats'?" said Nellie. "How the hell is she supposed to know ballet slippers? She hasn't been out of this house in seventy years."

Jane shook her head. Nellie might be exaggerating her cousin's closeted life, but in the end, she was right. Ada wasn't the type of person to identify someone by clothing style or comparisons to anyone outside of her world.

"She moved like a cat," said Jane, remembering the tabby that had sidled up to her on the porch yesterday. "A quiet surprise."

Ada nodded.

"That's the woman who wanted to marry my brother. She came over here and fussed over him. All the girls wanted to marry James. He liked her all right, but he didn't want to marry her. She doesn't come over here anymore."

"She doesn't stop in? To see if you need anything? To help you run the house, pay your bills?" asked Jane.

"Don't need her," said Ada, picking up her knife. "I got a lot of pumpkins to finish."

"Who bought the pumpkins? Where do you get your food?" Jane felt herself losing what Detective Oh called "dispassionate remove."

Remember, Mrs. Wheel, there is a balance of concern and commitment in every interaction. If you seem to care too much, you make the other person wary of weighing in too heavily. If you keep a distance, a quietude, the person with whom you converse will want to add more to the transaction, to make it weigh enough. Your dispassionate remove will draw someone out enough to give you what you need, he had told her. And right now, she was all passion and weight, and Ada, just as Oh would have predicted, retreated into carving another jack-o'-lantern.

Jane sat down opposite Ada and picked up the knife that Nellie had left.

"Ada," Jane said, "I love Halloween and I love jack-o'-lanterns. May I come back and help you with the carving?"

"Yes," said Ada. "Cousin Nellie, will you come back?"

"Yeah," said Nellie, "I guess I can come." She offered it up like a challenge. "If Jane will drive me out here, I'll come."

Jane looked at Nellie's jack-o'-lantern. The snaggle-toothed frown seemed familiar. The eyes, though, were almond shaped with brows cut out arching downward to emphasize the frown. The nose was a flattened oval, small, delicate even. Jane was surprised. She remembered Nellie's efficient, fast pumpkin carving from her childhood—a smile or a frown, a tooth or two, then three quick triangles for eyes and nose. She seemed to have gotten more creative in her old age.

Jane stood to leave. Nellie finished her inspection of the pantry. Ada embraced Nellie, still holding her knife, making Jane cringe. It didn't seem safe to leave this woman here by herself. Breathing deeply, hearing Oh's voice in her head, she kept her voice calm and undemanding.

"Ada, are you sure you're all right here alone?"

"I'm not alone," Ada replied.

Jane nodded, Nellie sighed, and they moved toward the front door.

Jane, thinking of the past hour step-by-step, stopped at the dining room table and turned back toward the kitchen.

"How did you finish carving that pumpkin?" she asked her mother.

"What are you talking about?"

"When we went upstairs, you had only carved the mouth of that pumpkin. Remember? I told you to leave the knife. And we were together the rest of the time in the house, except when I went back to the study to—"

"Get your sweater?" asked Nellie. "The one you never wore in here in the first place?"

"I was gone a few minutes, not long enough."

"I didn't have time for that carving nonsense. I had to check on her food supplies."

"Who carved that pumpkin?" Jane said, turning around to Ada who stood in the kitchen door. "Who carved that pumpkin?" she asked again, louder, facing Ada. "The one Nellie began?"

Ada turned to look at the kitchen table, covered with newspapers and pumpkin seeds. Nellie's jack-o'-lantern frowned at them all.

Ada turned back to Jane and Nellie.

"That's how Brother James does the eyes. He loves the carving. That's who carved that one. Brother James."

10

Jane allowed her mother to drag her out of the house, but only because she didn't want to upset Ada. If she wanted to return, and be welcomed, she had to remain calm and not frighten off the woman.

"Start talking," Jane said to Nellie. "I want the secret, the truth, the whole story. How could you have a cousin who lived less than twenty minutes away from us and not even tell me or Michael? Why in the world would you keep this a secret? What was the point? If I live to be as old as Ada, I will never understand you, I swear, Mom, I am—"

"You're one hell of a detective, aren't you? Asking so many questions you don't give me any time to answer them," said Nellie. "Just hold on to your horses. Calm down and drive us out to Swanette's and I'll tell you."

Jane didn't think she needed the "dispassionate remove" for Nellie. Her mother knew how to throw her off balance no matter how calm Jane might remain. She didn't bother with a deep breath or a soothing tone. Instead, she started the car and waited.

"My ma didn't want us to know our cousins. She didn't get along with her brother—he was James, too, but she called him

'Jimmy.' And she couldn't stand Jimmy's wife, Margueritte. That might be why they fought so hard—over Margueritte. I don't know. Ma wouldn't talk about it to us kids. She said they were crazy and their kids were crazy and she didn't want me and Veronica playing out there. We did the bare necessities as she called it—we visited on their birthday sometimes because it was Halloween and they made a big deal out of it. Me and Veronica always wanted to go. They had caramel apples, for God's sake, and about a million pumpkins. Uncle Jimmy grew them. He owned and farmed all the land around the house. Uncle Jimmy was okay, he'd hook up the hayrack to the tractor and take all us kids for a ride. And Aunt Margueritte was okay to us, too. She could cook—made candy and cakes and all kinds of fancy stuff our ma never made. I remember she'd take flowers from her garden and dip them in sugar somehow and decorate all her cakes and pies. But they never talked, Ma and Margueritte. Even as kids we noticed they never said a word to each other.

"Ada and James were sort of strange kids. They didn't look alike even though they were twins. Ada was nice and all, but she was an oddball. Always wearing dark glasses. Like now, I guess. Probably because she couldn't hear very well, but in those days, they didn't do a lot of testing. I still don't know if she's ever been to a doctor. I heard Ma tell my dad once that Ada needed help and it wasn't right that because Margueritte didn't believe in doctors Ada had to suffer. James was just mean. He was a nasty kid, except to Ada. He treated her like a pet. No, that's not even right. He was mean to animals."

Jane pulled into a gas station on the outskirts of the small business district. After filling up the tank and running inside to pay and get a couple bottles of water, she got back in the car, handed one to her mother and nodded.

"What?" asked Nellie.

"Keep talking," said Jane.

"That's it. That's the story."

"I swear to God I will make you hitchhike back to Kankakee."

"What else is there to tell?" asked Nellie, opening up her water and taking a long drink.

"You knew James was dead. That's why you were giving me the eye when we went upstairs. What happened? And who pays the bills? How does she get around? She can't hear well. I don't think she sees all that well, either. Dark glasses—that's why the lights are so dim. It doesn't matter to her, she just knows the place by heart."

"Look, we didn't know James was sick. Ada has a phone but never calls anybody, never answers it, probably can't hear it. It was like she said. James told her what to do when he died. She made the call to the undertaker, I guess, whoever James had made his plans with, and he was taken away and cremated and returned to her before we even found out. That's the right thing, you know. I want to be cremated, did I tell you that?"

"A million times. So how'd you find out he died? Did she have a service?"

According to Nellie, not only was there no service, there was not even a death notice in the paper. Edna, from the diner across the street, noticed that no one was mowing the lawn or watering the herb garden and just thought things looked weirder than usual, so she went over and banged on the door.

"Ada told her that James was gone and Edna should call me and tell me. Lucky she did it, because she didn't even realize that *gone* meant *dead*. She just figured he'd left Ada there alone. He'd go off and do odd jobs and Edna told me she thought he had been married for a while when he was young. I didn't ask questions, I never wanted to know anything about that. I steered clear of Cousin James. Anyway, your dad and I drove out and saw her and she told us how Brother James had died and all, introduced us to the urn, just like she did today. I thought your dad was going to pass out," said Nellie.

"What about the rest? How does she live?"

"Dad arranged to have all household bills sent to us. He pays her heat and electricity, which isn't all that much. He found an account book that James had kept and saw that he had put money away in Ada's name. Came from selling all the farmland around the house. Now Ada just owns the house, the lots on either side, and she owns the lot next to Edna's—the parking lot for the café. Money's enough to cover property tax for the next ten years if she lives that long. I send out groceries, they're delivered once a month."

Jane smiled. So Nellie hadn't just been snooping in the kitchen. She had been making a list.

"What are you grinning about? It's no big deal."

"It is a big deal. It's a good thing to do. That's why she was so happy to see you."

"Nope. She likes me. She always liked me. But it doesn't have anything to do with groceries or bills. She doesn't even know we do that."

Jane swung the car into Swanette's long driveway.

"Come on, Mom. She's a little eccentric, but she's not a complete simpleton. How does she think the bills are paid, who brings the food?"

"Brother James. Who else?"

Jane hit the automatic childproof door locks from her side

this time, locking Nellie in. She wasn't going to let her mother leave her hanging while she exited on a good line.

"Unlock the damn door. Swanette's got a lot of work in there for us to do."

"What do you mean, Brother James?"

"I had your dad drive me out there after the first grocery delivery because I got to worrying she might not find the bags, you know, maybe she wouldn't even open the door. I had no way of checking. So when we got there, I had to walk in just like today, because she didn't hear us knock. She didn't seem surprised. Didn't seem lonely or scared or anything. Was in a fine mood. And before I could ask her about the groceries, she told me that James was taking real good care of her. Brought her everything she needed. Even bought the right kind of oatmeal and flour. So, Dad and I decided there wasn't any harm in letting her think James was doing the grocery shopping."

"You let her believe that her dead brother goes to the Jewel for her?"

"What's the difference? Let her think what she wants. If you ask me, real life isn't all it's cracked up to be."

"Did you hire that woman to keep an eye on her?" asked Jane.

"Nope. Maybe Edna asked her to look in."

"Yeah, she seemed pretty surprised to find out there were relatives. She might be stealing from her. Somebody is. I think there were some books missing in the study."

"Well, let's get on that. I don't want anybody taking advantage of her. She's a kind old thing." Nellie seemed to hear herself say this and added quickly, "Even if she is nuttier than a fruitcake."

"So Dad pays the bills. You order the groceries. And the spirit of Brother James is playing her guardian angel."

"Yup."

"Okay," said Jane, unlocking the car and opening her own door, "but there is still one thing unaccounted for . . ."

"Okay, Walker, Texas Ranger, what's that?"

"Who carved that pumpkin?"

Jane had noted earlier that Tim had left his speedy little Mustang at home. Instead, he had made this house call in his truck. Was he hoping to haul out some good stuff before he even signed a deal for T & T Sales? Jane knew that compartmentalization was not usually her strong point. Her mind was more likely to race, three or four vintage bicycles at a time, around tracks paved with whos, whats, and whys. But she was able, when faced with a house like Swanette's, to put aside everything but the stuff. The sheer number of items packed into that house, crammed into the closets and alcoves, shoved onto windowsills and hidden under beds, might give her a break from puzzling over what was going on over at Ada's, which was certainly linked to someone hiding behind her brother Michael's image on the Internet. If she could throw herself into straightening out Swanette's mess, her mind might be refreshed enough to think clearly about the situation at Cousin Ada's.

"Tim," Jane called, walking in through the side porch. Tim had the radio blaring from the kitchen, but he wasn't in sight. Nellie had preceded her and, she assumed, had disappeared upstairs to begin dusting and mopping and scolding Swanette for letting this house go to the . . . well . . . if not the dogs, then the packrats. "Tim," she called again, thinking she might lose her voice from all the shouting she had had to do today.

"I'm in the back bedroom," called Tim.

Jane didn't notice any furniture items missing. Tim couldn't have culled any pieces yet—she could hardly move through the room.

"This must have been the niece's room when she lived here. Swanette described her as quite the teenybopper. Look at the great condition of all these magazines," Tim said, pointing to the stacks of *Teen* and *Sixteen*. "And there's a slew of celebrity photos, too. A lot of them autographed, although they might have been studio signed."

Jane recognized Tim's chatter. He wasn't really talking to her, he was just doing a kind of running inventory, the kind of out-loud thinking one did when faced with so many inanimate objects that, inanimate though they might be, screamed loudly for attention and assessment.

"Where's Swanette?" asked Jane. At the same time, Nellie came clumping down the stairs asking the same question.

"She found a ring of keys and thought some of them might fit the padlocks on the coop and the sheds, so she was going to check. She thinks the good old furniture might be out there," said Tim. "A lot of this stuff is all very cool, but it's mostly kitsch and a lot of junk. You are going to love it here, Janie."

"I'll go see if I can help her," said Jane.

Tim tossed her the keys to his van and asked her to bring in some folding tables he had in the back. He wanted to actually start staging a room by sorting the wheat from the chaff, setting out the good stuff on the tables so they could see what they were dealing with. Jane wasn't sure where they'd find the space to set up even one table.

"Swanette!" Jane called. The padlock was still in place on the door to the old chicken coop directly behind the house. There was a shed about twenty feet away and Jane cut across to it. As she got close, she could see the padlock dangling. *Goody,* Jane thought, *I'll get to see the good stuff before Tim.*

The door was partially closed and Jane swung it back on its hinges to let in as much light as possible. She should have stopped to get the flashlight out of her car or one of the big torches she knew Tim kept in the van.

Jane's eyes adjusted quickly enough to see the chairs stacked one on top of another. They did look good. Six, maybe eight, really good carved-walnut dining chairs.

"Nice," said Jane out loud. She scanned the shed. It couldn't have been more than twenty feet by thirty feet, but it was packed efficiently from top to bottom. There were some boxes to her immediate left that were partially unpacked. A wooden crate had slats pried off it and was almost empty except for some newspaper-wrapped objects at the bottom. Jane stepped into the shed a few feet, to see what the back corners held, and stopped short, barely preventing herself from tripping over a stylish low-heeled pump.

Just as one is disconcerted when one sees another in an unfamiliar situation—a running buddy out of his gym gear and dressed in a three-piece suit, a teacher out of the classroom—Jane was momentarily confused. Why would a single modern shoe be in this shed packed with items clearly over a hundred years old? It only took a second for her to shake herself out of the fog and follow the shoe, to the foot to the leg to find Swanette crumpled on the ground. Jane awkwardly felt for a pulse. Knowing she wasn't an expert at it, she was relieved to find a faint ticking beat. It wasn't too late. She slapped her pocket and realized her cell phone was in her bag, still in the car.

She screamed at the house, knowing that the radio would drown her out. She hated to leave Swanette alone, even for the minute it would take to get to the door and yell for Tim to call the ambulance. Standing, she turned to find Nellie, her mother in the form of a shadow, right behind her. For once, she was grateful that her mother hovered over her every move.

"Stay with her and I'll run to the house to—"

"I'll go. I'm fast," said Nellie, and sure enough, she sprinted for the porch, yelling at top volume for Tim to get on the phone to 911.

"Swanette," said Jane, "it's going to be okay."

Was it a slight movement in her cheek, a tic, a twitch? Her mouth moved, lips pursed.

"Blue . . . no . . . blue . . . one blue . . ."

Even as Jane shushed her, she was pleased to hear her talk. This had to be a good sign. Had Swanette had a heart attack? A stroke? Had she tripped over one of the boxes?

"Head . . . Oh . . . head oh . . . dad? Head . . . crosswor . . . good . . . aitch is for . . . so many . . ."

Was Swanette trying to tell her something or just wandering?

"Don't try to talk, Swanette," Jane said, trying to sound soothing. She wondered if Swanette knew she wasn't serious. Jane did want her to talk, to tell her what had happened. Blue? Head? What was that about? "Shhh," Jane lied, "the ambulance is on the way."

Then Jane noticed two things. Later, she would be hardpressed to remember which she saw first. There was a wound on the side of Swanette's head, just above her ear. There was a darkened area, swelling and the beginnings of a bruise, but the bleeding had slowed to a trickle. Jane had seen more than her share of dead bodies, but she realized she had little experience with what she hoped was a nonfatal wound. Could this have happened in a "slip and fall"? Jane doubted it. It appeared to Jane as if someone had hit this poor woman hard on the side of the head.

The other thing Jane noticed was more of an oddity, but equally chilling. Swanette, with her impeccable taste and stylish clothes, was wearing a pair of dark slacks and a cropped navy blue jacket over her turtleneck. Although Swanette had been surrounded by all the dust and filth in the house and now the shed, Jane noted that her jacket had remained impeccable except for where it now touched the dirt floor and except for a small place on the jacket sleeve. Near the inner elbow of the jacket was a clump of a stringy viscous substance. At first Jane thought it was just a gross little something, nothing unusual to find on a farm-shed floor, until she leaned in closer. Small, flat ovoids, caught in the strings, all beige and shiny?

Were those pumpkin seeds?

11

The ambulance careened down the driveway. Jane was always taken aback when professionals arrived on a scene. The flashing lights, cryptic radio communication full of static and staccato commands, slamming doors, squeaking wheels, the clear loud voices of the EMTs all contributed to a hyperrealistic scene that played out in a most unrealistic way. Too many movies, too much television. All that time watching fictional events unfold made real events recede into a kind of alternative universe.

Since no one knew what had happened, no one could be very helpful with information. Tim estimated that Swanette had been out of the house no more than thirty minutes, no less than fifteen. Jane looked into Swanette's purse, still in the house on the kitchen table, and found her cell phone. Scrolling through the phone book, she found office girl Christine's number and asked Nellie to call her and tell her what had happened.

"Just say that Swanette fell and is being taken to the hospital in Kankakee. No speculation, just the facts. Ask her if she knows how to get in touch with Swanette's niece," said Jane.

"What the hell am I going to speculate on?" asked Nellie. "What do you know?"

Jane shook her head. She didn't know what she knew. Without thinking, she had plucked the pumpkin seeds and strings from Swanette's jacket and wrapped them in a handkerchief. They were in her pocket right now. She didn't want to take the chance that the hospital staff would remove her clothes, shake off the seeds and pumpkin debris and it would be lost altogether. If she hadn't been so worried about Swanette, she might have made Tim laugh by suggesting they run the seeds through the lab to check out the pumpkin DNA and see if it matched up with Nellie's pumpkin at Ada's house. Did Swanette's accident have something to do with the massive pumpkin carving that was going on at Ada's?

A police car had arrived and an officer took their names, addresses, and asked them questions about Swanette and their reasons for being there.

"I don't get it. You're here to buy all this stuff?" Officer Cord asked.

"We're here to sell it," said Tim.

"But it's not yours to sell, right?"

Tim explained his duties as someone who conducted a house sale and showed Cord the contract that Swanette had signed sometime after Jane and Nellie had left that morning. Jane noticed that Tim had agreed to have the sale ready to go in two weeks. She pointed to the date and raised her eyebrow at Tim.

"I was counting on you to help me," said Tim.

"Still," said Jane, "I'm not sure the two of us—"

"I thought Nellie might work with us," said Tim.

"I'll bet you did," said Nellie. "You got a lot of nerve, Lowry, to think you can make me work like a dog in that—"

"I pay pretty well," said Tim.

"I'll think about it," said Nellie.

One of the paramedics came over and announced that they were ready to leave for the hospital in Kankakee.

Jane looked at her mother.

"Yeah, I'll go," said Nellie, "I'll make sure they don't screw anything up. You can come and meet me at the hospital. Now just wait a minute."

Nellie ran into the house, grabbed Swanette's purse off the table, and held it up so Jane could see it. "Her insurance information," Nellie said.

Jane watched Nellie argue with the driver all the way to the ambulance, and even out of earshot, the body language was clear. She wanted to ride in the back with Swanette, and they wanted her up front. Jane watched her mother climb into the back and the driver throw up his hands. The other paramedic, the one who had been tending to Swanette, smiled and shook his head and climbed in after Nellie. They were going to get along.

Cord was putting away his notebook and Jane, silently arguing the pros and cons of mentioning any suspicions to him, decided it was better to bring up a question now than to try to start from scratch later.

"Officer, I'm not sure that this was just a fall," said Jane.

Cord looked very much like he was trying not to look amused.

"Amateur detective, are we?" he asked.

"I heard one of the paramedics say that her EKG looked good. I saw nothing in the shed that she might have tripped over. She was groggy, but agitated, like she wanted to tell me something. And she had a huge bump on the side of her head, like she had been struck."

"Or like she struck her head when she fell?"

"I just have a feeling . . ."

"Do you think Mr. Lowry here might have wanted a better deal to sell her stuff—" Cord began to say.

"Oh no," said Jane. "Not at all, I—"

"Well, we'll get to the hospital and see what the lady has to say about all this when she feels better," said Cord. He looked in Tim's direction. "And we'll hope that she wakes up feeling better soon, right, Mr. Lowry?"

"Oh, for God's sake," said Tim. He stopped himself. "Yes, Officer, we do. Swanette is a lovely woman and I was nowhere near that shed, I was busy inside. Mrs. Wheel has a notoriously overactive imagination. Likes to play cops and robbers and doesn't always think before she speaks."

Jane nodded. "Mr. Lowry is right. I don't know what I was thinking."

Cord nodded and left for the hospital.

"Are you out of your mind?" said Tim.

"It was silly of me not to realize the position I'd put you in by raising the question. You saw how humbled I got . . . enough to convince him I'm just an armchair detective out of control," said Jane. "But she was attacked."

"I didn't hear anyone drive in," said Tim. "Hey, look at your dog. Rita's crying her eyes out over there."

Jane looked over at Rita who had run over to the spot where the ambulance was parked. It was the last place she had seen Nellie . . . and now she sat whimpering at attention.

"Look," said Jane, "you had the radio on so loud you wouldn't have heard a tank roll in. Did Swanette mention anyone who might be coming out? She had been trying to call a handyman, right? Did she ever get him?"

"No," said Tim. "That's why she was so excited to find the ring of keys. The only reason she wanted him was so he could let us into the outbuildings."

Jane began walking toward the shed and motioned for Tim to come along. She stopped at the doorway.

"I saw those chairs and noticed the box and that crate, then I saw Swanette's shoe right about there," Jane said, pointing, but she did not go in. The police might not have wanted to tape this building off as a crime scene, but she was determined not to disturb the spot any more than necessary. Tim stepped around her and into the shed before she could stop him.

"What's the difference? Both paramedics have been in here. They rolled the stretcher in . . . you and Nellie were both in here. Let's look it over thoroughly."

"We need more light," said Jane.

"That's why you've got me," said Tim. He took a flashlight out of his back pocket and handed it to Jane. She shone the light on the spot where Swanette had lain on the ground. The other boxes and crates, still sealed, were tightly and neatly packed. Jane moved the light back and forth over the floor space carefully.

The wooden shipping crate that Jane had noticed before had letters stenciled on the side. Two slats had been pried off. One lay flat on the ground as if it had been bent back from the box. The other one had been entirely removed.

"Where's that board?" asked Jane.

Tim had gone to his truck and gotten another light, a lantern with a large rectangular base. He stood behind Jane and began imitating her slow steady sweep with his light.

"Is that it?" he asked.

Jane stepped farther into the shed. Tucked in between two boxes, just to the side of where she had found Swanette, was the piece of wood. Jane left it.

"He could have come in behind her. The slat was probably on the floor in front of that crate. He could have picked it up and whacked her with it while she was turning around, which would explain why she was on her side, facing that way," she said. "Maybe he got scared or heard our car coming up the drive and just stashed the board there. You wouldn't notice it if you weren't looking. He might have figured he's coming back . . ." Jane and Tim both glanced over their shoulders when Jane said that. "No . . . he's long gone by now," Jane added. "All the ambulance activity would have covered his getaway."

"Two questions," said Tim. "Probably more to come, but first, why *he*? Why always, always *he*? And second, where did *he or she* come from? If it happened while you were coming up the drive, you would have seen the car. *He or she* couldn't have come from anywhere on foot, there's no place. Which of course begs the question, where, after coming from nowhere, did *he or she* get away to?" Tim turned so he could keep one eye on the door behind them.

"Stay right here," said Jane, "I think I know. And don't touch that board."

She left Tim in the shed and walked farther down the drive to the pole barn, situated directly behind the house. At first glance, the layout of the farm—the house, the barn, and the outbuildings—led one to believe that there was only one way in and out of the property. As you drove down the driveway, the natural place to stop for access to the house was between the sheds on your left and the house on your right. There was a large area used for parking—Jane, Tim, and Swanette had all left their cars there and proceeded into the house through the kitchen door. There was a walkway that wound around to the front door, but the path, carelessly landscaped with a few bushes and flowers, looked like it was seldom used.

Because visitors obviously parked by the kitchen door, Jane hadn't really paid attention to the rest of the driveway, which, she now noted, continued on to the barn located behind the house. Trees in the backyard partially hid the barn from view. If a car had driven all the way down the driveway, not only would Tim not have heard it arrive because of the radio—he likely would not have seen it, either. Even if he had bothered to look out the window where he was working in the back bedroom, his view would likely be of the large trees, which, although on the verge of shedding their leaves, had not yet lost their brilliant fall foliage.

Jane stood at the barn where the driveway seemed to end and, as she had guessed, saw that the gravel continued around the back of the barn. Walking around the structure, she saw the drive go on, narrowing a bit, but it remained drivable, bordering the now-spent cornfield. Jane figured the road was used primarily by farm machinery. Since the cornfields went on as far as she could see, it was safe to assume the service road did as well, and likely was accessible from the other direction, probably from one of these confusing country roads marked with a number, a letter, or known by the name of the farmer who owned the biggest property along the way.

It was a back entrance and exit, easily used by anyone who knew his *or her* way around. In fact, if Jane had her directions right, and she almost always did, this route would be a shortcut if you were coming from the main street that was Herscher's downtown. Anyone familiar with the territory could arrive at Swanette's farm without people in the house seeing a vehicle—coming or going.

Jane tugged on the door to the pole barn, but the padlock held it firmly closed.

"Jane," yelled Tim. "Where are you?"

She called back, gave one more tug on the door, and ran back to the shed.

"Don't leave me here holding a flashlight and take off like that. When that little compact fluorescent goes on over your head, I want in on the idea. The jerk who beaned Swanette, he or she might still be around, yes?"

"Nope," said Jane. "Left by the service road and long gone for sure. Let's check these other buildings. Someone didn't want Swanette or anyone else in them, so let's get busy and find out why."

"Swell idea, Sherlock, but I left my giant padlock cutters in my other trousers. How do you propose we get in?"

"Keys? You said Swanette found keys," said Jane, once again shining the light over the interior space. She held out little hope of finding them, but she didn't want to miss the obvious easy solution to getting into the sheds.

"Don't bother. While you were out surveying the roads, I shined light into every corner of this place. I even broke your rules and got in there on my knees and looked into the nooks and crannies, such as they are. No keys," said Tim. "In fact, that's your proof that someone knocked her out. She left the house with a giant brass ring, must have been five inches in diameter, with a slew of keys. It would be hard to miss. It's not here."

Jane backed out of the shed. She ran over to the other shed and the chicken coop, checking the locks. She had looked at them earlier when searching for Swanette, but hadn't pulled on them to see if they really were locked. Maybe they just looked secure and the doors could be opened? The chicken coop was definitely locked. The second shed had what appeared to be a dummy lock. Jane could see a sturdy padlock was in place, but the latch was not threaded through the loop in such a way that the lock really prevented opening the door. The wood on the door frame was rotting, causing it to sag, and the two parts of the latch just didn't match up enough to get it to work. Whoever wanted to keep others out of the shed was counting on them seeing the padlock and not really trying the door. Jane tugged on the handle. The sagging wood frame did make the door seem fast. She lifted up as she pulled and inched the door open.

The space was larger than the other shed. It was also electrified and Jane switched on the overhead light.

Crude, hand-built shelves lined three walls. Perhaps at one time fertilizer, gardening tools, old clay pots, tangles of hoses occupied these shelves. Jane pictured them lined with Mason jars of various sizes full of nails, screws, and bolts, but now, less practical objects were on display.

"This is how you ought to fix up your garage, Janie," said Tim, always one to give credit where credit is due. "This is some system."

The shelves were crammed with vases, dishes, small lamps, small appliances, primitive farm objects—at least that's what Jane assumed the various large forks and blades were—cast-iron pots and pans. And those were just the things Jane could take in at a glance. There were objects behind objects, so a complete inventory would take some time. At first, Jane couldn't understand what Tim was admiring. As far as she could tell, there was no rhyme or reason to the objects collected on the shelves, in their order, their type, their size, their use . . . then she noticed the placards with numbers. Each item was tagged with at least one number, each shelf was marked with a date.

"These dates go several months back," said Jane. "And there are a few cards here with addresses. Do you think someone was selling this stuff online, then not mailing it out?"

"No," said Tim. "Look at this address card. It's a public storage facility. I recognize the address . . ." Tim said, trailing off, picking up the cards on the shelves, reading them and replacing them. "Listen: 'From locker number 4826/WeStoreIt/K3.' That's a storage rental place in K3 . . . Kankakee. What I think these cards tell us is where the objects came from, not where they were supposed to go."

"I think you're right," said Jane. "'Ada's basement canning locker,'" said Jane, reading off a card in front of two giant blue jars, labeled THE QUEEN in raised glass letters. "I have jars like these."

Jane and Tim strolled the shelves, picking up the cards and reading them. Jane noticed that Tim held on to one of the cards as he walked on, then replaced the card in front of a few items farther down on the shelf.

"No," said Jane. "These ivory glove stretchers . . . that's where that card goes."

"Sorry," said Tim. He stepped back and put the card down, picking up one of the stretchers. "Not ivory, honey. I think this pair is bone, look at the striation here . . . and this pair is Bakelite, I think, or something like it."

Jane picked up the blunt, scissorlike object and stroked its smooth butter-colored surface. She put it back on the shelf and read the card. "'Trunk number 3, A attic.'"

"Got a notepad in your pocket?"

Jane told Tim to copy down as many of the item numbers as he could. Tim could check the numbers against some of the item numbers on the online auction site they'd found where Honest Joe had posted items. Jane would have to settle for a small sampling from the shed. There were hundreds of objects and the overhead lights in this shed would be little help when they completely lost the daylight.

Right now, Jane wanted to close up the house and get back to Kankakee to see how Swanette herself was doing. Just locking the doors, however, didn't feel like enough to secure the property. If someone had been using this farm as a storage facility, a staging place for Internet sales, they had been doing it right under the nose of Swanette's mother-in-law. It was simple enough since the older woman never left the house and surrounded herself with so much stuff that she wouldn't be aware of the controlled chaos in the out-buildings. Swanette wasn't allowed into the house and the other areas were locked up. Who else had access to the property and was likely to use the service road? The nurse who came from town prob-ably knew about both entrances to the property. The handyman who had the keys to the sheds was the likely person to also hold the key to Michael's twin. Wasn't he? So . . . if *whoever* had been doing *whatever whenever,* wouldn't it all be even simpler with no one at all living on the property? Especially at night?

Jane went to her car and fished out her address book from the big leather bag she hauled around with her. Although Tim had been after her to get a BlackBerry or whatever newest incarnation of electronic assistant he was currently touting as a brilliant invention, Jane clung to the beat-up leather book that not only held all of her current information, but had all the pages from her past life, as well. When Jane had worked as a creative director for a Chicago advertising firm, she took on a lot of the setup arrangements for various commercials, finding that she liked supervising the produc-tion details. Paging through the *L*'s she found the company she was looking for—Len's Industrial Lighting—and punched in the numbers.

Len himself, who felt he owed a great deal of his success to Jane's championing him as a lighting designer on several night shoots she supervised, assured Jane that they could handle her emergency. Their main warehouse was located in a south suburb of Chicago, and Len promised he could have a truck on the road in thirty minutes.

Within two hours, before the true blackness that is nightfall in rural America descended, Len would have technicians set up a "night shoot" at Swanette's farm. Jane was certain that two large trucks full of equipment, a trailer, and enough bright lights trained on all the outbuildings and house to film a commercial would protect the goods stored within. Len promised her someone would stay with the equipment for as long as she needed.

"It is the light we shed on the problem, Mrs. Wheel, that aids us in the solution," said Bruce Oh, when Jane called to ask his opinion of the plan.

"It's only a temporary answer, though. I'm not sure how long I can tie up Len's crew," Jane told Tim, when they met in the hospital parking lot. On the way into Kankakee, after phoning Bruce Oh, she had called her dad, hoping Nellie had checked in with him. He told her where to go when they reached the hospital, but had no new information on Swanette's condition.

"Not to mention the fact that lighting up the night sky for the town of Herscher might not be universally appreciated. Sooner not later, a neighboring farm is going to wonder what's wrong with the nocturnal rhythms of their livestock," said Tim.

"Really?" asked Jane. "You think the roosters will crow all night?"

Tim shrugged. "Depends on how much light spills, I guess."

"You're making stuff up, aren't you?" asked Jane, checking the directory next to the elevator for Family Waiting Area Two.

"It's about time you two got here," said Nellie, jumping out of her chair. "I thought you'd be coming right along behind me. They kept asking me questions and I—"

"Is there family? Has someone been called?" asked Jane.

"Christine is here and she had an old number for the niece, but it doesn't work anymore. I think Christine's the one who should call the shots here."

"What shots need to be called?" asked Tim. "Is she—"

"No, Lowry, she isn't dead, but the doctors look pretty serious and asked me a lot of questions before Christine got here and was able to give them information about her medical history and stuff. Hell, I don't know anything except that she always ordered tuna salad on white bread every Friday."

"Okay, then, she's probably Catholic," said Jane. "She was having lunch at the EZ Way back when you couldn't eat meat on Friday. We should probably tell the nurses so they can alert a priest."

"Yeah," said Nellie. "That's a smart idea. Unless she's a Methodist who liked my tuna fish."

Christine walked into the room. Jane marveled at how put together the woman was. Matching sweater and skirt, sensible low-heeled shoes, gray hair wound up in a neat bun. She even wore lipstick. Jane, at least thirty-five years younger, wore beat-up jeans, broken-down leather hiking boots, and imagined her hair sticking straight up out of her head. Even though she kept telling herself that she had escaped her small town and found adventures in the big city of Chicago, every time she returned to Kankakee, she found herself outclassed. Usually it was Tim Lowry who made her feel frowsy . . . this morning it had been Swanette, now it was Christine, too.

"She was mumbling, then she just slipped off," she told them, shaking her own head. "Unconscious, I'm not sure what to do."

"What's to do but wait, right?" asked Nellie.

"Oh, there are forms and things I guess I have to sign," said Christine, sighing. She looked at Jane and must have seen a puzzlement on her face, because she went on as if she were answering a question voiced aloud.

"Because I have power of attorney. When Swanette had a hysterectomy several years ago, Lee was already dead, and she asked John and me to be the executors of her will, and gave us power of attorney since she was going under and all. John's office drew everything up. Her surgery turned out fine, but then she just asked if we'd mind keeping everything current, since she didn't have anyone else. I expect she figures her niece is dead. She dropped off the face of the earth about twenty years ago and Swanette hasn't been able to track her down. She's the only relative and from Lee's side of the family, too.

"Swanette didn't have a soul, except us girls," said Christine. "And John. He tried to be a friend to her, too. I always said John had the gift of being sort of a husband to the girls that didn't have any or had lost theirs. I don't mean I thought . . ." Christine smiled for the first time. "No hanky-panky or anything. I just admired the way he could be a friend to my women friends."

Since Christine talked about her husband in the past tense, Jane assumed she had been widowed. When Nellie asked how he was doing, Jane saw all of the put-together-efficiency of Christine disappear. When she shook her head and shrugged, Jane saw every worried line in her face, every sad shadow emerge.

"Doesn't know me at all," she said. "According to the support group, I'm lucky. At least he likes me. Even flirts with me now and then. Just has no idea that he was married to me for sixty years."

"What exactly did the doctor say about Swanette's condition?" asked Tim.

"Listen to me," said Christine, apologizing. "Poor girl. She slipped off to sleep. A serious concussion and some swelling in her brain, they think. They just won't know anything until she wakes up. I signed the DNR form. It's what she wanted me to do when she had her surgery, so I figured nothing's changed on that."

"I don't want to seem crass here," said Tim, "but are you the heir?"

Christine looked blank for a moment.

"Well, I guess I am," she said. "We went over the charities she'd like some of her things to go to . . . we had to discuss all this when she signed the papers on the independent-living apartment. We joked about it. I'm about six years older than Swanette and I told her we all had to get ourselves some younger friends. Here she is counting on me and I could drop dead in a minute."

"Yup," said Nellie. "I guess that's one good reason to have children."

"Nellie, you are the funniest person I know," said Christine, actually laughing out loud. "I wish mine lived as close as Janie. You are a lucky woman."

"Yup," said Nellie. Only Jane saw her eyebrows rise and the one corner of her mouth go down when she said it.

"I asked because of the sale," said Tim. "I could go ahead with it. At least the preparation and staging of all the stuff. She went over the house with me and there wasn't anything in there she wanted to keep . . . at least nothing in our preliminary walk-through. I don't know about the outer buildings, of course. I'm not sure if—"

Jane cut him off. "This is the least of all of our worries right now, we know that, Christine. But maybe Tim and I should continue working out there and then we can decide if we really hold the sale when all the prepping's done. Swanette signed the contract so we know it's what she wanted, and that way, when she wakes up, it'll be one less thing she has to worry about."

"That sounds fine to me," said Christine. "If you need me to sign off on that, too, I will."

Jane wasn't really sure how she felt about continuing to prep for the sale with Swanette lying unconscious in the hospital, but she had to cut Tim off before he mentioned that the outbuildings contained more items, maybe items that did not belong to Swanette at all. The fewer people in on that bit of news, the better. Jane was already planning to bait a hook for Honest Joe, who very well might be the one storing stolen goods, even some from Ada and Swanette, and then selling them on the Internet. If whoever was behind the Honest Joe name thought that she and Tim were preparing to hold an estate sale, one that included selling their own stolen goods, wouldn't they come out of the woodwork and try to claim their stuff?

On second thought, maybe Jane didn't need much bait. If someone had attacked Swanette in the shed, hadn't the bad guy already come out of the woodwork?

12

"You do know, Bruce, that I am not one to criticize, but I find your partner's methods . . . well . . . haphazard, to say the least," said Claire Oh. "So if Jane Wheel is saying that this estate is in *disarray*, I interpret that as *disaster*. I hardly think a day will be enough time to assess the value of the items."

Detective Oh wanted to believe his wife's concern was simply over the amount of time he had assigned to the task at hand, but he knew better. Even though Oh's wife, Claire, was a dealer in fine antiques, an art historian, a professional appraiser so much higher on the collector food chain than Jane Wheel was or ever aspired to be, Oh found it fascinating that she seemed interested in competing with Jane. Claire was not really worried about the amount of work or the time allotted; she was upset that there was a large farmhouse filled with antiques and Jane Wheel and Tim Lowry had already seen them.

Did it matter that Jane would not covet the same Philadelphia card table that would make Claire's heart beat faster? Bruce Oh had watched Mrs. Wheel in action. She would not caress the wood of an antique game chest; instead she would pull a vintage board game off the shelf, its broken box mended with peeling tape, carefully lift the lid and hold a pair of yellowing Bakelite dice in her hand. She would squirrel away the worn decks of cards with pictures on their backs of a little cartoon man with a loaf of Butternut Bread tucked under his arm, beaming as if she had struck gold. Bruce Oh would not raise this issue now with his wife. He would not tell her that she and Mrs. Wheel valued different objects. He had learned that it was not about who collected what . . . it was about who got there first.

When Mrs. Wheel phoned and presented her plan to catch Honest Joe, he had asked her three questions.

"Are you sure you are laying a trap for an Internet con man?

"Or, Mrs. Wheel, are you attempting to catch someone who is guilty of assault and possibly murder if the farmhouse owner, Swanette, does not awaken?

"Might Claire be of assistance?"

Oh knew that Tim Lowry was perfectly capable of assessing and pricing antiques. But Mrs. Wheel had answered yes to the first two questions and he felt that the best way to help her catch the bad guy, bad guys, or bad persons, this time around, was in a more tangential fashion.

Mrs. Wheel had come up with a perfectly plausible plan. He would simply be on call to aid and assist. What better way to be on call than to stand behind the expertise of his wife, who would arrive at the farm as a master appraiser, arousing no more suspicion than any other antique dealer who might consult with Tim Lowry on a few unusual items. He would simply play the bemused husband, a retired professor who tagged along to browse the library for any valuable first editions.

When he had spoken with Mrs. Wheel last night, despite her concern for her friend whose medical condition was still uncertain, she seemed confident that she would soon confront the scoundrel with whom her brother had been confused. The Herscher post office box, the fact that someone might have had access to photos from a relative's house—Oh was a bit confused about the Nellie-Ada connections since Mrs. Wheel had gone off on several tangents herself when speaking about her mother's secretiveness about Cousin Ada—but it seemed that Mrs. Wheel felt that a photograph of a young James Speller might have been somehow doctored and used for a seller's Internet profile, causing the identity confusion with her brother Michael.

Mrs. Wheel had also managed to tell him a great deal about mysterious pumpkin carving, missing correspondence from Cousin Ada's desk, a caregiver who came and went, and finally, she had mentioned something about rookie baseball cards that she had found at her brother's house.

"I didn't think about them as important before. I mean, I still don't, but you know, you always told me to list everything that made me uncomfortable when I'm working on a case. And even though I know there's a perfectly logical explanation, I keep coming back to them, wondering what they were doing there, all open and unprotected, next to Q's stamps."

That was the last bit of information Mrs. Wheel shared. She said she looked forward to seeing Claire in action since there was more than enough furniture for her and Tim to work on. He could hear in her voice that she was tired. Too tired for any more discussion. She had said she was too tired to eat dinner, too tired to wash her face, too tired to sit down and watch the nightly news with her father. She was heading off to bed.

There was no reason to tell her, as tired as she sounded, about a feature story that had appeared in the *Chicago Tribune* that week.

Oh felt he was safe in assuming that she had missed it in her travels and was too tired to catch up with any newspapers this night.

Claire had pointed out the article to him on the "Con-Men Collectibles." According to the reporters who had contributed to the story, there were several areas of collecting that were vulnerable to fakery. Several patterns of Depression glass were being reproduced by companies who had bought the vintage molds; there was a kind of modern resin that resembled Mrs. Wheel's beloved vintage Bakelite; and old boards were being cobbled together to mimic antique furniture. In times of economic downturn, it seemed, people were more anxious than ever to believe they had found a valuable treasure so the con artists were coming out in full force.

The article also reported that there had been a series of counterfeit baseball cards flooding Internet auction sites. The phony collectibles had been traced to a businessman in California whose identity, pending further investigation, was being kept confidential.

Coincidences happened all of the time. There was no reason to upset Mrs. Wheel, to cause her a sleepless night. Detective Oh, however, was wide awake. After making plans with Claire for what time they would leave for Herscher, Illinois, the next day, he walked into his study and switched on his computer. Detective Oh had never before logged on to an Internet auction site, but how difficult could it be? He loved the game of baseball. With his own wife urging him to take an interest in her career and with his fascination with Mrs. Wheel's attachment to vintage objects of all kinds that she claimed told her stories, maybe it was time for him to start a collection of his own.

Baseball cards, perhaps?

13

Sunday morning. October. A comfortable bed. Coffee percolating. Was Nellie the last person in America to use a percolator? Jane might prefer the taste and jolt of strong drip coffee these days, but when she awakened to her mother's perfectly usable and shiny-like-new chrome pot gurgling out its caffeinated song, she felt happy enough to wiggle her toes and steal one more minute of eyes-closed reverie. In the moments before sitting up, fully awake, could she postpone thoughts of Michael's look-alike and Ada's ghost and the person who attacked Swanette? Nope. Apparently she couldn't. Eyes fully open.

As soon as she slipped on her clothes, Jane fished a notebook out of her purse. She had meant to write it down before she fell asleep. *Head, head oh, dad, crosswor, aitch* . . . that was what she remembered Swanette saying. It was probably meaningless, the unraveling of an injured brain. The most logical interpretation? Oh my head! Swanette had just taken a blow to the side of her skull . . . it seemed only natural that she would moan about her head hurting. But she had been so earnest, so intent on Jane hearing those sounds.

Nellie had already phoned the hospital. She poured Jane's

coffee, slid a plate of toast in front of her, and announced that there was no change in Swanette's condition.

"Still sleeping," said Nellie.

"Who did you talk to?" asked Jane.

"Christine spent the night there. She made a schedule with the other girls and they're going to take turns at the hospital so she won't ever be alone. Zarita's on duty tonight," said Nellie.

While Jane listened to her mother, she knelt down next to Rita, trying to coax her away from Nellie's side. The dog would not be moved.

"Those girls are something," said Don from behind the *Sunday Journal*.

"Don't you think it's odd to call them 'girls'?" asked Jane. "Haven't they earned the right to be called 'women' by now?"

"Oh Janie, they've earned the right to be called anything they want," said Don. "They call themselves 'the office girls.' Seems to me this girls-women thing is more about what you want to call them, not about what they want to be called."

"Did you know that Christine is Swanette's heir? I mean if they don't find her niece?" asked Jane.

"So?" asked Nellie. "Don't go looking for trouble with them girls. They all spent time with John, asking him for legal advice and all. Christine never minded sharing her husband with Swanette."

Jane had just been thinking out loud. She hadn't suspected Christine of a thing.

"Sharing her husband . . ." Jane repeated out loud.

Don set aside the newspaper and added cream to his coffee.

Tim knocked at the kitchen door, then entered quickly before Nellie finished with her, "Who is it, what do you want?"

"What do you say, Tim, *girls* or *women?*" asked Don.

"I stick with *lasses*," said Tim. "Or *Fräuleins* or *mesdames*. I find going Continental keeps you out of trouble."

Jane wasn't sure how long Tim had actually been outside the screen door, but long enough, she was sure, to have gotten the gist of the conversation. He was born with the "jump right in" gene. He helped himself to toast and opened the refrigerator door, searching for jam.

"Here," said Nellie, reaching in from behind him and pulling out strawberry jam and apple butter. "Do you always help yourself in other peoples' houses?"

"Nellie, my lass," said Tim, "you are definitely not other people."

Jane planned to ride out to the farm with Tim where Bruce and Claire Oh would meet them. Don and Nellie were going to the hospital to check on Swanette, and would join them afterward.

"You don't have to get involved in this, Dad," said Jane. "It's your day off."

"I wouldn't miss helping out Swanette for anything," said Don. "She's a good old . . . *Fräulein*. And then we can go into Herscher and check on Ada. Sounds like somebody might be taking advantage of her."

"Besides, how would I get out there to work if your dad didn't drive me?" asked Nellie.

"You're taking me up on my offer?" asked Tim. "I had a feeling you couldn't resist the opportunity to work for T and T sales."

"Oh, I can resist all right, I just want to make sure you don't rob poor Swanette blind." Nellie looked over at Tim in time to see him wince at her words.

"Oh hell, Lowry, I know you wouldn't steal from her. I'm just kidding. Can't you take a joke?" said Nellie. She crossed over to the

stove and mixed leftover scrambled eggs into Rita's food and set it
down for her new best friend.

Jane pinched herself under the table. Nellie just apologized,
in her own way, to Tim for a thoughtless insult. She cooked extra
breakfast for a dog. What was next? Pigs flying and ice-skate rent-
als in hell?

"Before we all go our separate ways this morning," said Jane,
still trying to figure how much she could say while still keeping
Michael out of the question, "I wanted to ask you about Ada and
her brother."

"I told you about them yesterday," said Nellie.

"Yes, but I want to know more about Jim Speller," said Jane,
clearing plates and joining her mother at the sink.

"Dead and good riddance," said Nellie.

"Nellie," said Don.

"I don't give a damn, I can say what I want. He was a bad man.
Mean to the people around him, tormented his folks. Nice enough
to Ada, I guess, which keeps him from being a complete devil, but
he was no good."

"The man's dead," said Don.

"So what?" asked Nellie. "Somebody dies and suddenly everything they did or everything they were is okeydokey? We have
to whisper about them and shake our heads and think the best of
them? That's a crock. Somebody's a son of a bitch in life, death
don't change that. Just makes Jim Speller a dead son of a bitch."

"Tell us what you really think," said Tim.

"Here's something I know about that man. He married some
woman he met a couple towns over and didn't tell Ada. Moved her
into the house and everything. He kept her there on and off for two
years, telling the wife that Ada was crazy and couldn't be told about

her, so the wife had to keep hidden in their part of the house. He made her keep her own place and went there most of the time, but still lived at the house with Ada, too. His wife came and saw us that time, you remember it, Don."

"Yes, but she wasn't a stable woman herself, Nellie. . . ."

"Would you be? She did come to the tavern one day. He had thrown her out. I don't even know how she found out I was related to them. Her name was Martha something. Well, Martha needed money to start living on her own again. She said she was—" Nellie stopped and glared at the ringing telephone.

"Pregnant," she said, finishing her sentence before growling a hello into the receiver.

Jane looked at her dad. "Said she was?"

He shrugged his shoulders.

"We took her at her word. We realized later she could have been lying, Jim Speller could have even put her up to it. He and Ada owned all that land out there, worth a fortune, but he was still a schemer. Always sponging money and coming up with ways to steal a buck. He was the kind of guy who got a kick out of the *taking* more than the money," said Don. He looked over at his wife who was still on the phone.

"You know your mother's a softie. She gave her some money and Martha said she was going back to her place and decide what to do, but just wanted to get far away from him. She said he told her he didn't want a kid and blamed her for getting pregnant on purpose."

"Why did you think she was unstable?" Tim asked.

"Well, she was so upset, I guess, and to tell you the truth, I thought anybody who'd marry that guy must have something wrong with them," said Don. "Probably not fair, but even looking at the guy made you nervous. He had these mean eyes and he'd stare you down." Don gave a kind of shudder. "He gave me the willies."

"If she had a son, maybe he came back here . . ." said Jane.

"I saw Martha around once or twice after we gave her the money," said Don. "She hung out at Lucky's in Bonfield. I was out there for a liquor dealer's meeting when I saw her in the parking lot. She was getting into her car when I was parking. I asked Lucky what he knew about her. He said she came in once in a while, but he never saw or heard about any kid. And she turned her head away when she saw me, that's for sure. Ashamed of lying, I figured."

Nellie's phone conversation was almost all one-sided. She nodded several times, muttered yes twice. Before hanging up, she said, "We're on our way."

"Swanette's not doing so well. Christine said one of the doctors told her something looks worse than last night. I don't know what, but she's upset."

"Should we go with you to the hospital?" asked Jane.

"No. Christine said just Dad and me. They don't want a mob up there. But she said you kids should just keep working out at the farm. She said she was sure her husband would agree with her that it was the right thing to do. Christine wants it cleaned out. Whether Swanette wakes up or not, it's got to be done."

Nellie leaned over and gave Rita a strong pat and looked into the dog's eyes. She seemed on the verge of saying something important, but then, thinking better of it, just shook her head. Within a few minutes, she and Don were on their way to the hospital.

Jane grabbed her bag, locked up the house, and she and Rita climbed into Tim's truck. She had made both Don and Nellie promise that they would call her cell the minute they had any news from the hospital. She took out her phone, just to make sure she had a signal, and was surprised to see that she had missed a call yesterday.

"You should set that thing on the loudest ring plus vibration. And you should make a rule to check it regularly. What if it were Charley or Nick? You never hear it," said Tim. "That's why I encourage Nick to keep changing your ring tone . . . to keep you on your—"

Jane held up her hand to shush him as she dialed up voice mail.

"Janie, it's Swanette. I went out to the shed. There is so much stuff here. I'm not sure where it all came from. Books and collectibles. There could be jewelry and coins, stuff that she wouldn't . . ." That was all.

Jane pushed 9 to save the message, then checked the time it was recorded. Swanette called while Jane was in the car with Nellie, returning to the farm from Ada's house. Jane's phone was probably buried in her bag at the time. She and Nellie were yelling at each other. Or maybe the call came when she had run into the minimart to buy the bottled water at the gas station. If she had heard the phone, taken the call, would she have suspected something was wrong? Would she have cursed her cell phone for dropping the call or would she have been worried enough to call the police? An ambulance? No, of course not. If someone cried emergency at every dropped call, the sirens would never stop. But maybe she would have called Tim. He could have run out and found Swanette and gotten help. How much time did they lose? Jane turned into Swanette's driveway five minutes after the gas station. Whoever hurt Swanette might have still been in the shed, then waited until Jane and Nellie went into the house before leaving by the service road behind the barn. Jane talked to Tim and looked around for what? Five minutes?

Ten minutes? Then she went out to the shed and found Swanette unconscious. Would that fifteen or twenty minutes have made a difference?

Jane realized while she was calculating the minutes that she had missed with Swanette yesterday, Tim had been talking. She had caught a few words about furniture styles and vintages but it took her a minute to get on track with his train of thought.

"... if it was from the early part of her marriage. But then you got those handmade footstools. They're neat, they really are, but the primitive stuff doesn't gel with any of the Victorian froufrou. It's a little like she was keeping shop or like that one sale, remember? When the woman told us she was the caretaker of all the family jewels, except instead of jewels, she had her aunt's clothes from the twenties and thirties, her mother's rosaries and medals, her grandmother's Victoriana, her dad's tools, her brother's comic books, her uncle's World War II memorabilia ..."

"Are you talking about Swanette's mother-in-law?"

"Who else would I be talking about? You know, in the living room, where she held court, judging from the bed set up there and TV and all, she liked the more ornate Victorian stuff. Those big chairs and the ottomans? The velvet pouf with the tassels? Also, there's a trunk full of linens under that picture window that appears to have been hers, maybe handed down from her mother. But then there's a cheap rattan trunk full of T.J. Maxx irregulars. There's a lot of silver, too. All of a vintage that makes sense given her age. Then there's a boatload of cheap silverplate. Then there's the bedroom that Swanette says her niece lived in and that's got all the vintage teenage stuff, like it's been frozen in time ..."

"We come in from the outside and see it frozen in time, but

people who are living in it? It's not frozen, it's a part of their every-day life, it's what—" said Jane, breaking off.

"What?"

"The house is just what Swanette's mother-in-law lived with. Within. It was her life and it was in flux, not frozen. If her nurse or the handyman or whoever was in the house, moving stuff around, rearranging, bringing stuff in and taking stuff out . . ."

"What are you talking about?"

"If I wanted to steal stuff and sell it, just to get along, you know, like a part-time job? What better steady income than finding an old lady like Swanette's mother-in-law, who is surrounded with stuff? But instead of scaring her off and robbing her, why not let her belongings provide a steady stream of product for your sales? Sell her antique linens, and just bring in a bunch of cheap stuff to fill the trunk, so nothing is ever really missing?

"I mean, it wouldn't work for anyone who was with it, but it would work with someone who was already nutty. I mean, Swanette's mother-in-law was an invalid who wouldn't even let Swanette in the house. No one who had her best interest at heart could get close enough to keep an eye on her valuables. And Ada . . . Ada's library?" said Jane. "If books were missing outright, Ada might notice, even with her bad eyes. But if one or two disappear and the spaces are filled in with fakes? Maybe it's only a hundred or two hundred dollars a book, but still, with a whole library to pillage?"

"Could be a living," said Tim, nodding his head. "A modest living."

Tim turned into Swanette's drive and whistled at the equipment set up on the grounds. "Are we back in Hollywood? Looks like they're shooting a major movie here," said Tim.

"Yeah, Len's a good guy. Until he needs this stuff for a paying job at the end of the week, he's willing to leave us the lights and the trailer. Since the barn has electricity, they were able to rig it all up without an extra generator. The tech pried open the door to get in and connect everything."

The technician who had set up the lighting was presumably still sleeping in the trailer parked near the road. Jane reminded Tim to go out and introduce himself and warn him that other people would be out and about on the property as the day wore on.

"And I have to remember to tell everyone else about him. If Nellie gets here and sees a stranger, she might try to whack him with a board herself, so let's make sure everybody knows who's around. Len said he was sending one of his best guys . . . Dave, I think he said his name was. I assume he'll be here while the equipment's here for the next day or two," said Jane.

Tim eased the truck into the parking area between the kitchen door and the row of sheds. Already parked closest to the house was a Mercedes, the color of coffee with an indulgent dose of cream.

"Whose car? Pretty fancy for a lighting guy," said Tim. "Hey, you know whose car it looks like . . . ?"

"I meant to tell you before we got here," said Jane. "I know you don't really need any help, but just go along . . ."

"Almost right on time," said Claire Oh, appearing at Jane's side as soon as she and Tim got out of the car. How did she manage that? Tall and impeccable, Claire had a talent for showing up. She didn't arrive, she materialized . . . usually in the very spot you thought you wanted to be. If there was a glass case at a flea market and you just knew it held a silver bracelet, obscured by tarnish, with a designer signature undetected by the seller, Claire Oh would be the buyer in front of you, boxing you out of your closer look and pointing to the very item herself, asking if she could see that dirty little piece in the corner. Openmouthed, you'd watch her lay it across her elegant wrist with a scornful look, and then ask for a better price since she'd really have to clean it up before she let her niece have it for her dress-up box. Before the transaction was finished, Claire would have the seller convinced she was lucky to have gotten rid of the thing, and Claire would be pocketing a delicate multistrand bracelet that would clean up to reveal two Tiffany signatures and, in a week, appear in Claire's own locked case, wearing a two-hundred-dollar price tag.

Jane thought she heard Tim groan at the sight of Claire, but tried to convince herself that she imagined it. It's not that Tim wasn't fond of her. He admired her, actually, or at least claimed that he did and encouraged Jane to take a page from her book. *Think upscale, like Claire Oh*, he often told Jane when he caught her running her fingers through a tin of buttons, or paging through a 1930s high school yearbook, reading the signatures of graduating seniors. So why wouldn't he be pleased to see her here at Swanette's when they had so much stuff to sift through, so many pieces of furniture to touch and turn upside down and scratch their thumbnails against? So many pieces of costume jewelry to study through a jeweler's loupe, searching for that elusive hallmark, that coveted signature? Claire would be an enormous help, wouldn't she?

"Darling, Tim, so good to see you again," Claire said, offering him a perfectly made-up cheek. "Jane told me you've got your hands full."

"Did she?" asked Tim, glaring at Jane.

"I thought perhaps while Detective Oh and I puttered around and went into town to talk to Ada, you and Claire might get a good start on—"

Jane stopped and looked at the two of them. Claire and Tim were giving each other such frozen smiles that Jane could picture their lips and teeth cracking and falling from their faces. This was ridiculous. There was a full house and at least three outbuildings and a huge barn filled with stuff. Surely there was enough to go around. About to say just that, she opened her mouth, but before she could begin, Tim turned his frozen grin on her.

"So generous of you, Jane, to think of me and realize I'd need some help. Let's see . . . we give me first refusal on everything since it's my sale, and then, it would have been you next, of course, because you're my partner and you found the deal for me, but since Claire drove all the way down here, let's give her second dibs, okay? Then you? Or maybe Nellie, then you? That seems only fair."

Jane nodded, conscious now of her own frozen smile. She probably deserved that. But Claire wouldn't want the same stuff as Jane, would she? If there was a stash of old wooden knitting needles sitting in a blue jar or a tin of buttons or a bag of old quilting scraps or rolled balls of fabric for rug making? Claire Oh wouldn't care about that junk, would she? Tim knew that, but he also knew where to aim the arrow—it was the whole first-look thing. Tim didn't want Claire to see anything first, even if she didn't want another set of Spode for one her clients. That's why Tim resented her presence. In the long run, he knew it would help to have her here. It was just hard to share that first look. Jane knew that Claire wouldn't want any old typewriter-ribbon tins, but having them tossed aside by her first, into a pile of stuff that Claire would mentally label Jane's junk, somehow took a little of the shimmer off the discovery, didn't it?

"Mrs. Wheel?" Jane turned around, so happy to see Detective Oh that she had to fight an urge to reach out to him. Although she had taken his arm on occasion and he had patted her shoulder once or twice, their relationship was one of intellectual oneness mixed with what felt like awkward physical adolescence. Jane was drawn to his voice, his face, his eyes. She often wanted to reach out and touch one of his vintage ties, which she knew he consented to wear only to please Claire, but Jane held herself back, fearing that even rubbing fabric worn close to his heart would be too intimate a gesture.

"Shall we all begin inside?" he asked, and led the way to the porch and kitchen door.

After the initial glaring period, Tim and Claire lost themselves inside the farmhouse, Tim pointing out some of the better pieces he had seen the day before. Claire had taken out a leather folder filled with custom-engraved index cards and began writing notes, placing them on tables, chairs, and small chests. Jane, from the kitchen, could see her gliding from piece to piece as Tim pointed out spindles and pulled out drawers to illustrate his conjectures.

Bruce Oh stood at the kitchen sink, looking out of the window toward the barn.

"The service road goes back around behind . . . there?" he asked, pointing.

Jane nodded.

He turned to his left and moved to the other window, which faced the driveway where the cars were parked and the two sheds and the chicken coop were lined up, each around twenty-five to thirty feet apart from each other.

"If Mrs. Swanette was struck in that shed," he said pointing, "you are correct that it would have been easily accessed from that road. Easy to get to the buildings, easy to leave without being seen."

"Tim had music on and it was so loud, he wouldn't have heard a vehicle drive onto the property—even here at the kitchen door, let alone back there behind the barn. And if Tim wouldn't have heard it, Swanette's mother-in-law, living in that interior room with the television on, wouldn't have heard the comings and goings out on the property. These windows are warped and haven't been opened in years. Tim and I both tried them yesterday. Whoever was doing whatever with all of that stuff in the barn and the buildings would have been able to come and go whenever they pleased," said Jane.

"Let's go look at the building where your friend might have been attacked," said Oh.

Jane wanted to correct him and say that there was no "might have been" about this, but she knew that in his own careful way, Oh was right. Until they found proof that someone was in the shed with her, or until Swanette woke up to tell them what happened, they had no proof that she didn't trip or fall ill.

The morning light illuminated the shed much more brightly than the late afternoon light did yesterday when Jane found Swanette unconscious. She got down on her knees to show Oh exactly where Swanette was lying and where Jane had seen the slat from the crate. It was still there, between two other tall sealed boxes. Oh nodded at Jane's observation that it might have been used as a weapon, but he didn't remove it.

"Tim said she had a large ring of keys . . . and we couldn't find it anywhere," said Jane. She also told him about the phone message from Swanette that she had just heard. "I haven't seen any coins and she specifically said coins and jewelry, but I haven't had time to really look at anything."

"Presence rather than absence makes for better proof, Mrs. Wheel," said Oh. "Although it seems logical that her assailant would have taken the keys and anything valuable that she had stumbled upon, having something gone or missing is simply not as definitive as finding something here that proves that someone else was with her in the shed and was responsible for her injury."

Jane reached into her jacket pocket and pulled out the pumpkin seeds that she had removed from Swanette's arm.

"Not only is this something concrete that proves the presence of another, I think it connects everything to Ada's. That's where the pumpkins were, but also, that's where the Internet auction complaints were—on the desk—and where the books are missing from the study," said Jane.

"And where the ghost lives," said Oh.

Jane nodded.

"I believe that I would like to visit the ghost," said Oh. "Tim Lowry, my wife, and your mother will be inspecting everything here. The three of them together are almost as good with the concrete objects as you, Mrs. Wheel. I find that my strength usually lies in the invisible. May we visit the ghost?"

Jane nodded and carefully rewrapped the pumpkin seeds and put them back into her jacket pocket. They had become as much of a good-luck talisman as one of the buckeyes from Cobb Park. Jane knew if she found out who had finished carving that pumpkin, she would find the person who was using her brother's photograph to run crooked auctions and who was storing his phony or stolen goods right here on Swanette's farm. Honest Joe was going to turn out to be Michael's doppelgänger who was going to turn out to be stealing from Cousin Ada and who was going to be running his operation from Swanette's barn and a Herscher post office box.

Oh said he would get the car keys from Claire and drive them into town. Jane took her time leaving the shed, since she held on to the belief that if she just looked hard enough, she would find that *presence* of proof that Oh said they needed. This particular outbuilding contained only packed boxes and crates. Jane realized that there was a definite progression in these buildings. This shed contained packed crates and boxes. The next building over had objects all unpacked and arrayed on shelves. In the barn, where she had just stolen a glance now that it was opened by Dave, the lighting tech, objects were not only displayed, they were tagged and coded with dates and numbers. If she were to number these buildings one through three, the sequence would go from stored goods, to examined objects, to sale items. So this was the building where they received objects and sorted them for sale? Jane picked a cardboard box off the shelf that was nearest to her and stripped the thick tape from it. On top of the box was written "Kitchen" with a date underneath, about five and half years earlier. Jane unwrapped the newspaper from a stainless steel ladle. Nothing special about it. Jane set the box back on the shelf and pulled another one close and saw that the handwriting on this box was totally different. In broad black marker was written "Cottage Linens." Jane opened up the carton to find pale blue sheets and pillowcases, clean and decent, but again, nothing special. These were, indeed, the slightly worn sheets you might earmark for your summer cottage.

If Swanette had really seen valuable goods in the house, her attacker had removed any of them that had been stored in the shed. And Oh had suggested they needed to find something instead of speculating about what had vanished. Jane pulled and turned some of the boxes on the shelves. Most were marked—"Living Room," "Kit's bedroom," "Jillian's Office." Who were those people? Kit and Jillian? On the carton marked "Jillian's Office," Jane saw an address and underneath was printed, "For Storage."

When people moved and packed up their goods, they often

labeled the boxes by room. That was the logical way to know where everything should be put when they arrived at their new place.

Okay. What was unusual in this shed about all these packed cartons? The boxes were so random. There were no two boxes that had the same handwriting, the same type of marker. One box came from a self-moving company, another from a private moving company. There were boxes that had hauled bananas to grocery stores and cartons that had held twelve bottles of wine. Some of the boxes had advertising on the side and no two were the same. Why did that seem so odd? Jane thought about all the times she had moved in college and afterward into her first series of apartments. How had she packed her stuff? Even if she did travel lighter in those days, there were books and records and clothes. Yes, fewer McCoy flowerpots and vintage typewriters, but still objects needing to be packed.

Like everyone else she knew, Jane had gone into the grocery store and asked for boxes. Clerks usually sent her to the produce department where she got four boxes freshly unpacked of broccoli or green beans that had just arrived. She remembered that the produce guys told her that they usually broke down the boxes immediately, so she was lucky that she had just come in after a delivery and was able to grab the broccoli group.

That was what seemed unusual. Swanette said that she believed her mother-in-law was the "keeper of the stuff" for her family; that she had all of the handed-down memorabilia and objects that her family had left behind when they passed on. Swanette told Jane that was what had filled these outbuildings. Those treasure boxes were what prompted the heavily padlocked doors. Looking over all these cartons, Jane agreed that they were packed as if they were being put away for a while. In fact, this shed could be anyone's storage locker containing the extra stuff that hadn't been unpacked during the initial stages of the move, except for the fact that each box seemed to belong to a different person or persons. Jane looked at Kit's box and Jillian's box. Totally different handwriting and markers. One box came from a Tulsa supermarket and the other was a purchased U-Haul medium-sized carton.

"Kit and Jillian don't even know each other," Jane said when Oh came back with the car keys.

Oh looked at the shelf to which she pointed.

"Interesting, Mrs. Wheel," said Oh. He scanned the shelves she had been studying. "Although . . . perhaps they just marked their own boxes with their own markers?"

"And purchased separate rolls of tape?" said Jane, pointing to the clear tape on one, and tan strapping tape used on the other. "Nope. These boxes are definitely one-offs. It's as if someone took one carton off every moving van rolling its separate way down the highway."

"Interesting," repeated Oh. "Shall we visit the ghost now?"

14

Jane tried to describe Ada in the precise manner she knew Detective Oh appreciated. She told him she dressed in black, maintained an erect posture, hadn't had a haircut in a long time, if ever, and tilted her head to the right when she listened to a question.

"Does she look directly at you when she speaks or does she seem to look into the distance?" asked Oh.

That was a new one.

"Actually," Jane said, "she did seem to be looking over my shoulder, although I'm sure she doesn't see or hear well, so that just may be a kind of mannerism that developed because of her limitations."

"Yes, that's true," said Oh. "However, when one has difficulty hearing, I find that one looks harder at the speaker. Even those who don't read lips seem to concentrate on a speaker's face especially hard when they are trying to hear. If Cousin Ada's sight is also impaired, that might explain her lack of focus, but . . ."

Jane waited for Oh to finish his thought, but instead, he began a story.

"When Claire and I were first married, we took a trip to Canada and attended a theater festival where we watched one or two plays each day. Shakespeare, mostly. It was a trip that Claire thought would be good for us. She could go off and visit galleries and antique dealers when we weren't sitting in an audience, and I would be kept busy with lectures and classes between the performances. She was correct . . . it was a most enjoyable vacation. I learned a great deal about stagecraft as well as Shakespeare's plays. A lighting designer spoke to our group one day and he announced that all lighting design came down to one tenet. 'My job,' he said, 'is to light the actors well enough so the audience can hear them.' Of course, someone in the audience who heard but did not listen shouted out, correcting the speaker that he must have meant to say 'see them not hear them.'

"The designer smiled and shook his head and said that he had spoken correctly. Lighting on stage allows audience members to hear the actors as well as see them. And the hearing is much more difficult if the lighting is not right." Detective Oh nodded. "That stuck with me, Mrs. Wheel. I see light now as the key to hearing as well as to seeing."

Oh had driven into the town by following the service road behind the barn, all along the now-spent fields, and turned onto the county road, taking a good minute, minute and a half, off the already short trip to Herscher's main street from Swanette's farm. Oh had driven conservatively, though. Jane was certain, with a little more speed, at least two more minutes could be shaved off the trip. Jane had directed him to park across from the diner, in front of Ada's house.

Jane was looking up at the gabled structure where her second cousin had spent her isolated life. The house seemed to give off darkness even now in the bright morning light, and she waited for a moment before speaking, hoping Oh's story would make enough sense to her that she wouldn't have to break down and ask him what the hell he was talking about.

Waiting worked. The house, Jane thought, if only its outlines were rendered with slightly more curve and slant and bend, would be a dead ringer for a cartoon Halloween illustration. Jane realized she was tilting her own head, staring at the house while she had listened to Oh. And now, as clearly as if she were next to her in the car, Jane heard Ada's voice admonishing her to turn off the light, that it was unnecessary in the house.

"Ada is looking at someone else, listening to someone else. Is that what you mean?" asked Jane. "Do you mean she's looking into a kind of light so she can see? Or hear?"

"If someone tells you that they live with a ghost, Mrs. Wheel, it's always best to believe them."

"I believe that Ada thinks her brother is taking care of her," said Jane. "For her, Brother James is quite real."

"I believe in ghosts, Mrs. Wheel," said Oh, opening his door and stepping out of the car. "Have I ever told you that before?"

Jane didn't answer.

"And I believe if Ada is listening for others, certainly others are listening in this house. Shall we go in and give them something to listen to? To think about?"

Just as she had watched her mother do yesterday, Jane knocked loudly, then opened the door, calling out to Ada as they entered. Jane pointed out the vintage garlands of black cats in the dining room to Oh.

"Ada's got a small fortune in vintage Halloween decorations," said Jane.

"Are you here to steal them?"

Jane and Oh both turned around.

A small sturdy woman, dressed in blue jeans, a plaid flannel shirt, with her brown hair pulled into a high ponytail, stood with arms crossed, waiting for an answer.

"I'm Jane, Nellie's daughter. Nellie is Ada's cousin and we were here yesterday. . . ."

"Aha, so it was real. Ada told me her family had been out to see her and carve pumpkins, but I just thought she might be dreaming it all up. I'm Linda Weller. I live out in Limestone down the road, but I come in once a week to check on a few people around here. I'm a kind of visiting nurse."

"Do you work with someone else? A partner? I met a woman yesterday when I was here who says she checks in regularly . . ." said Jane.

"Nope. I work alone, strictly volunteer for some of the old-timers around here. I grew up down the road and I remember coming here every Halloween, and my older cousins remember this place for all kinds of holiday stuff. Hayrides and Christmas caroling and stuff, but for me, this was the Halloween House!"

"I'm really confused," said Jane, adding to herself, *and a little worried*. "A woman came into the study while I was admiring the books and acted like she was a regular visitor, and I mentioned her to Ada who said no one came to see her, she didn't need a nurse."

"That's right. And when she comes downstairs in a minute, I stop being the nurse. I don't know who you met here yesterday, maybe one of the neighbors. But today, I'm Linda, here to buy some pumpkins. Some weekends, I stop in to see if she's got jam for sale or salad greens. In the winter, I ask if I can shovel snow or help out for a dollar or two. She just thinks I'm a hobo or something," Linda said, laughing. "One time, she actually made me cart out ashes from the fireplace, then gave me a silver dollar for my trouble," said Linda. "Told me to go buy myself a meal at Edna's Diner."

"It seems you have found the cleverest way to be kind," said Oh, extending his hand and introducing himself as Jane's friend Bruce.

"Look, I don't need to monitor her blood pressure or run labs on her. She wouldn't take any medicine anyway. She'd just cook up some of those herbs out back. I just feel it's my duty, you know. As a neighbor. And other people do for her, too, because the walk's almost always shoveled before I get here and her groceries are delivered. I can see she's well nourished and seems healthy as a horse."

"Who does she say takes care of her?" asked Oh.

"Her dead brother, of course," said Linda. "You must know she has a ghost living here with her."

"Does she hear and see well enough to live here alone?" asked Jane.

"If somebody gave her a battery of tests, I think the official answer would be no. But she gets by. Like I say, she's got someone bringing her food. Edna's even given her free run of the diner kitchen if she's hungry. Every once in a while I get by with bartering something. Like, I'll bring in a bushel of apples I'll say I picked and could she give me some mint from her garden or something. She figures I stole some apples and she takes them and I watch her bend over and pick that mint and she doesn't ever moan or groan. Heck, I can't even tie my shoe without thinking I broke something. And she hears more than you think she does. Sometimes I think she just likes being the spooky old lady in the haunted house . . . you know . . . like she's just acting in a play or something."

They heard Ada descending the stairs so they all came out of the dining room so she could see them head-on and not be startled.

"I'm here to buy a pumpkin," said Linda, loudly.

"Of course you are," said Ada. She came close to the three, patting Jane's cheek firmly. "Nellie's girl, Jane," she said.

"Yes," said Jane, "and this is my friend Bruce."

Ada nodded and motioned for them to follow her into the kitchen.

The long table was covered in old newspaper and, as it was yesterday, laden with several pumpkins carved in various stages of expression. *There are more pumpkins today*, Jane thought. She noted three additions at the far end whose mouths were all finished with snaggle-toothed frowns, but with no eyes, making their expressions all the more grim. *They really don't like what they can't see*, thought Jane. Several knives lay on the table, along with a small keyhole saw and several long scoops and instruments with curved blades. Jane spotted an entire set of Bakelite-handled wood-carving tools in a leather pouch that was unrolled next to a pumpkin with a particularly menacing grin.

Ada did not stop at the table, but instead walked through the kitchen, past the deep farmhouse sink and the gigantic butcher block, so used and worn that its wood top undulated like rolling hills. A large platter was balanced on this wide oak piece of topography and on it were heaped small mounds of roasted pumpkin seeds glistening with salt. Ada pointed to it as she passed and all three of them obediently took small handfuls and popped them into their mouths. Continuing through the back porch where a tangle of rubber boots looked as if it had been planted as a single boot a hundred years ago and had since grown roots and branches of work shoes and Wellingtons, Jane, Oh, and Linda Weller followed Ada, a stately, if sinister, mother duck leading them into the backyard.

Although Jane had been awed by the vintage Halloween displays inside the house she had not anticipated the jaw-dropping effect of Ada's backyard.

"Cut or solid?" asked Ada.

"One of each, maybe," said Linda, walking toward the rows of picnic tables and benches where more than a hundred pumpkins were carved and displayed. Eight tables were lined up with their sixteen benches forming rows in front of them. Every available surface was covered with carved pumpkins. They grinned and frowned, leered and ogled. Some looked as if they had a million questions to ask and more than a few looked as if they wanted to provide the answers. One of the picnic tables had large bottle and birdhouse gourds carved with leaf and geometric shapes interspersed with the pumpkins, but it was the jack-o'-lanterns that were the stars.

"Halloween's a week away, yes?" asked Oh. "Will these creations last?"

Linda Weller may have been right about Ada's hearing being somewhat selective because, despite her back being to Oh, she heard his quiet question and turned to face him. "These are today's pumpkins. For sale if people want them to burn tonight or for a party. Doesn't matter if they last until next week, since they can come and buy more all week. These are just for the early birds," said Ada, "the people who like scary nights."

Her usually solemn face cracked into a sly, guarded smile. "Some folk around here celebrate Halloween more than one night."

"She looks exactly like my mother," said Jane softly.

"Speak up, Nellie's girl," said Ada.

"You look like Nellie," said Jane. "You look like Mom."

Ada turned back to the pumpkins.

"Phone's been ringing. I don't answer it, but it's people wanting their jack-o'-lanterns for their parties and such. I know it when the phone starts ringing when the leaves are falling. So pick while you got a selection."

Linda Weller asked Ada if she could help her get one down from the pile of uncarved pumpkins on the other side of the yard. Jane started to go over to assist Linda, but Bruce Oh shook his head and put his fingers to his lips.

"This is Ms. Weller's method for examining your cousin," said Oh, whispering.

How old was the woman? Seventies? Eighties? Her face was weathered and her long dark clothes suggested an old crone, but Jane watched her actually hoist a pumpkin from the top of a small mountain without a wince or groan. Linda Weller was right. Ada did not seem to suffer from any age-related aches or arthritis pains. She also followed Linda's directions as she pointed here and there, asking to see that "tall one" or the "round fat guy" on the other side. So Ada wasn't blind . . . at least she could see well enough out here in the bright October light. Maybe her visual limitations were exacerbated by the dim gloom of the house's interior as well as the dark-tinted lenses she wore. And she heard Jane's comment that was very nearly whispered. Maybe Oh's explanation of light helping one to hear was true for Ada.

"Who do you employ to carve these many pumpkins?" asked Bruce Oh.

"Anybody who wants to come and help with the carving is welcome," said Ada. "Ma always said to leave the doors open during harvesttime." Ada turned toward Oh, but included Jane in her look. "But it's a family business," she added. "Most are done by the family."

"So you have family members who come to help you?" said Oh. "That is excellent teamwork."

"My cousin Nellie and her girl came to me yesterday," said Ada. She nodded then caught herself. "You came to me yesterday," she said, looking at Jane.

"That's right," said Jane. "Mom and I came to visit you. Mom carved a pumpkin and I got to see your beautiful house."

"You like old houses?" asked Ada.

"Very much," said Jane. "So does my friend."

Jane had planned to ask if she could show Detective Oh the study. She wanted another opportunity to look around for any more papers that tied this house to Honest Joe's auction site. The key to that particular puzzle had been in front of her on the desk just yesterday.

Ada waved her hand and Jane took the gesture to mean she could show Oh the house. This time when she went into the library, she would not only search the desk more thoroughly, she would pay special attention to the bookshelves to determine all the actual books that were missing. She could look up those titles and see what they were worth and, as she—

"I am a collector of books, Cousin Ada," said Oh, "and I would love to visit your library. Mrs. Wheel tells me it is most impressive."

"You two go on in. This one"—she nodded her head at Linda—"takes her time deciding. Makes me set up a dozen before she makes up her mind."

Walking back through the kitchen, Jane stopped Oh.

"Did you notice that before?" she asked.

A wooden pie safe stood against one wall. Its punched tin panels were original, Jane was sure, even looking at it from across the room. On top of it sat a large pumpkin . . . the biggest one by far in the room. Only partially carved, it had eyes, both with half-moon pupils carefully cut, a conventional triangle nose, and half of a large leering grin. The tableau of pumpkin on top of cabinet was not so arresting because of the partially finished face, but because a large butcher knife stuck out of the mouth. One might have guessed that the person carving it had been interrupted and simply put it up out of easy reach so he or she could come back and finish the job. The knife, however, was not placed into the pumpkin's flesh from the outside. The handle was inside of the large mouth, the blade sticking out dangerously—as if the pumpkin were being carved from the inside out.

Jane thought she saw Oh shudder, but she knew she might be projecting her own shivers. She had never seen a creepier Halloween display.

Her cell phone rang then, and she fumbled for it in her pocket. Usually annoyed at the interruption of a mobile phone, she realized that this time she welcomed the distraction. She pointed out the door to the library and told Oh she would follow. Oh touched one ear briefly and Jane nodded. It was his reminder that there were ghosts listening to them. She would plan carefully what she wanted them to hear.

Bruce Oh nodded to himself once inside the wood-paneled library. It was every bit as majestic as Jane Wheel had described. Clearly, the person who had arranged this space, used it for private study, for work and contemplation, had revered reading and writing. The inkwells on the desk, the pearl-handled magnifier on the dictionary stand . . . each object was the most exquisite one for its job. Those qualities of precision and beautiful design were what Oh admired about the antiques his wife bought and sold and the objects pointed out to him by Mrs. Wheel. *If we only possessed the correct tools and the most perfect*, he thought, *we would require so few things.*

The detective took out his notepad and began jotting down the titles that he could see were written on the sham paper covers. *Six, maybe seven, books*, he thought, although without climbing up the curved library stairs parked by the far end of the cases, he couldn't be sure about the highest shelves.

Oh heard Jane come into the room, but did not immediately turn away from the bookcase. He was counting books, trying to figure out if there was any type of pattern to the placement of the substitute paper books. Perhaps he should move the ladder into position and check the uppermost rows.

"Would your cousin mind, Mrs. Wheel, if I climbed up and—" Oh stopped when he heard a sharp intake of breath that did not sound at all like Mrs. Wheel. Turning to the doorway, preparing to introduce himself as the curious friend who had innocently wandered in to admire the book collection, he automatically slipped his notebook and pencil into his pocket.

No one was there.

Oh stood still, waiting to see if the dim light was playing tricks on him and a person actually did stand in the shadows on either side of the door. Willing his eyes to readjust to the dimness, he could see no one in the room other than himself. He turned slowly around, looking for the standard comic device of a pair of shoes at the bottom of the heavy drapes to indicate someone hiding behind them, but the drapes hung straight, admitting no light from the window and revealing no hidden visitors.

Oh continued turning in his slow circle until he was back gazing at the bookcases, his back to the door, the position he had been in when he had first heard what he knew was the sound of foot-steps, what he was positive was a breathing being behind him.

He turned around again slowly. This time, Mrs. Wheel stood in the doorway. He knew, hearing her light step, hearing her soft breathing, that she was not the person who had been in the room with him only moments ago. How had he even believed for a moment that the heavy step and the far from delicate inhalation and exhalation had belonged to his dear friend and partner? No, his visitor had been the opposite of Mrs. Wheel. He . . . or she . . . had been a larger and more formidable presence, the ghost who had lumbered in to surprise him at his task. Detective Oh wanted very much to meet this ghost, and felt certain he would, but the confrontation would have to wait.

Mrs. Wheel, here and now and very much alive, needed him.

Oh tried to remember if he had ever seen Mrs. Wheel cry. He knew she had closed herself up in her car and wept after a friend's funeral. He had witnessed that from a distance. He remembered being impressed with the immensity of her emotion, matched by her need to express it privately. Had she ever openly cried in front of him? He couldn't recall a time.

It looked as if she were wiping away tears now, though, as she stood in the library doorway.

"Swanette died," said Jane, loudly and deliberately. It was as if she were still speaking in the voice she used for Ada. "A few minutes ago."

"Shall we go to the hospital?" asked Oh, stepping away from the library steps he had been about to test.

Jane shook her head.

"Mom and Dad are with Christine. That's her best friend who has power of attorney. My dad said she stayed groggy for a while last night, in and out of consciousness. The doctor said if she woke up and stayed awake, she'd . . . I guess she talked to Christine who was by her side all night. But she didn't make sense and drifted off and lapsed into a coma. 'Brain activity ceased,' they said, and"— Jane's voice caught—"then I guess they just unhooked everything and let her slip away."

"Have you called Mr. Lowry?"

"No need. We'll tell him when we go back there. Christine told my folks that we should keep on doing what we're doing since now the farm would have to be sold. Dad said Christine is overwhelmed with all of the responsibility. As he put it, Christine isn't any spring chicken herself and her husband is incapacitated. He was a pretty important lawyer in this county, so she knows people to advise her, but still . . . it's a lot on her shoulders," said Jane.

"And the grief makes everything weigh so much more," said Oh. "It will balance . . . the tasks ahead of her will help manage her sadness . . . but right now, the weight is crushing."

"I think we should talk to the police. Even if they didn't believe me before, they'll have to pay attention to murder. That board in the shed . . . it would have fingerprints . . ."

"Let's assess the situation today and talk to the police tonight or in the morning, Mrs. Wheel," said Oh. "That will give your parents and their friend Christine some time to rest and recover."

Jane's cell phone chimed. She looked at the number and shook her head. "I don't know who it is, but it can't be anyone I want to talk to."

Bruce Oh slightly raised an eyebrow. Jane saw it and knew that he wouldn't say anything, would never interfere with her feelings, but as sure as that eyebrow moved a centimeter, she knew that he wanted her to answer her telephone.

"Yes?" said Jane.

"Can you hear me?" asked Tim. "I'm using the house phone. My cell couldn't hold a call and—"

"What is it, Tim?" asked Jane.

"Honey, I heard. I know about Swanette. But you better get back here."

"What's the matter? Has something . . . ?"

"Claire and I are fine. I just want you to get back here. It's important, not life threatening, not break-every-law-to-get-here-urgent, just important, okay?"

Jane nodded, then, remembering she was on the phone, told Tim she would leave right away. "Let me tell you what they said about Swanette," Jane said, and repeated to Tim what she had just told Oh.

"We need to have the sale as soon as possible," said Jane, before hanging up.

Linda Weller came through the kitchen door balancing two pumpkins. Both were small, one had a smiling face and the other was uncarved.

"Ada passed her physical, so I'll be leaving," she said. Looking at Jane's face, she added, "Are you okay?"

"Did you know Swanette Flanders? She lived in town here, but had a farm where her mother-in-law had been living until a few years ago?" Jane didn't wait for an answer. "She just passed away."

"No way," said Linda. "I saw her at Edna's place last week. She was as fit as . . . What happened to her?"

"Murdered," said Jane.

"Mrs. Wheel," said Oh quietly, "perhaps you should wait for the police to determine what exactly happened."

Jane looked at Oh, then back to Linda Weller, who stood, openmouthed, holding a pumpkin under each arm.

"Murdered," Jane repeated.

15

Jane and Oh drove back to Swanette's farm in silence. Jane had promised Ada that she would return and Oh had received Ada's permission to return, as well, to examine her library as both a scholar and a collector. Ada seemed genuinely pleased that someone was taking an interest.

"My mother and father made that room. They said we didn't need a school outside this house if we had all the important books in the world right here. My father said an education was a private business between a person and his books. If a person was smart enough to want to be educated, he was smart enough to educate himself," said Ada, taking a deep breath when she finished, as if she hadn't made such a long speech for a while.

"Your father sounds like a wise man," Oh had told her.

"A wise man," she had repeated, nodding.

Jane pulled into the parking area at the farm, noting that there was a new vehicle next to Tim's truck. The white midsize had a small rental logo on the bumper sticker.

"Tim," Jane called out as soon as they entered through the back door, not seeing either Claire or Tim in the kitchen or adjoining parlor. Jane turned around and went past Oh to get back to the kitchen door. She started to feel panicky, remembering the last time she had gone out to the shed, but before she left the porch, three people came out of the other shed and walked toward the house.

Tim and Claire were listening to the third figure, a man, explain something. Jane could hear him saying, "Okay, I'm an idiot, I admit it, but if you tell me one more time exactly how idiotic I am, Lowry, I'm going to . . ."

Jane ran to the threesome and hugged the idiot so fiercely that Oh, watching, winced. Jane, so glad to hear her brother Michael's voice and see him, safe and sound, and on her turf, that she didn't even notice, until backing out of her uncharacteristically emotional embrace, that her brother was sporting a swollen black eye.

Before she could begin the questioning, Michael put his hand on her shoulder and suggested they all go inside and sit and he would explain everything.

"Perhaps we can all have some tea or coffee, Mrs. Wheel. I think we could all use something to revive us," said Oh. He looked at Claire who nodded and walked ahead. In the few minutes it took them to catch up to her in the kitchen she had already set a large kettle of water on to boil and was rummaging through the kitchen cupboards in search of tea or instant coffee. Tim had cleared the round oak table in the kitchen except for his own equipment . . . a basket with tape, markers, scissors, tags, and a plastic price-tag gun for attaching price tags to linens and clothes.

Michael extended his hand to Bruce Oh and introduced himself.

"Oh, I'm sorry," said Jane, "I'm just so surprised to . . . what the hell happened to your eye?"

"As Tim has been pointing out to me for the last twenty-five minutes or so, I'm an idiot. And I have a black eye because someone punched me, and because I was an idiot . . . and greedy to boot . . . I deserved to be punched. And I believe I was also told I was a lucky idiot to have come out of the encounter with only one black eye."

"Someone thought you were Honest Joe again, right? I warned you, I—" Jane began.

"Before you, too, get to the idiot part of your speech, I beg you, please, stop and let me just tell this, okay? And although out of sequence, I do want you to know, up front, this was not a case of mistaken identity. The guy who punched me knew exactly who I was and meant to punch me, Michael, and did just that." Michael barely smiled, rubbing his purple cheekbone.

Claire didn't bother to ask who wanted tea nor did she offer a selection from the boxes she found. She rinsed out a Hall Autumn Leaf pattern, Aladdin-style teapot she had found in the cupboard, filled the ceramic insert with some loose black tea, and filled the pot with boiling water, setting it on a hammered-aluminum Wendell August tray to steep. She found the matching sugar and creamer, filled them with some old sugar cubes she dug out of the pantry and the fresh cream Tim had brought, along with coffee and soft drinks and snacks, with the hope that they wouldn't have to leave the property for coffee breaks.

When Claire set the tray down, along with some pink Lu-Ray cups and saucers, Jane knew, that under any other circumstance, she would be delighted to attend this hodgepodge vintage tea party. Who knew that Claire would appreciate the quaint kitsch of the vintage kitchenware she was using to serve the tea? Jane had Oh's wife figured more for modern Paul McCobb designs or maybe some fine English bone china.

"Not to worry, Tim, I used the rummage ware for us and put the good things in the dining room," said Claire.

So much for Jane Wheel's and Claire Oh's moment on the same page in Ye Old Stuffe catalog, thought Jane.

"Remember the box of baseball cards you found next to Q's stamps?" asked Michael. "Okay, I bought those from a guy about a month ago who had—"

"You wanted me to think Nellie had let you save your stuff and not mine, didn't you? You said—"

"Jane, I didn't say those were my childhood cards. When you asked about them, I said Mom liked me best. You just assumed that meant she kept my stuff for me," said Michael. "My sister," he said, explaining to Claire and Bruce, "has always equated old stuff with old love or something like that . . . ever since her teddy bear got left behind when—"

"Okay, okay, go on . . ." said Jane.

"I, for one, would like to hear the rest of that saga sometime," said Claire.

"Anyway, I met this guy at a golf outing for work. We got to talking baseball and childhood heroes at the nineteenth hole. . . ."

Jane saw Bruce Oh taking notes and looked at his notepad. He had written *19 holes? Not 18?* Jane smiled for the first time since seeing her brother's black eye.

"The guy tells me that he's been collecting great baseball cards and he had some really valuable cards and lots of multiples of them, since he could never resist one when he found it for sale. I told him I might be interested in buying some of his spares if he ever wanted to part with them and one thing led to another and one drink led to another and pretty soon I had made a deal to look at his collection. We exchanged numbers, and the next day he called me, sounding really upset. He told me he had been doing some gambling lately, sports betting, and he had just lost a huge bet and didn't have the cash. He was just in a panic and then he remembered we had talked about the cards and he offered me all of these great rookie cards and said he'd take a loss if I just got him cash right away and he said he was sure I could sell the spares on eBay and double my money, but he just didn't have the time to do that himself. If he didn't pay off his bookie, he was going to be in big trouble.

"Monica would have killed me if she knew I was taking money out of our savings to buy baseball cards, but I figured I'd just take a look at what he had and maybe make some money on the deal. Phil, if that was his name, met me at a coffee shop, said he didn't want to do anything at his office and didn't want anybody to be able to find him until he had the money, and even though I didn't think I'd ever do anything like this . . . you know, make a cash purchase for something like . . . oh God, I saw those cards and my brain just went to mush. I don't know how to explain it, but I knew I had to have them, it was like I was drugged or hypnotized or . . ."

"Meiji period Japanese porcelain," said Claire.

"Harvey Probber furniture," said Tim, nodding.

"Bakelite buttons," said Jane.

Oh, seeing the puzzled look on Michael's face, explained. "Those are the objects that drug them."

Michael still shook his head.

"It just means they understand your need for the baseball cards," said Oh.

"Well, even though I had taken this money out of our savings account, I never meant to spend it all. I thought I might buy a Mantle and maybe a Nolan Ryan . . . I don't know. But when I saw them and he told me what they were worth individually, I knew he was on the mark since I had looked a few up myself on the Internet. I figured I could triple my money by selling off the spares."

"Oh, honey," said Jane, laying her hand on Michael's arm. "How much did you pay?"

"Six thousand. Cash."

No one spoke as Tim, Claire, and Jane all remembered their own purchases of desire . . . when need and greed obliterated common sense and practicality.

"It would have been a bargain if—"

"Fakes?" asked Jane.

"All but two, and together they might be worth around five hundred."

"Sounds like maybe this other guy should have the black eye," said Tim.

"If I could find him, he'd have worse than that," said Michael. "The number he gave me was a cell phone—no longer in service. No, it turns out the guy wasn't even part of the golf outing I was on. He was waiting to play alone and got picked up as a fourth before I got there, so I didn't even know that he wasn't part of the party I was joining."

"He was clever, this Phillip," said Oh. "Con men are wonderful listeners. He had time to observe, pay attention, and fill himself in on who he was supposed to be associated with, he saw you arrive late, and knew that you wouldn't have noticed he was an outsider."

"The black eye, sweetie," said Jane. "Get to the black eye."

"I put a few cards up on eBay, hoping to get my money back fast—before Monica even noticed it was gone. Then yesterday I went to a card shop where they sell all kinds of memorabilia. They were having this parking lot event. A bunch of dealers had card tables set up and stuff. I started talking to this guy who was looking for a birthday present for his dad. I told him I had a lot of great cards. He said if I had a Stan Musial Bowman rookie card in good shape, he'd buy it for a thousand cash and I had one and we made the deal right there. Problem was, I wasn't a dealer and shouldn't have been dealing like that anyway, right in front of all those professionals who were set up . . . and this guy takes the Musial right over to a dealer who starts laughing and pointing out that it's a fake. I was still browsing, hadn't even gone twenty feet away, and this guy comes up and slugs me. People wanted to call the police for my sake, but I didn't want the police involved—hell, I wasn't really the injured party—so I gave the guy his money back and apologized. One of the dealers took pity on me when he heard me tell my story and looked over the cards. He's the one that authenticated the two that were real. I got a quick education and this," Michael said, pointing to his eye.

"I called Monica and told her I had to come and help you on a case, that you needed a lawyerly take on something that had to be kept confidential—a last-minute thing—and since her two sisters had come for a week and I was clearly the fifth wheel around the place, she told me I should definitely come. They were all at Disneyland for the day when I stopped at home to fill a bag. I've got some flexibility at work, especially since I can handle most of this week's obligations from my laptop. I felt like a thief sneaking out of town like that, but I figured maybe you'd be able to track down my scam artist at the same time you found out who this Honest Joe guy was. Maybe I'd be able to help you since I'm the one that looks like him and all," said Michael. "And by the time I get back home, this," he said, pointing to his eye, "will have faded a bit."

Jane looked at her baby brother who was a head taller and who had always seemed more adult and sophisticated than she had—even though she was the alleged big sister. At this moment, he looked like her baby brother again, waiting for her to come up with a plan. She patted his arm and looked at Oh and Tim to help her deliver the news.

"No chance, Mike," said Tim, draining his tea and getting up to rinse out his cup. "That guy is in another town selling cards or stamps or Beatles cards or whatever to some other sucker right now. Most people don't even report a scam like this because they're embarrassed about being taken. I can't believe you could ever find him. Am I right?" he asked, looking at Detective Oh.

"As a rule, yes, I'm afraid Mr. Lowry is right," said Oh. "In this case, you might be lucky. You can report your encounter, and since you still have the cards, you might be able to recover your bad investment if they catch your 'Phil.' If you report it, it will help warn others and alert potential victims. You would have the satisfaction of stopping him from doing the same to another," said Oh.

"Satisfaction plus six thousand dollars would be better, but if I have to settle for satisfaction, so be it," said Michael. "It's not like I didn't deserve it. I was greedy and—"

"No one deserves to be cheated," said Jane. "Just because you love something or long for something or just because you get excited at discovering a treasure, that doesn't make you less of a deserving person. It's easy to get fooled or not see a chip. . . ."

"Or a tiny hairline crack that renders worthless a vase that would have been worth thousands that you thought you were lucky to spot at an estate sale where they had no idea of what it was . . ." said Claire, staring at a space above all of their heads.

"Professional hazards," said Tim. "We all have a kind of hysterical blindness when we see something that's too good to believe. We know in our brain that something too good to be true usually is exactly that, but our hearts always win and we stick up our bidding paddles or grab something and pay and then run away like a thief, and when we get to the car, realize we overpaid or missed a flaw and we feel like such idiots. . . ."

"Thanks," said Michael. "I didn't think that I could smile again after this mess, but being an idiot in the company of idiots is more comforting than I would have imagined."

Jane stood at the sound of a car pulling into the drive. From the kitchen window she could see it was Don and Nellie arriving, and Jane realized Michael was about to pay triple for any idiotic act he felt he committed. Nellie would be relentless when she saw that black eye. When Jane once experimented with an extremely short haircut, Nellie never left her alone about it. A black eye would, as Don might say, wind her up like an eight-day clock.

Rita, who had been standing watch on the porch, ran over to Nellie, and Jane watched her mother crouch down like a woman half her age and give the dog a thorough rubdown. Nellie was full of surprises, Jane thought, as she watched her parents making their way to the door. Nellie walked three steps ahead of Don, talking to him over her shoulder the whole time. Rita walked at Nellie's heel.

"Michael, have you talked to Mom and Dad?" asked Jane.

"Not yet. There was no answer at the house or on your cell so I called Tim's store and the girl who answered the phone said you and Tim were working out here and gave me directions to this place. I figured you and I could cook up a story to satisfy Nellie," said Michael, still sitting with his back to the door.

"Start cooking then, because I'm ready to hear it," said Nellie, pushing open the screen door.

Jane got up and went over to give her parents, her dad anyway, a hug. They looked like two people who had been keeping a vigil at a hospital, tired and spent. Don returned the hug, but Nellie bobbed and weaved away from Jane like a featherweight boxer and eyed her son, Michael. She showed no surprise at his appearance at Swanette's farm.

"What the hell happened to you?"

Don came around and patted his son's shoulder, giving Michael's eye a quick glance and wincing. Jane understood the language of that wince. Whenever Nick scraped his knee, jammed his finger, twisted an ankle, or was on the receiving end of a rough foul in a soccer match, she felt the same physical recoil from her son's pain. She actually felt herself physically caving in to the blow when she saw him struck. She could see Don was experiencing the same sensation.

Nellie, however, had a different method for dealing with the illnesses and injuries of and to her children. For as long as Jane could remember, when either she or Michael had a fever or a banged-up elbow, Nellie would stare them down, daring them to feel the pain. She battled their aches with a fierce anger. If Jane said her leg hurt, Nellie's reply was always the same.

"Everybody's leg hurts."

Nellie would perform the required bandaging with a gentle hand, but her eyes stayed angry. When she was small, Jane thought her mother was angry at them when they allowed themselves to get hurt or sick, but she realized now, watching Nellie, that her mother's quarrel was with something much larger. She was a tigress defending her young from a hurtful world, a cruel universe. That pothole in the street that had knocked them off their bicycles? Nellie would smooth it out with her bare hands if she could, and beat the daylights out of the city worker who had not made a proper job of fixing it the first time around.

"Who did that?" asked Nellie, staring at his eye.

Michael hugged his mother even though she never unfolded her arms to hug him back. Bruce and Claire Oh made themselves busy clearing away the cups and tea things, but Tim stayed planted right where he was. He loved each and every episode of the Nellie show and wasn't going to move from his front-row seat for what promised to be a memorable viewing experience.

"Michael was a total idiot, Mom. He was carrying the baby and ducking low into a doorway to protect Jamey and didn't notice a low beam over the door after passing the baby under. He wanted me to cook up a story that was more exciting and heroic, but I told him honesty's the best policy. So what if you seem clumsy, right? Better just to spit it out and get on with things. Let's just be thankful he still got to make the trip out here for work, so we all get to be together," said Jane.

Tim looked just like a judge at an athletic competition, ready to hold up a card marked with a very low number.

Michael nodded, content to let Jane take the questions. They both knew there would be questions.

"What the hell kind of doorway? Were you visiting midgets?" said Nellie.

"Little people," said Tim, unable to stop himself from the automatic correction.

"Should stay out of other people's business," said Nellie, dismissing Tim. "What the hell kind of a doorway—"

"That's enough, Nellie. It's been a hell of a morning. Let's have some coffee and figure out what everybody's doing next. How long can you stay, son?" asked Don, putting an end to the awkward tension.

Everyone got busy then. Jane made a pot of coffee. Tim dug

out the few snacks he had packed. Nellie filled a bowl with water for Rita and set it out on the porch and Don explained what he and Nellie had been doing all morning at the hospital. Sitting, waiting, and more sitting.

"So Swanette's sale and accident and . . . everything . . . has taken over here, hasn't it?" asked Michael. "I can see there's been no time for any progress on Honest Joe."

"Not an accident," said Jane, "and I wouldn't say no progress. I know that Honest Joe is somehow working out of Cousin Ada's house; I saw his mail there. I just don't quite know whether he's a *he* I haven't seen or he's the woman who pretended to be looking in on Ada yesterday or someone else entirely," said Jane. "Everybody seems to know that they can go in and out of Ada's house at will, during the carving season anyway."

"Who's Honest Joe?" asked Don, at the same time Michael asked, "Who's Cousin Ada?"

Explanations were exchanged and Jane saw that Michael was as befuddled by the news that Nellie had somehow managed to hide a first cousin from them all these years as she had been. Nellie ran water into the sink, preparing to wash dishes, and listened to Jane explain Ada then allowed Michael to give a short history of his mistaken identity without interrupting with any questions.

Bruce Oh asked for paper and Tim pointed him to his box of supplies. Oh took out a blank piece of paper and began carefully drawing what looked like a map of Swanette's property.

"We only have the rest of today to accomplish what we need to do, since by tomorrow morning we will need to cooperate with the police. I believe by tomorrow they will agree to open an investigation and our opportunities here will be limited."

Everyone nodded and all except Nellie gathered behind Oh

to hear his plan. Nellie kept her silent post at the sink, washing out the cups and saucers.

"If you and your wife are willing to help," Oh said, looking at Don, "I think you would be most useful beginning the inventory in the outbuildings. You can leave the objects there, but take down their numbers and descriptions and any dates, and Mr. Lowry and I, here in the house, will use our computers to look up these numbers, seeing if we can link them to auctions. Claire will continue going through items in the house . . ."

"Bruce, I'm happy of course to do whatever you need me to do, but I'm noticing a pattern here that's very strange. For every set of vintage linens, there's—"

"Some inexpensive country-look set from Target or somewhere, right?" Jane interrupted. "Tim and I noticed the same pattern. We think somebody, probably the caretakers here, the health-care worker and the handyman, maybe together, were selling off the real stuff and supplying Swanette's mother-in-law with cheap knockoffs. That way she didn't know she was being robbed and her real vintage goods supplied a steady stream of income. Since she was old and frail, it was only a matter of time before they'd get to move out the bigger pieces, the real antiques. In the meantime, they could keep her trust, and take stock of all she had. They could even run their business out of the outbuildings. And if, together, they're Honest Joe, they could be stealing from Ada, too. Some of those tags could have referred to Ada's things," said Jane, remembering "A's Attic" and "A's trunk" written on some of the identifying note cards. "As long as they stoked Swanette's mother-in-law's anger and paranoia, which kept Swanette out of the house, they could run the show here."

"You think the two people here were Honest Joe?" asked Michael.

"It's possible," said Jane. "Probable. But I think they were inconsistent. I think sometimes they confused the phony goods, the contemporary stuff, for the real items and when those got sent out to the winning bidders, those people felt tricked and cheated. They worked on an auction site that provided an option for the seller to provide a photo, and somehow, they used a photo of you or someone who looked enough like you to be your twin. Who knows how they got it or why? They could have lifted it from a box of photos at Ada's house. Maybe it was just a joke or something. But those customers who bought fakes from the sites where your double appeared? They were the ones that confronted you, Michael."

"Inconsistent? Confused? Why do you think they were so innocent?" asked Tim. "I think they knew what they were doing, just got greedy and decided they could sell fakes as well as they could sell the real stuff."

Jane nodded. She was trying to make it sound less ominous in front of her parents, but she believed the same thing. Whoever was stealing from Swanette's house got greedy . . . so greedy that when Swanette was on the verge of finding a stash of valuable objects in the outbuilding, Honest Joe had knocked her out and left her for dead.

"You got one part of your story screwed up," said Nellie.

Her mother had been quiet for so long, Jane thought she had stopped listening. Nellie had, in fact, finished the cups and saucers and had moved over to a shelf next to the kitchen window. She had taken down a photo album, one of several that were lined up together, and was paging through the old book, seemingly lost in her own thoughts.

"First of all, they weren't just stealing from Swanette's mother-in-law." Nellie grabbed a napkin to mark her place in the photo album and moved back to the sink where many of the dishes she had washed and dried the day before were still piled up on the counter.

"Sixty, seventy years ago when people were collecting plates like this out of their laundry detergent boxes or sending away for stuff or using their trading stamps to get stuff, people were brand loyal. Pattern loyal. They had their favorite and stuck to it. They didn't collect one of everything; they tried to collect a set. I remember my own mother, trudging from store to store trying to find certain brands that would sell out when a special piece of china she didn't have yet was included. Not everybody had a car back then, so she'd be walking twelve, thirteen blocks out of her way to find the right box of soap. This junk here in this house? There are partial sets of a bunch of stuff. It's not the new stuff, either; it's all really old. It's just that one person the age of Lee's mother wouldn't have stood still for all this stuff . . ."

"Swanette said that her mother-in-law was the caretaker of things from her whole family, that she had her aunt's stuff and her own mother's . . ." said Jane.

"Nope," said Nellie. "I saw some of them boxes upstairs. They were labeled as coming from different relatives and the stuff inside all made sense, it went together. But all these different patterns of glass and such? These people were stealing from all kinds of other people."

Jane looked at Oh.

"This is what I was talking about with the boxes in the shed. Different handwriting, different types of boxes, different tape and packing styles even. It's as if they just took one box off the back of every moving truck," said Jane.

Michael stood, and when he scraped his chair back, Jane looked up and noticed for the first time how tired and pale he looked. Before, concentrating on the deeply colored bruise, she hadn't really paid attention to how fragile her brother appeared.

"Michael, you must be starving. You were at that card show yesterday and took the red-eye, then drove here from O'Hare? How long has it been since you've eaten a meal?"

Michael shrugged. "Weeks?" he asked.

"We'll go into town and get food and bring back sandwiches from Edna's Diner," said Jane. "Everyone can get started here and we'll be back quickly. In fact, I want to time the shortcut using the service road anyway," said Jane.

Oh nodded. He had completed his map and Jane saw that he had rendered Swanette's farm in a charming freehand style, listing everything he remembered from this morning's tour. He had only spent minutes in two of the outbuildings, but he was able to list the types of items and the manner in which they were coded and inventoried. Jane was sure that by the time she and Michael returned, those who were working here at the farm would have clear connections to auction sellers.

"Michael, you took those baseball cards off eBay, right? Those phonies?" asked Jane.

"Canceled the auctions before I left town."

Jane and Michael started for the door, but as if both were taken with the same thought, they each turned to Nellie.

"You're not mad at me, are you, Mom?" asked Michael. She had said very little directly to her son as she listened to all the explanations and speculations, except for pointing out to the group what had seemed obvious to her about the thousands of items crowding the house.

Jane also asked a question, although she had decided long ago that Nellie was always mad at her, so that was an obvious query she never bothered to voice. "What's so interesting in that album, Mom?" Nellie rarely sat still for long. But during the entire process of Claire angling for a peek out at the shed and Tim trying to keep her in the house so he could watch her and Don conferring with Oh about the way he wanted the item numbers recorded, Nellie had continued to sit in the old mission-style rocker and page through the worn old photo album.

"Mom?"

"I'm just looking at some old pictures," said Nellie. "Don't you always say that old pictures deserve to have some attention paid?"

Jane did always say that when she was explaining why she brought home old family photos of people she had never met, but she had hardly expected her mother to have listened to her let alone remembered her words.

Michael was still watching his mother when she finally looked up and gave him half a smile. "No, I'm not mad. I'm glad to see you, but I want to see the kids, too. They all right?"

Michael nodded and bent over his mother to kiss her cheek.

Jane smiled, oddly able to enjoy one of the rare tender glimpses into her mother's heart, even though it wasn't directed at her. She forgot to be jealous and was simply pleased to see her brother and her mother pictured, for a second, in such a warm tableau. She wasn't prepared, however, to see what most people would identify as a tear in her mother's eye. Nellie wasn't someone who produced tears. Nonetheless, Jane was sure she saw it. It was minute, but it was a tear. As quickly as Jane registered the sight, Nellie blinked hard and bent her head back over the album, refusing to look up again as Michael took Jane's elbow and steered her out the door.

16

Jane backed out of the parking place she had claimed between Tim's truck and Michael's rental and drove around all the cars to the barn, turned behind it, and drove down the service road, slowly and quietly at first, then, once clear of Swanette's house, she stepped on the gas, kicking up gravel into the cornfield.

"I'm not that hungry," said Michael.

"I just want to see how much time I can take off in getting to town the back way," said Jane. "I'm just curious. If I'm right about this, Honest Joe and/or Honest Joanne have been working their business between Ada's and Swanette's places. I'm guessing they did the paperwork at Ada's since the post office is in town, unless they drove to another town for mailing out stuff. Might make somebody suspicious if someone kept mailing stuff out in a little town like this . . . the postal workers would know who was dealing on auction sites . . . and . . ." Jane's voice trailed off, but it was clear she hadn't really been talking to Michael. She was just trying to work it all out.

"Janie, I'm sorry I busted in here with my hard-luck story at a terrible time."

"Why, Michael? You can probably help, it's going to take all of us tonight to carry out—"

"I mean right after Swanette died. Makes my stuff seem even stupider. Tim told me when I got here what was going on. . . . Mom and Dad had just called him. I'm sorry, that's all. I know you were trying to help her."

"Yes. I still am. I'll explain just how we're going to do that when—"

Jane turned onto the main road and looked at her watch. She set her tripometer and nodded at Michael. "This is going to cut off more than half a mile. Someone could have been at Ada's the whole time I was there yesterday with Mom, listening to everything that was going on, left the same time as we did, and beat us here with minutes to spare. It doesn't help that I stopped at the stupid mini-mart."

"Hey, you can't blame yourself for Swanette . . ."

Jane shook her head. "I don't. I'm just always amazed at the minute or two-minute decisions that change everything. Let's get those sandwiches, then maybe we can take a few minutes for you to meet your second cousin, Ada."

Michael started to ask Jane about their newfound relative as they entered Edna's Diner. A few people sat at the counter, a family with two small children occupied one booth, and another table was filled with men playing cards. Michael picked up a menu and began to study it. Jane walked over to the cardplayers.

"Bill?" said Jane, standing next to the old man she had met on Friday. "Bill, I met you in here on Friday, day before yesterday, and showed you a picture. Remember?"

"I'm old, but I ain't stupid, honey. I remember," he said, laying down his cards. "Gin."

There was some grumbling from the other men and a few

quarters changed hands. Bill's card partners got up to stretch and left their friend alone with Jane. Bill looked Jane up and down. "Got more pictures to show me?"

Jane waved at Michael to come over. "I want to introduce you to someone."

Bill shifted in his chair and turned toward Michael, who approached from the side. His eyes grew wide, then he began to laugh. "You could be him, son, you could be old Jim Speller except for the eyes."

Michael touched his bruised eye and shrugged. "I'm a fast healer. When this is gone, who am I going to look like?"

"Hell, it's not the shiner. Jim Speller was always getting into fights. If anything, that mouse makes you look more like him. Nah, it's your eyes. They're green."

Michael was wearing a light green sweater and his eyes had mellowed from a gray-blue into a green to match.

"What color were James Speller's eyes?"

"Green," said Bill.

"I think I'll order our food," said Michael, giving Jane the raised eyebrow that indicated she might be better at dealing with this crazy coot solo.

"Brown, too," said Bill. "Dark like yours, honey," he said to Jane. "One bright green eye and one so brown it was almost black. Drove people crazy when they were talking to him. Made some folks uncomfortable, but old Jim, he loved it. He'd stare right at you, dare you to look away from him. He was a character, all right."

"What happened to him?" asked Jane.

Bill shook his head. "Some people around here thought Ada might have poisoned him with those *medicinals* she grew out in her garden. But I don't think so. Ada was always peculiar, but she and Jim loved each other. He protected her, even if he wasn't always real honest with her. He sort of hid her away from the town and he hid his own business away from her."

"Did he hide his wife from her?" asked Jane. "Did he hide Martha?" Bill hesitated. Michael returned to ask Jane a question about the food, but Jane cut him off.

"Look, Bill, I know that Jim Speller had a wife named Martha who lived in a town near here. And I know he left her, maybe when she was pregnant. Or made her leave him. Do you know about it? It's my family. My brother and I are Ada's cousins and we're trying to help her. You can see we're related. You said yourself my brother looked just like young Jim."

"I used to run with Jim and he could be one mean son of a bitch. That's the truth. But we had fun, too. When I married my Helen, she didn't want me hanging around with him and I could see her point so Jim and me kind of drifted off. One night, though, I was out at the tavern with the boys when Helen was visiting her mom, and Jim comes in, buying everybody drinks, telling everybody they should be doing the buying because he got married. He bragged that he had the best setup in the world. He could run his family place and make money there, but he had a wife in another town who knew enough to keep her mouth shut and let him tend to his family.

"It was Martha he said he married, all right. She grew up in Bonfield, I think. Maybe Limestone. It was all a long time ago."

"Do you know what happened to her?"

"He'd bring her around the tavern and places for about a year, then after that, she just wasn't around anymore. Some people said old Ada found her and sealed her up in one of the secret rooms in the house, but I think she just left. No one would have stayed with Jim. His sister was the only one who could bring out anything nice in him."

Jane could see Bill was getting uncomfortable. His card-playing buddies had returned from stretching and refilling their coffee cups, getting desserts, and now were eyeing him, wondering what was going on, what was making him so talkative, and Jane could tell that this all felt wrong to him. Gossip was okay in a small town, but not gossip about the dead and gone.

"Thank you, Bill. This is going to help Ada," said Jane.

Bill shrugged and turned back to the cards, motioning his friends to sit back down at the table with their drinks and pieces of chocolate cream pie.

"I know you'll explain all this to me," said Michael, "but I am so lost right now. Or maybe she could explain it all to me."

Jane looked into the kitchen where the waitress was packing up the food Michael had ordered. "Why? What did she say?" asked Jane.

"Not a thing," said Michael, "she was too busy listening to you and the old guy. I thought she was going to fall over, she was leaning so hard in your direction. I can't believe she bagged up the right food. I told her we were in a hurry and she said they had premade sandwiches and salads. Some lunch specials left over, too. Is that okay?"

When the waitress returned with two full bags, Jane saw it was the same young woman who had been impatient to close the first time she had come into Edna's with Michael's picture.

"Remember me? I was in here the other day and asked you if you knew anyone who looked like this guy." Jane nodded her head in Michael's direction.

"Yup, and the answer's still no. But I know one thing about that old lady across the street now. I asked my boyfriend and he says she's pretty crazy, and around Halloween, she gets even nuttier. He says bad things happen to people who mess around with her."

"Yeah?" said Jane.

The waitress nodded.

"What's his name?" asked Jane.

"Who?" she asked, her attempt at a menacing stare dissolving into a confused look.

"Your boyfriend," said Jane. "Anyone who knows anything about Ada is someone I might like to talk to. You know, keep this quiet, but there was a . . ." Jane hesitated, then leaned forward and lowered her voice. "A murder might have been committed just outside of town. There's an investigation going on right now. Don't say anything, but anybody who knows anything about weird goings-on is going to have to come forward . . ."

"Will you get us a bunch of extra napkins, please," said Michael.

The girl hurried back to the kitchen, and Michael leaned over and whispered into Jane's ear, "You might be the detective, but you're not such a great judge of character. I told you she's an eavesdropper, which means she's a gossip, too . . ."

"Here you are. And some extra ketchup for the meatloaf."

Jane looked guiltily at Michael and nodded before turning back to the waitress.

"What I told you is confidential," Jane said. Turning to Michael, she indicated the house across the street.

"Let's go meet Ada."

"Man, Q would love this house," said Michael as they stepped onto the porch. "Look at those spiderwebs. They are works of art."

"Don't put your hand in them, most of them are real," said Jane, knocking then opening the door. "Cousin Ada doesn't hear too well. You have to plant yourself right in front of her. She doesn't see that well, either, and I'm afraid when she gets close to you, she might act a little strange. I mean stranger than usual. If she thinks you're her dead brother, just follow my lead, okay?"

"I came here to solve my problems back home and it's working. I don't even remember why I got on that plane," said Michael.

When they stepped into the house, Michael and Jane were greeted with a moaning sound. At first, Jane thought it might be some kind of Halloween recording, some scary haunted-house sounds that Ada might be playing. But this sorrowful wailing was real and close by. Jane motioned for Michael to follow her as she walked through the hall into the dining room, calling Ada's name out loudly.

They found her in the kitchen, sitting at the table, knife, as usual, in her hand. But she wasn't carving a pumpkin. She was holding a paper cutout of a black cat with a devil's mask and shaking her head, crying. Before Jane could catch her attention, Ada put the cutout on the table and stuck the knife into it, ripping the cat down the center with a jagged tear.

"Holy Toledo, Ada, that's worth hundreds of dollars," said Jane. "Ada," Jane shouted, "Ada, don't!"

As Jane approached her cousin, Ada looked up, still sobbing, and dropped the knife.

"Ada, don't tear up your decorations. They're valuable. All of these," Jane said, gesturing around the room. "People collect these pieces."

"No," said Ada. "It's not mine. Somebody took mine and put this one up instead."

Jane picked up the torn paper and felt it between her thumb and forefinger. Ada was right. It wasn't an original Dennison cut-out. It was a flimsy paper copy.

Jane looked closely at the black cat. It wasn't even that great of a phony. Someone had just color-copied the original, then pasted the copy onto a thin piece of cardboard, coated it with a shiny Mod-Podge kind of material, and stuck it up on the wall. This wasn't the work of a counterfeiter—someone who was trying to fool vintage collectors with carefully, if cheaply, made phonies. This was done by someone who thought he didn't have to work very hard to fool Ada. Whoever had done this assumed her vision was poor enough that she'd never spot a fake among the originals. Oh had said earlier that effective con men were great listeners. *But they make mistakes,* Jane thought, *by underestimating their mark.* Ada might have compromised vision, but every other sense in this woman's body was finely tuned to every object that held a place in her world. Jane was certain if she took away one of the green glass salt cellars in the dining room hutch, Ada would spot its absence the next time she walked through the room. Something would be wrong—placement, color, shape—and she would know.

I'm like that, thought Jane. *I know when things are missing, when things are added, adjusted, rearranged. Even when I can't say what it is, I know when things are not right.* Jane took Ada's hands in her own and coaxed the old woman to look up at her. Her thick glasses, so darkly shaded, added to her ominous look. In such a dark house, why did Ada wear tinted lenses?

"I'll find the real decorations, Ada. I'll find your cats and your pumpkins and—"

"Mama's," said Ada. "I know what Ma's things are and people shouldn't take away those things."

Jane nodded. Ada looked past Jane then, and saw Michael. Jane felt Ada's hands stiffen and she withdrew them and stood up. Age had no effect on Ada's spine or posture, and when she rose to her full height, she was formidable with her long hair fanned out behind her. Jane didn't see Ada pick up the knife, and until the old woman lunged at Michael, the flash of silver in Ada's hand didn't resonate. It was a reflex, Jane told herself, just pure reflex that made her jump up and use her own arm to knock Ada's hand aside, causing her to drop the blade. Ada's fist connected with Michael's chest, though, and she said in a low growl, "You're not my brother."

Michael took Ada's hand in his own and shook his head.

"Where did you get my brother's face? What did you do to it?" Ada said, softer and sadder. "My brother is dead, isn't he?" Ada unclenched her fist, but Michael still held it.

"I'm Michael. I look like your brother, but I'm not your brother or pretending to be him."

Jane watched Ada's body relax.

"I thought you were the ghost, and my brother doesn't come to me looking like that . . . I thought . . ."

"Ada, someone has been playing awful tricks on you," said Jane. "Not us. This is my brother, *my brother*, Michael. Nellie's boy. And I'm Nellie's girl."

"Why would anyone play tricks like that?" said Ada. "Halloween? Ma gave wonderful treats. No one should be playing those tricks."

Ada was calmer now, but she still stared at Michael.

"You're like my brother," she said. "But you don't have the eyes."

"So I've heard," said Michael, giving Ada a big smile.

"Heterochromia," said Ada.

"What?" said Jane. "What did you say?"

"Heterochromia. That's what Brother James had. Pa wanted us to know the real word for it. It meant that his eyes were different."

"And your eyes, too? Is that why you wear dark glasses?" asked Jane.

"No, no, no," said Ada, smiling, truly relaxed now. "My eyes are your eyes."

She removed her glasses and Jane and Michael saw that she had deep brown eyes, almost black, like Jane's own.

"It was Mama's idea that I wear these glasses. Brother James was my twin and Ma said it would be better if everyone saw our eyes as the same. James wouldn't wear dark glasses. He liked heterochromia. He said it made people remember him better. Mama said, though, that it would make us even more twin if people thought my eyes were like Brother James's."

"So you tricked people," said Jane.

"Just a little," said Ada. "But I never stole from people."

"Heterochromia," said Michael. "I never heard of it. Do you have a dictionary or an encyclopedia, Ada?"

"My father's library," said Ada.

Jane thought there would never be a better time to tell Ada that there had been some tricks in the library, too. When she took down one of the paper "book covers" someone had slipped in to fill the gaps where the missing books belonged, Ada's face grew mournful.

"Father wanted his books to stay together. He told us they belonged together. One led to the next one, he said."

"I'm going to try to get them back. We think someone has been stealing from a lot of people and trying to sell their good things. We're going to catch the thieves. Maybe tonight," Jane said, in a whisper. In fact, Jane had dropped her voice so much that both Ada and Michael strained forward to hear her. Louder, she added, "We're going to recover all the stolen property tonight. We hope. Tim and I are going to send everyone home and we'll stay and work all night if we have to," Jane said, now projecting her voice so Ada would understand.

Before Michael could ask what she was talking about, Jane took Ada's arm and asked if she would take them out to the back-yard to see the pumpkins. Ada nodded, and turned away from the books, leading the way to the back door.

"Who carved all these jack-o'-lanterns?" asked Michael.

"Everyone comes and carves," said Ada. "When we were children, the town was invited. And even when Mama and Pa were gone, we invited everyone. From the diner, the children from school. Their teachers would bring them. Brother brought friends, too, from his work."

"Work? Didn't James run the farm and manage the property? Did he have a job, too?" asked Jane.

"He managed this property and other property. Ma and Pa owned buildings in other towns where people lived. Apartments. Brother James checked on all the buildings, kept it all up. He carried keys on a big brass ring and checked on things. He sold the buildings, so I'd have money to keep me. I have the house and I have—" Ada stopped herself.

"Brother James is dead?" she said to Jane, who nodded.

"Who is living in my house with me?" Ada asked.

It was a simple question, but so odd and unafraid. Jane felt cold all over.

"Is someone in your house now?"

"Someone is always in my house," said Ada.

Jane looked at Michael who, although fascinated by the conversation, looked as hungry and tired as he had before they had come to town. Jane knew they had to get back to the farm. She didn't like leaving Ada, but knew Ada would refuse to leave the house. Jane felt that no matter who was in that house, any intruder would be more interested in Jane's claim that all the valuables would be discovered at Swanette's tonight. Ada and any other real ghosts might have the place to themselves this evening.

Ada bent down to her herbs and picked a fistful of green and yellowish stems and handed them to Michael.

"Boil these and soak a piece of new wool in the tea. Put the compress on that eye, the bruising will be gone in two days," said Ada.

Michael thanked her and impulsively hugged the old woman. She hugged him back, but in a no-nonsense Nellie-like manner. She broke away and patted his arm and touched his eye briefly and gently. Then she went into the house, leaving Jane and Michael alone in the backyard—alone except for a hundred leering faces staring them down.

"Must be something when they're all lit up," said Michael.

Jane nodded, but her mind was somewhere else.

"In the library, I didn't notice if you looked it up? Heterochromia?"

"I didn't have time," said Michael, as they walked around the house and crossed the street to Jane's car. He unwrapped one of the sandwiches and started eating. "Either this is the best tuna salad I've ever tasted or I've never been hungrier."

"Heterochromia," said Jane. "You've never heard of it before?"

Michael shook his head.

"I'm not sure. I feel like I've heard about it somewhere," said Jane. "It's driving me crazy."

17

What had begun as a warm autumn Sunday had turned into something else entirely. Late afternoon, as the sun dropped lower, the temperature followed.

Claire Oh retrieved her own blue knit jacket from her car and buttoned it up as she worked her way through the drafty house. Nellie had found an old Pendleton plaid wool jacket in the hall closet. It had a forties-style nipped-in waist and shoulder pads, giving Nellie the look and style of a spunky starlet from a Frank Capra movie. Tim had put on one of the sixties-style crocheted ponchos he found in the teenage niece's closet. Every time someone looked at him, he smiled and flashed the peace sign. Don found a down vest in one of the sheds. Oh had shown up that morning wearing a tweed wool sport jacket and seemed to remain comfortable. Michael, spoiled by California, had brought a Patagonia fleece in his duffel, prepared for a Midwestern October chill. Jane went from closet to closet, marveling at the different eras of vintage clothes, trying to find something that would warm her, but had no luck finding a decent-fitting jacket.

She was shivering in her denim work shirt when she walked out to the camper van at the entrance to the driveway. No one had seen Dave, the lighting technician, all day, and around dusk, when they were breaking for some food, Jane realized that she needed to tell him what was going on at the property that evening.

Jane knocked on the door, but there was no answer. She walked in and was astonished at the efficient outfitting of the small space. The rear half of the camper was all storage with specially fitted boxes for the lights that were set up on the grounds. When they were taken down, they would all fit neatly back into their crates. But the front half of the van, behind the driver's seat, was a delightful space, intimate, personal, and comfortable. A small tabletop could be folded down from where it was latched to the side wall. A swivel recliner, complete with a clamped-on reading lamp, fit neatly behind the driver's seat. A built-in LED TV screen was hung opposite the comfortable chair. Another small drop-down table was built over a space where a small refrigerator and microwave sat.

Jane loved tiny efficient spaces, and when she saw one, she immediately dreamed of clearing out all of her things and living in one room with just what she needed. She knew that urge would pass, but it was a pleasant brief sensation—the belief that she could be a minimalist. Dave could have been out for a walk, but it was more likely he had ridden his motorcycle into town. Jane had noticed earlier that a small trailer was hitched to the camper and she had seen that it held a Harley. It made sense that whoever drove the equipment down for a shoot might need alternative transportation, since the van, with all the tools and spare parts and extension cords, would need to remain with the equipment.

Jane took her notebook from her pocket and left Dave a note.

No lights tonight until we give a signal. I'm leaving a walkie-talkie
here—switch it on after dark, and wait for anyone to ask for lights. We're

doing a little detective work, and we don't want to alert anyone to our presence until we're ready.

Thanks—Jane Wheel

Jane wasn't totally pleased with the note, but couldn't think of a better way to explain on a tiny piece of paper. She should have made a point to meet Dave and talk to him in person earlier in the day.

When she got back to the kitchen, still feeling unsatisfied with her communication or lack thereof with Dave, she opened a small closet next to the pantry that she had pegged as a utility closet. Hanging inside was an old broom, its bristles stiff and bent. On another peg was a hand-knit gray-cabled sweater with an oversized collar. Also on the hook was a wide wool scarf. Jane slipped the sweater on and buttoned it all the way up to her neck. It was perfect. The buttons, she was especially pleased to note, were large butterscotch Bakelite discs in perfect condition. In the big pockets, she found some fingerless gloves and slipped them on. Her teeth still chattering from her walk out to the trailer, she layered the scarf around her shoulders and around her neck for double warmth.

I wonder if this is what Swanette wore when she worked outside in the fields. When she drove the tractor. Jane smiled and pictured her, an educated career woman Monday through Friday and a laborer in the fields on the weekends. Jane remembered all of those office girls as smart and educated, their manners and vocabularies so different from the usual factory workers at the EZ Way Inn.

Vocabulary?

Jane took out her small notebook and flipped back over the notes she had jotted down the past two days.

"Hey, sister, peace," said Tim, swathed in poncho, coming into the kitchen with another box of green glass he had dug out of a closet for Nellie to wash. "Nice sweater. Very British old-money-walkies-with-the-dog-in-the-garden-maze and all. All you need are some Wellies, and then you could be one of those tough old birds who lives alone in her cottage by the sea."

"Do you remember what I told you Swanette said when I found her in the shed? I know I wrote it down here."

Tim came and looked over her shoulder. "Head. Head Oh. Headoh," said Tim, hesitating over Jane's handwriting. "See, honey? Sounds too much like *hetero*. It couldn't have been me."

"Hetero . . ." said Jane. "Of course. Swanette did crosswords, had a big vocabulary, would know the proper word for—"

"Jane," called Nellie from the living room. "It's almost six twenty-eight. You wanted to know when it was six-thirty."

Whenever Jane needed to keep track of time and was anywhere near Nellie, she counted on her mother as a safer bet than the clocks at Greenwich, the chimes of Big Ben, or any timer, wristwatch, or cell phone alarm. Nellie ticked to an inner clock that, once set, surpassed any other man- or woman-made devices.

Jane called everyone into the living room.

"I'm going to have to take a call in a few minutes. Charley and Nick call on Sundays around now, and I can't reach them, so I have to pick up when it rings. After that, I am turning off my cell phone. Everyone turn off your cell phones. Take these walkie-talkies that Tim had—"

"Do you use them at the big shows?" asked Claire.

"Essential. Kane County flea market or, hell, even the shows at the Merchandise Mart—they're too big and I can't risk a dropped call when I need to get my client in front of a piece I know is going to sell immediately—"

"Hey!" said Jane. "This is important. We have planted it all over town, at Edna's when we ordered food, at the minimart, and with Ada's ghost, that Tim and I will be working here alone tonight to sort out all of what we believe are the stolen goods. When the news gets to the people who have accumulated all this stuff, they know that tonight's the night they have to act.

"Dad, I need you and Mom to drive off, following the Ohs, then you can double around to the service road and park inside the barn. The doors away from the view of the house are open. You and Mom and Rita will take the barn. Claire and Tim will stay in the house. Detective Oh and I will be out in the shed where Swanette was attacked."

"What about me?" asked Michael.

"Chicken coop?" Jane asked. "Will you be all right out there?"

"I don't like all this, honey," said Don. "Putting together puzzle pieces is one thing, but this is police work."

"You're right," said Oh. "I have discussed everything with Detective Cord, who might not totally approve, but was persuaded to give us one night to try our plan for capturing the thieves. He and his people are on watch. The two tractors out in the cornfield, you might remember, were not there earlier. There are officers stationed in both of them with a clear eye on the property. If anyone hears anything or sees anything, call for lights into your walkie-talkie."

Jane looked at her father who didn't appear any happier. She understood. He loved the idea that she was happy and brave and successful at her new career, but he didn't really want this backstage look at what might turn into a dangerous finale. After all, wasn't Swanette struck from behind in the shed because she *stumbled* upon something? Hadn't they advertised that Jane and Tim had *found* something?

Jane had told Oh her concerns about leaving a note for the technician, Dave. What if he didn't return in time for the "lights" signal? Oh had sent word to the police that this could be a problem and they were scouring local taverns and roadhouses, looking for a young man on a Harley, to alert him to the plan. If they didn't find him, one of the police officers would station himself in the camper.

Jane's cell phone rang then, and she waved to everyone, knowing that Oh would lead all who were supposed to drive off and repark in a few minutes. She clicked her phone on as she walked into the visitor's parlor and made herself comfortable among piles of hand-crocheted pillow tops and top-stitched velvet crazy quilts.

"Nick? Oh sweetie, I miss you," said Jane.

Although Nick didn't say in so many words that he, too, missed his mother, Jane could tell by his excitement over their excavation work and his minute descriptions of the dig that he was as excited to talk to her as she was to him.

"Mom, I'm coming home next week," he said. Was his voice deeper? "I thought I'd never want to come home, but I'm really ready. I even miss school!"

Jane wrapped one of the quilts around her ankles. She knew that in just a few minutes she would be planted outside in the dark waiting for someone dangerous to creep up onto the property, but right now, with her son's voice giving her wonderful news, she felt completely safe and protected. Too soon Nick said he had to go so Dad could have a few minutes. The entire crew used the same phone, the only one that worked, on Sunday nights to call home, and Jane knew that Charley tried to respect everyone's need to connect and catch up with family.

"Charley," said Jane, "oh Charley, you've been gone forever this time."

"Jane."

Jane heard something. In the same way a deer senses a storm, a rabbit freezes at a circling hawk, Jane knew something. Her world was about to change.

"Nick says you're coming home next week. I'll be . . . I've missed you so much," said Jane.

"Jane, this is all wrong, the totally wrong way to say anything about this, but I am no good at timing," said Charley, keeping his voice very low. "Nick's coming home next week."

"And you'll follow?" said Jane. "Soon."

"The institute has asked me to stay on as the director. As the permanent director. I've thought of nothing else all week, I've been over and over this and I know I can do great work here."

"Quite a commute, between Evanston and South America," said Jane, trying to keep her voice light.

"I'm staying here," said Charley.

"Your classes, your work here, Nick, me . . . What happened to our decisions, the ones we make together . . . ?" Jane said, trying not to open up a conversation that she would then have to abruptly end, proving to Charley that he had made the right decision, that it was she, Jane, who always put her work first.

"I'm calling Northwestern this week. They'll either give me a leave for this or I'll quit. Jane, you know when you were working in advertising, you were really good at what you did, but you always said it wasn't your work. *Your real work.* Well, I've found my real work. The place, the country, the people . . ."

And then Jane knew. A key turned in a lock inside of her head, a door opened, and light flooded in. Charley had fallen in love.

"Jane?" he said, sounding younger than Nick. "I'm sorry."

"We'll sort it all out," said Jane. "When can you call again, alone, so we can go over the fine print?" Jane asked, surprising herself with her own sense of calm. She heard the cars pulling out of the driveway and knew that in a few moments, she would be on duty in her field of choice, doing her real work.

"Charley?" said Jane, realizing that she did have one question that she needed answered immediately. "Does Nick know?"

"God, no," said Charley. "Jane, nothing has happened here. Nothing. But I—"

"But it will," said Jane.

They agreed to talk midweek, before Nick came home, so that they would all be on the same page. Jane actually used that phrase, *on the same page.* She was about to be lost in a whole new book, one written in another language, one that she did not understand or speak, and yet she had pulled that particular cliché out . . . *the same page. Ah well,* she thought, *it matches the fine print.*

"Mrs. Wheel?" said Oh. "I am sorry, but if you're ready, I think perhaps we should find our places."

It was like a play. Jane sensed that more than ever. It always had an unreal sense, this detective work. But today, Oh had explained lighting design and discussed theater work with her, and now Charley had involved her in a timeworn scene she had witnessed on the stage, in front of movie screens hundreds of times. They had had their ups and downs, she and Charley. She had practically thrown away this good man when her life was in chaos a few short years ago, but hadn't they come together, stronger and more in synch than ever? Or had Jane just thought that because she had everything she wanted? A best friend in Tim. A partner in Oh. Where did Charley fit in? A husband who traveled and was fulfilled by his work and who basically left her alone to . . .

To what? Find Bakelite buttons? What was it again she did

for a living? Oh yes, she scavenged junk that others threw away, and once in a while, she solved a crime. And when she was staring at other peoples' old stuff, she knew that she wore blinders, she saw nothing else. If asked, would she be able to describe Charley's face as well as she might the hand stitching on a quilt, or a Heisey glass pattern?

"Mrs. Wheel? Is anything . . . is everything . . ."

"Yes. Anything. Everything. But I'm ready."

Jane Wheel then did what she always did very well. She wrapped up her personal life in a vintage blue handkerchief, tied it with a yellow grosgrain ribbon, and put it away. It was not so easy this time to make a neat little bundle. She could feel the *what about . . .* and the *who will* and *how will I* pieces of this spilling out and hissing at her through the dark. She tucked in the ends and sealed the imaginary package even tighter. She would have much to deal with when she unwrapped it again, but for now, there was a story right here, right now, that needed an ending.

10

Neither Jane nor Tim had found any trace of the jewels or coins that Swanette had mentioned in the phone message. Whoever had hit her could have taken whatever it was she had discovered in the shed. But since all the boxes still seemed so neatly packed and stacked, it was likely that Swanette thought she had glimpsed something, made the call, and was struck. The person who hit her might not have had time to ferret out what Swanette had described or thought she had discovered. Now in the fading light of the day, as she and Oh settled into the shed, Jane decided to search until she found some object for which someone might be tempted to kill.

Oh lost himself in the corner shadows, shining his flashlight on each box on the shelf in front of him. Although Jane had no reason to hide—she was supposed to be there, working away, pricing items for an estate sale and/or cataloging stolen goods—she, too, used a small light to examine the boxes. This plan would work best if any visitors believed she and Tim had remained working in the house.

"Mrs. Wheel, I think you are right about these boxes belonging to different people. Your observations about the handwriting, the labeling style . . . it all makes sense. But what puzzles me is the accumulation of such a variety . . ."

"I know. I said before it's like one box off several different moving trucks and who would have the inclination or the access . . . I mean, as a thief, I want stuff I can get rid of for quick money, right? Jewels or art or electronics? Why would I ever want a box of . . . ?" Jane paused while she reached into the carton she had just slit open with a box cutter marked "Extra Kitchen" in bold marker and pulled out a handful of serving utensils. Nothing special . . . a large slotted spoon, a ladle, a cold-meat fork, a spatula. She held up the spatula and rotated it in front of her face. "There is nothing special about this, no Bakelite handle, no red-painted wooden handle, just a utilitarian stainless spatula that you might keep around as a spare. I see these at garage sales all the time . . . actually at the end of garage sales. Objects too good to throw away, but too ordinary to collect. So people put them out at their sale and they don't sell and then what happens to them? Packed up, donated, or stored—" Jane stopped.

"Stored and . . . ?" Oh said, prompting. The detective knew when he was out of his depth. Tracing the life cycle and storage of a spatula clearly fell under Mrs. Wheel's purview.

"This is the kind of thing that goes into the kind of box with stuff that's too good to throw away, but not good enough to miss," said Jane.

Oh nodded, realizing that she couldn't really see him in the gloom of the shed, but knowing it didn't matter. Mrs. Wheel would continue her "aha" moment, with or without an attentive audience.

"Have you ever moved?" asked Jane.

"Sorry?"

"Moved residences. Moved from apartment to apartment, house to house?" asked Jane.

"We lived in the city in an apartment before moving into our home, yes," said Oh.

"Did you pack up yourself, then hire movers?" asked Jane.

"Yes."

"In your new and pristine home, did all the stuff you brought with you overwhelm you? Did you put boxes aside, maybe into your basement, to unpack later, then realize after a few months you never missed what was in them?"

"Not exactly, but I understand where you're going. Claire had some things. I travel rather light, Mrs. Wheel."

"Right, but most people don't. Ada's brother James . . . our ghost, I guess . . . had a job other than taking care of Ada. He took care of some small apartment buildings owned by their parents. To her knowledge those buildings were sold some years ago, but James could have kept the keys or copies of them and even if someone changed all the locks on all the apartment doors, does anyone bother to change all the locks to the basements or the padlocks on the storage lockers? In these little local apartments? And Swanette had a ring of keys with her when she was attacked. Maybe the handyman she hired to help care for Lee's mother, her mother-in-law, was a friend or partner of Brother James. There must be someone involved who inherited the business—and maybe even the keys—from Brother James.

"When Charley and I moved to the house we live in now"—Jane paused for just a moment, considering her use of *we* and wondering how difficult the habit would be to break—"I packed up boxes of stuff I had accumulated and had the movers take it down to the basement. There are probably still boxes there that had been in the storage area of our apartment that I hadn't wanted to go through before the move. People cart boxes and boxes from place to place until they have absolutely no memory of what they have stored, what they've sold at a garage sale, what they've given away. It's a big, clunky, cardboard-box trail we leave from place to place as we move through life," said Jane. Remembering that she was talking to Bruce Oh, she added, "Most of us, that is."

James Speller, Jane was certain, took the occasional box from a storage locker. Maybe, at first, it was stuff that was left behind when people moved on. It might not have been actual stealing. But somewhere along the line, either he or whoever he partnered up with realized they could sell things on the Internet . . . all kinds of random objects. And they might only find one box out of ten that held something valuable, but if they were just doing it as a side business or for a little extra income, it was a pretty safe way to procure inventory. Just take the oldest, most battered box at the bottom of the pile in the storage locker.

"I think," said Jane, "that for old James, this little side business was fine as is, selling the occasional box lot of stuff. After he died, though, whoever helped him with it got greedy. They wouldn't have his paid-up lifestyle—the property he and Ada owned outright plus the interest income from all the land deals he made selling off parcels of the original farm. Whoever he shared that ring of keys with still needed to keep the selling going, and needed to make more money. The books from Ada's library would bring bigger money, and some of her antiques—the Halloween decorations for sure. There's a big market for them."

Jane stopped talking and Oh shined his flashlight her way. She pointed toward the barn. Both heard the hum of a motor. Both heard it stop. Someone had driven onto the property and parked behind the barn. Whoever had stored their stuff here, whether it was honestly acquired or not, had come to make his claim.

Jane had advised Tim to keep the radio on in the house, allowing noise to filter out into the night through a few open windows. Tim and Claire also had left all the lights on. Claire had changed into a pair of dark trousers, as close to Jane's old dark jeans as she could get, and she had pulled her hair back with one of Jane's barrettes, so that her silhouette, if glimpsed from outside, might be confused with Jane's. Claire was a head taller than Jane, but Jane didn't think anyone on a mission would notice that detail. The hope was that if Tim and Jane were assumed to be in the house, the person who had assaulted Swanette would once again slip into the dimly lit shed, hoping that the weapon used was still in place.

Jane and Tim had made sure, while spreading their story around town and proclaiming it from every corner of Ada's house, that they said the police had no idea how Swanette might have been attacked, but that once they found a weapon, they would be able to find the murderer. The police had actually removed the suspicious slat earlier in the day, sending it off to the city to be checked for evidence that it had been used to strike Swanette. Another slat had been pried from a crate in the barn and been wedged into the corner. If someone entered the shed to retrieve what he believed was his weapon, Jane and Oh were ready to surprise him with a light show and a quick call to one of Officer Cord's men with an arrest warrant. Jane wasn't sure what Oh had said to persuade Cord to allow them their night, but she was once again grateful that Oh had been a police officer himself, that he understood procedure and the territorial nature of a crime. Perhaps if Swanette had actually—

Jane stopped her runaway train of thought and froze. She still held the box cutter in her right hand and silently, with her left, she picked up the meat fork that she had laid out on top of the box. Oh held the walkie-talkie. She and Oh were on the opposite side of the shed from where the original wooden slat had been tucked away. Someone was coming in, and if they were correct in their speculations, that someone was coming to fetch the piece of wood. Without saying anything to each other, without even exchanging looks, they had flicked off their small penlights. The nearly full moon came in through gaps in the sides of the building, illuminating a slice of earthen floor in front of them, in front of the door, which opened slowly, creaking slightly on its hinges.

Jane kept her eyes on that slice of light, watching for shoes, for feet. As someone stepped in toward the corner, Jane held her breath. They were timing the call for lights to the moment when the intruder actually laid hands on the board. Anything else he touched or tried to take away from the shed might be robbery, the act of a thief, but someone trying to remove an alleged murder weapon was the perpetrator they were trying to catch tonight.

Jane heard no movement or sound from Oh, but was aware of a voice in the distance calling for lights. Nellie's voice, to be exact, screaming, "Turn on the goddamn lights!" The person in the shed froze for just a second then began to back away toward the door. Jane jumped out and kicked it closed, her box cutter raised over her head.

Light, as well as the buzz and hum of a generator, flooded the property.

"Please don't hurt me. I haven't done anything."

Jane and Oh remained where they were, staring at a man who looked enough like Michael to indeed be his twin brother.

"Joe?" asked Jane.

"How do you know me?" the man asked, near tears. "Please put the knife and fork down. You look like you're going to eat me."

"This is just a formality, sir, but I would like to search you. May I have your permission to make sure you're not carrying a weapon?" asked Oh.

Jane was impressed with the wording of her partner's request. No longer a policeman, he made no mistakes that would violate the rights of Joe, who right now, since he had been thrown into shock by the lights a beat too early, had done nothing more than trespass. Jane felt certain he had been going toward the wooden slat, intending to take it and destroy it, but her hunch was not going to be what Cord needed to make a case.

"I got nothing to hide," said Joe. "Search me."

Oh patted him down and Jane suggested they all get out of the shed, onto the well-lit grounds, before the area police descended upon them, guns raised.

"What are you doing here, Joe?"

He shrugged. "Just looking around, that's all. I heard there was going to be a sale and I collect all kinds of stuff, and sometimes if you come early where they're setting up a sale, you can get bargains, so I just thought I'd come out and look around."

"In the dark?" asked Jane.

"I got a light," said Joe, pointing to the flashlight he had dropped. "And I figured I'd scout around before going up and knocking at the door. There are lights on up there in the house."

Despite the tension of the moment, Jane was amused when she looked toward the house, then did a full circle turn toward the barn, the fields, and the other small buildings. Family, friends, and police officers were moving in from every corner—all abandoning their posts since they had caught someone in their trap.

Nellie was walking the fastest, of course, and got there ahead of the rest.

"How the hell did you get my son's face?" she asked, more rumination than question. To Jane's ears, Nellie sounded mildly curious, but not surprised.

"Let's see those eyes," said Nellie, flashing the light directly in Joe's face.

One clear blue eye and one dark brown eye blinked back at them.

"Holy jeez," said Don. "Did you know that you got one brown eye and one blue eye?"

As unhinged as Joe seemed in danger of becoming, he sighed. "You'd be surprised how often I'm asked that."

Michael just stared.

Jane was conscious of trying to keep her mind orderly. When these climactic moments happened, it always seemed that all events and facts flew around their heads, confusing the main issues and diffusing the solution to the crime. Despite Jane's attempts at holding on to the reins, one question formed in her mind that had less to do with Joe and the police approaching cautiously with weapons drawn and more to do with her own mysterious mother. How did Nellie know to look at Joe's eyes?

Had she mentioned that Honest Joe's Internet offers had featured a twin to Michael with different-colored eyes? No, because she hadn't known that. Even if she had mentioned the eyes somehow being different, there was something about the way Nellie zeroed in on Joe's face and nodded to herself, as if she had suspected what she would find all along.

Head. Head. Oh. Hetero. Heterochromia. Two different-colored eyes. Jane now knew the term for it and knew why it had sounded familiar. She had heard it before. An actor who was a recurring spokesman in one of the commercial campaigns she produced had heterochromia. *Ben Crumb.* Jane had finally remembered both his name and his eyes. He would pop a brown contact over his blue eye before the shoot began, but Jane always found him more interesting, more arresting, before he "evened himself out" as he referred to it. Central heterochromia. Swanette probably had turned when she heard something, someone, and she had tried to tell Jane that the person who hit her had heterochromia. But only Jane had heard her struggle with the word and she hadn't even put it together until now. Why was Nellie nodding like Detective Columbo, like she knew all the answers to all the questions, all along?

Oh took care of arrangements with the police. Cord sent the two officers who had come in from their posts in the field to check out the area behind the barn where Nellie had heard the car pull in.

"You weren't supposed to call for lights that soon, Mom," said Jane. "We heard the car engine, too. We wanted to wait until he had actually picked up the wooden slat—that would have meant he was trying to remove what he thought was the murder weapon."

"We heard the engine, heard it stop, and I counted to forty-five. I figured it might take him that long to creep over to where you two were, but I wasn't going to give him a second longer and a chance to use that club again," said Nellie.

"I agree with your mother," said Don. "We shouldn't have been doing all of this cloak-and-dagger work anyway, and we weren't going to take a chance of anyone getting hurt."

Cord came over to them shaking his head. "Car's gone. His partner got away."

Honest Joe looked up from the porch steps where he had been sitting, handcuffed and curiously calm.

"I didn't come here in a car," he said.

"We're in the middle of nowhere," said Tim. "Out for a night hike?"

Claire had gone back into the kitchen and Jane could see her put the kettle on the stove. That was getting to be a familiar sight. Michael was sitting at the kitchen table. He had relaxed some after his initial shock at meeting his doppelgänger, but still looked shaken. Don and Nellie, Tim and Oh, they were all out here still surrounding Joe. So who was walking toward them from the road?

"I rode here with him," said Joe, pointing to the stranger.

"Dave, the lighting tech, I presume," said Jane, extending her hand.

"Jane Wheel, the love of my boss's life, right?" said Dave. "He's always talking about how you made his business for him, hiring him when he was just starting out. And you're pretty, too, just like he said." Dave looked around, realizing for the first time that he had a bit of an audience. "Did I do okay with the lights?"

Dave had gone into town on his motorcycle and met Joe at a roadhouse where they talked over beers and sandwiches. Joe asked for a ride out to the property so he could ask Jane Wheel about the sale and Dave didn't see anything wrong with giving him a lift. Figured the guy seemed to know about the farm and all the stuff that was going to be for sale. Len had told him that the whole lighting thing was probably for one of Jane Wheel's "junkapaloozas" or something. It all made sense by the third beer.

"Did Joe ask you if you would be able to drive him back to town?"

"Nope," said Dave. "I would have, though. Once I turned on the lights for the night, I really didn't have anything to do. I could have taken the ten minutes or so to bring him back to the bar."

"Or he might have arranged for another ride home," said Jane. "And when the lights went on and the commotion started, the driver left the same way he came."

"I didn't arrange anything," said Joe. "I just wanted to see what was out here, that's all. I heard there was lots of stuff and I thought it was my chance to be the first guy here. That's all. Haven't got a partner and I didn't ask for a ride," he said. "Except from him," he added, pointing to Dave.

"And you were planning to return home by what vehicle?" asked Oh.

"I've walked that far before. I just live over Edna's and it's less than a mile from here."

Michael had come out to the porch, holding a mug of tea. The autumn coolness that had led to their search for jackets earlier had turned into a real chill.

"You'd walk that distance in the dark?" asked Michael.

"Do it all the time," said Joe. "Nothing to be afraid of out here. You talk like a city boy. City people have to be afraid of the dark all the time. My mom always said that was why cities had all them bright lights. People who lived there were afraid of the dark." Joe had remained sitting on the porch steps, but had turned to look at Michael's face. "You look like you're afraid of the dark."

"Damn right," said Michael, looking as if he might want to add more, but stopping himself.

Cord motioned to Oh who raised an eyebrow in Jane's direction. The three of them retreated a distance from those on the porch.

"Under the circumstances, I could just barely hold him for trespassing. Keep in mind that someone in your employ brought him here. He could make a case that he thought that gave him permission to look around. He entered an unlocked structure. He didn't touch anything, pocket anything, and didn't go for the wooden slat we placed..."

"He didn't have time," said Jane. "He would have."

"Mrs. Wheel," said Cord, "I'm not saying I don't believe your instincts could be correct on this, but under the circumstances," he repeated, "I'm not sure anything that happened here tonight makes a case against this fellow."

Jane nodded.

"You're right. I appreciate your support on all of this, and I wish we had led you to a real suspect, but you're right. Under the circumstances, tonight was a bust."

Oh tried to look into Mrs. Wheel's eyes to see what was truly posted there. He had never known her to give up this easily.

"If Swanette had actually—" Cord began, but Jane stopped him.

"I'm willing to admit that tonight did not go according to plan, but I'd just as soon not reveal anything about the plan to Joe over there. I'd rather just give the gentleman what he came for."

Jane smiled at the puzzled look on Cord's face.

"To make sure he doesn't feel 'entrapped' or anything," Jane said, pulling the word out of her limited cop TV show vocabulary and hoping that it fit this occasion. "Not that he'd have a case since he didn't do anything he can be held for, but we'll just let him look around at the stuff. I might be wrong in some of my suspicions, but I can spot a picker and that guy really does want a look around at the stuff. Let's give him the preview."

Oh nodded. *Very nice.*

Jane left Oh to talk with Cord in police-speak about what would happen next. Based on Jane's limited experience with the police, nothing would happen. Someone would have to be hit over the head with a board to convince the police that a violent crime was committed. *Oh wait,* Jane wanted to say, *someone was.*

"Joe?" said Jane. "I'm afraid we've made a mistake."

Joe looked up at her. In the light from the porch, Jane could see his two different-colored eyes clearly enough to be momentarily disconcerted by them. She knew Michael too well to really be fooled by the face now that the first shock was over. Yes, Joe resembled Michael, but knowing someone, talking with someone, recognizing their expressions and foibles and flaws, allowed a sister such insight into a brother that she could never really think that anyone else looked like him. Not really. Resemblance and likeness were two different things.

Jane did notice something familiar about Joe that had nothing to do with Michael. He cocked his head when he listened. Now, as he looked at her, she realized it was the same angle from which Ada regarded her when they spoke.

Deaf, thought Jane, *or hard of hearing. At least in one ear.*

"You showed up here with all good intentions. Just wanted an early peek at the sale stuff, and then got caught up in something that doesn't really concern you. We should, at least, let you have your look around," said Jane.

Claire Oh now cocked her head at Jane and Jane knew her hearing was perfect. Claire just didn't believe what she was hearing Jane tell Joe. Even though Claire could never suspect this itinerant picker of posing the slightest threat to her own antiquing with her own deep pockets, she did arrive at Swanette's farm under the impression that she was being given an early look at the estate. Now some scruffy character in torn blue jeans was given the royal treatment by Jane Wheel?

"Claire, may I have a word?" asked Oh, suddenly beside her. Jane hadn't heard Oh approach, but she now heard Cord talking to his people out by the barn.

Jane had avoided speaking directly to Don and Nellie since the lights went on, except to remind her mother that she had jumped the gun in calling for them. She needed to dodge her dad's protective embrace and deflect Nellie's overzealous desire to participate. What Jane surmised was that Oh would suggest to Claire that she return to Kankakee with Don and Nellie and allow them to spend time with Joe on the property. Surely, as one picker to another, Joe would become comfortable enough to speak about his business, his greatest finds, his most recent Internet sales. Before the night was over, Joe would tell them everything they wanted to hear. But they had to make Joe comfortable . . . set him up with a meat-loaf sandwich from Edna's and some boxes to unpack. Jane had to persuade her parents to go home.

"Thank you for helping out here, but we've got it for the rest of the night. Looks like the show is over for now," said Jane. "If you would drive Claire back to your house and let her get some rest, we'll just follow along later. Michael's got his rental and Tim and Oh both have cars here, so . . ."

"Some detective you are," said Nellie. "You believe that guy?"

Jane looked at Joe who had stood up and was looking in the window of the house.

"Enough," said Jane.

"What the hell does that mean?" asked Nellie.

"It means I believe him enough to let the rest of the night play out here," said Jane. She realized that she was telling her parents the truth. "I don't totally trust him, any more than anyone should ever trust someone who's a picker, someone who wants what someone else has, but I don't feel threatened by him."

Jane was prepared for her father to be on her side and that it would take the two of them to force Nellie to go home. Nellie, however, didn't stand around waiting for them to persuade her. Instead she headed for their car, throwing up one hand in the air and waving without turning back to look at anyone.

"That's not like your mother," said Don, watching his wife retreat. "Jane, before I leave you and your brother here, tell me who the hell this guy is and whether he's the guy who hit Swanette, because I . . ."

Jane was no longer sure. As positive as she had been when she first saw Joe that he was the one who must be running the Internet scam, the one whom Swanette surprised in the shed, she had just watched him pop up from the steps when she said he could look around the farm. He was as eager as . . . Jane realized it as the thought formed . . . he was as eager as someone who had never been inside the house or the sheds. At least not on his own. Maybe he knew about it, the stuff stored on the farm, but he wasn't a person who had unlimited access. He might be the face of Honest Joe's Internet sales, but if he was, he might not even know it.

And if Joe wasn't old Brother James's partner in crime, who was he? James must have handed his ring of keys over to someone. It was unlikely that he shared his business with his sister Ada. He didn't have other family around. According to Don and Nellie, his wife left him or rather he drove her away when she got pregnant . . .

Unlike the cartoon incandescent bulb that instantly switched on over a character's head when an idea crystalized, Jane felt she was standing under the more ecologically sound compact fluorescent bulb. Awareness dawned with, first, a slight humming in her brain, then a pause while pieces fell into place, until, with an implied *ta da*, the light flashed.

Brother James had a son. Despite the gossip Don had heard from the Bonfield saloonkeeper, James and Martha had a son.

"Joe?" said Jane, watching the man as he reluctantly turned away from the window to look back at her. "Joe Speller?"

Joe turned from the window to look at Jane, who, with the others, stood at the bottom of the porch steps.

He opened his mouth, but whether he was going to agree or protest, Jane could not have predicted. His disconcerting unmatched eyes were wide and he lifted his right hand slightly, but before he made a sound, they all heard the shot.

Lying in bed at night in her Evanston home, Jane often heard noises that *could* be gunshots. Pops and bangs that turned out to be car noises and firecrackers were common enough, especially in the summer. It amazed her that, now, when she heard this true gunshot, fired from somewhere just beyond Dave's trailer, it sounded like nothing else. There was no confusion, no momentary *"what could that be?"* No wonder the sound of gunfire was so often described as unmistakable.

Oh shouted for everyone to get down and everyone—Jane, Don, Tim, Claire and Dave and Michael—dropped to the ground. Everyone except Joe, who, a second before, stood framed in the farmhouse window, was already down, crumpled on the porch floor, bleeding through his thin white shirt.

The silence was so profound after the initial noise that they all heard the car engine on the main road.

Oh was immediately on his phone, helping Claire to her feet, scanning the perimeter of the yard beyond the driveway and outbuildings, doing everything, it seemed, simultaneously.

Jane was the first to reach Joe. She removed her borrowed scarf and pressed it to Joe's shoulder. She had no experience with this and could only remember old Mrs. Tabor, her seventh-grade substitute teacher, who had decided that, in what Jane now realized was a period of undiagnosed dementia, instead of history, the class should learn basic first aid, repeating "pressure, pressure, pressure" as she pressed on the wound, using a giant teddy bear as a demonstration model.

"Joe," Jane whispered, "I think you'll be fine. Don't be scared."

It was the best she could do. His blue eye and brown eye remained open, but he was either wide-eyed unconscious or completely in shock. Jane didn't think the wound, which she placed around his right shoulder, was life threatening, but what did she know besides television and movies?

"That's right, Mrs. Wheel. Pressure," said Oh.

The ambulance arrived just after Cord, who had barely started up the road. An EMT relieved Jane and she realized how immediately she went from being necessary to just another outsider getting in the way of professionals. Michael and Tim were talking to police officers, Claire was out of view, and Jane saw Oh nodding as Cord ranted and raved about his own stupidity in allowing such amateurish goings-on. Jane thought it was probably not the right moment to remind him that it was she, not he, who believed this area was a crime scene in the first place.

"Who's missing?" said Jane aloud and immediately knew the answer.

Don was at his car, gesticulating to a police officer, and Jane knew, without being able to hear his voice or read his lips, what he was saying.

"Where's Nellie?"

She had gone off without a fight when Jane suggested they take Claire and go back to Kankakee. She should have been safely out of harm's way, sitting in the front seat, complaining to Rita about all the ridiculous human beings in her life. But Rita and Nellie were absent from the car and Jane could see Don was getting more and more frantic.

Jane turned to where she thought the shot had come from. Dave's trailer was parked at the very beginning of the driveway, just as one turned into it off the main road. He had turned the trailer and stationed it on the lawn, parallel to the road, which meant a car could have pulled up next to it and remained unseen from the house, which was set back several hundred feet from the road. If Nellie was sitting in the car, though, closer to the road and without the distraction of the group's conversation, she might have heard the car drive up. She might have heard the car, seen the person who had fired the shot hitting Joe.

And if that were the case, Jane had to ask herself, shuddering, WWND?

What would Nellie do?

19

Nellie, hearing a car slowly pull up and stop without turning into the driveway, closed the photo album she had been studying ever since she found it earlier in the day.

"What the hell is going on now?" she asked Rita.

A small woman to begin with, and shrinking steadily every year, Nellie was able to turn around in the front seat and, crouching on her knees, catch a glimpse of the front of the car behind the lighting trailer-van. She saw the car's headlights, dimmed to begin with, go out altogether, but could hear the vehicle still idling.

"I'll go find out who wants a piece of all this now," said Nellie. She hesitated for just a moment and reopened the album. Some of the photographs had been missing, but enough were there and enough were captioned that she had pieced together the family history. "Okay, Rita, just in case, let's mark the page."

Nellie fished out a package of Don and Nellie's EZ Way Inn matches from the emergency kit Don kept in the glove compartment, leaving the door hanging open so she didn't make any unnecessary noise. She opened the book, and bent up one match so it stayed outside the matchbook, dividing the cover into two halves. Unsatisfied, she folded the single match back in and pulled more matches forward, then tucked the cover in. Now all the print on the cover was blocked except for *Nellie's* and, below her name, *Inn*. "Let's see if the fancypants detectives can read this clue."

She put the matchbook in the album where the most interesting finds were, and laid the leather-bound volume carefully on the front seat. She squeezed open the door handle, put her fingers to her lips, and crept out. Rita began to follow, but Nellie turned and put her hand on the dog's head. "I'll be back."

Despite the lights provided by the huge floods directed at the house and outbuildings, the road itself was not lit and offered enough night, enough shadows, for Nellie to make her way to the other side of the idling car and crouch behind a few scrubby windbreak trees. She didn't know car makes or models, and noted this only as a nondescript four-door boxy little car. The driver was absent, but the driver's side door was open. Someone robbing the trailer? The car was parked close to the trailer door, close enough for someone to open the driver's side door and touch the trailer.

Nellie saw a figure do just that, open the back door and use the car as a step up to the ladder on the side of the trailer. This nut was climbing onto the top of Len's Mobile Lighting Van carrying what looked like a baseball-equipment bag.

Nellie needed to get closer to see if she recognized whoever this was, probably the partner of that crazy-eyed Joe, who Nellie was sure . . .

She couldn't see from behind the trees, not now that the climber was on top of the van. The best place to see what was going on was the base of the trailer, so Nellie crept between the car and van and slipped into the backseat of the idling sedan. Crouching down on the floor, she could look up and out the back door. The view was perfect. She watched as the figure, dressed in black and with a scarf wrapped around head and face, leaned over the trailer roof toward the house.

When she heard the shot, Nellie momentarily froze. Her husband, her daughter, and her son were in that group on the porch. Her family and that damn irritating Tim and that Detective Oh and his snooty wife, Claire, and some bozo from the lighting company. All of them were in the line of fire. And Joe. Then Nellie remembered that Joe was on that porch. Now everything she had only thought might be true became clear. Poor Joe.

Nellie stayed put, covering her head with a raincoat that was tossed on the backseat floor. If what she thought just happened, happened, someone was going to have to catch the killer. Might as well be her since she was already here.

20

Jane wasn't sure which—or whose—hysteria she should attend to first.

Don had threatened to hit the police officer who speculated aloud that Nellie was the only one of them who had had the opportunity, and therefore could have been the shooter.

Michael, seeing his look-alike shot, lying on the porch, reacted with a kind of twin-syndrome shock, and passed out cold.

Tim and Claire, assisted by Dave, who remained cool even though Jane was quite certain no commercial shoot had ever turned into this kind of literal shoot on his watch, were trying to stay out of the way of the police, while continuing to inventory what was in the immediate vicinity. This, and reviving Michael, put them into a kind of list-making, brow-mopping frenzy.

Detective Oh remained with Cord, nodding and listening to Cord give frantic orders to his people and making his own list at the same time.

And then, of course, there was Jane's own rising panic.

As unprofessional as it might have been to lie under the circumstances, Jane identified herself to the EMT as Joe's first cousin, his closest relative, and asked about his condition. Although he remained vague, it was a reassuring vague, and he did tell Jane he felt fairly certain that Joe's injury was not life threatening.

All of this activity, unfolding under the commercial lights, made the scene resemble a movie set all the more. Jane knew that the chaos would sort itself out, the police going their way, the ambulance and attendants going theirs . . . and all of the rest of them now banned from the farm, which would finally get its proper yellow wrapping to identify it as a crime scene.

Jane's panic was of the domestic variety.

Nellie.

Jane always tried to take a breath and solve the case of Nellie one non sequitur at a time. It was how she dealt with her mother's daily erratic behavior, harsh judgments, bizarre pronouncements, and general homespun voodoo.

And now, not for the first time, Nellie was missing. She had been kidnapped before, when thugs mistook her for Jane, and she was able to capture every one of the three while also cooking them a meal and diagnosing the leader's peptic ulcer. Jane wanted to soothe her dad by reminding him of this episode, but somehow, watching him near apoplexy, she knew this would not be the right thing to ease his mind under the circumstances.

"Dad, you have to take Michael home. Seeing Joe like that threw him," Jane said. "I think he realized that all of this mistaken-identity stuff was more serious than he thought."

Don shook his head.

"I'm going to go find Mom and bring her home," said Jane. "I promise."

Don took Jane's hand.

"She's a pain sometimes," he said, and she nodded. "But she's my pain and I can't live without her."

Jane had never heard her father say anything this simple, this dramatic, this true. He was the sentimental one and Nellie was the cold fish . . . that much she knew. But somehow, this direct declaration caught Jane by surprise.

Don finally agreed, after a struggle, to drive Claire and Michael back to Kankakee. Michael had wanted to stay with Jane, but she persuaded him that he needed to be with Don while she located their mother. Jane put her hand on her brother's arm.

"Take care of Dad for now and I'll bring Mom home later. She's following that car, I know it. She's impulsive, Michael, but she's too smart to get too close. We'll catch up."

Neither Jane nor Michael stated the obvious. The police had swept the grounds. If Nellie was "following" the shooter, was she trotting down the road? She didn't know how to drive. The car and Rita were both still here.

The likely scenario was that Nellie had been snatched because she witnessed the shooting. The riddle there was why wouldn't the shooter just do the convenient thing and shoot Nellie? Jane had wanted to comfort her father by explaining that if Nellie were going to be hurt, it would have happened then and there. She settled for telling him that if the bad guy had Nellie, he was going to keep her safe as insurance.

Don didn't answer back "until he doesn't need her anymore," but Jane saw it in his eyes.

"You two have to go home. If there is any kind of ransom demand or any kind of contact made, it will be through you and Michael at home. Mom herself might end up calling there—she could even show up there. Cord is sending a police officer to the house to stay until we hear something. And we will hear from her," said Jane. "Now go."

Jane and Oh had both spoken to Cord, who was sending people to cover all the roads into town, the service roads through fields, and also sending out Nellie's description as a missing person. At both Oh's and Jane's urging, he promised that all caution would be used in pursuing the shooter since . . .

No one finished the sentence . . . Nellie could be a hostage, but each of them said it silently. Cord patted Jane on the back and reassured her much the same way she had reassured her father.

Amazing how everyone pretended to believe everyone in times of crisis.

Dave was told he could leave the grounds, but the trailer needed to remain. He roared off on his motorcycle, presumably back to the bar where he had begun his evening. Jane couldn't decide if he was the coolest, most detached character she had ever met or if he had met a girl at the bar, but he couldn't get off the property fast enough. The police had been given a full description of Nellie, but Jane knew it was up to her. She had told Michael and Don that she would bring Nellie home.

And now to keep her promise.

"If Joe was the son of James Speller, that makes him Ada's nephew," said Jane, sitting in Oh's car, notebook in hand. "James's wife, Martha, left him when she got pregnant. She could have returned here with him as a boy and raised him, not telling him who his father was . . . or she could have told him he was entitled to something from his father's family and he could have come back to Herscher to sort things out . . ."

"His picture was on the Honest Joe Internet site, yes?" asked Oh.

"I don't think he had anything to do with that. Did you see his face when we told him he could look around here?" asked Jane.

"He was like a kid on Christmas morning looking in that window," said Tim, from the backseat.

"Either because he couldn't wait to see it all for the first time . . . or because he couldn't wait to get back and finish taking what he'd already started to steal," said Jane.

Jane reminded them how little they knew about Joe. He might look familiar, but neither the Internet image nor the resemblance to Michael told them anything about the man himself. Joe mentioned he lived over Edna's Diner. Could that be true? No one had reacted to Michael earlier in the diner.

"Mrs. Wheel, I believe that coincidences are a part of life, a regular part of life. In fact, I believe they happen quite frequently, yet few recognize their patterns. That is why, when they do, people are so surprised. In this case, however, I do not think it is merely a coincidence that Joe and your brother resemble each other," said Oh, starting the engine.

When Jane had walked her father to his car earlier, they found Rita, still waiting and whimpering. Jane opened the door and invited the bereaved dog to join her. "Let's go find Nellie," said Jane.

Rita hesitated, placing her paw on the photo album.

"It's okay, girl. You can come with me and we'll get Nellie."

Once again, the dog pawed the cover of the book. Jane picked it up, remembering that her mother had been studying it off and on all day. "Okay, we'll take Nellie's book, too."

Tim, now sharing the backseat with Rita, picked up the photo album.

"Nellie snagged this from the house, didn't she?" asked Tim. "I remember seeing it, wondering if it were one of the random collected volumes or actually a family book."

"The leather binding is familiar," said Jane. "I hadn't noticed until now. It's the same as all those leather-bound books in Ada's study. It's one more object taken from her house."

It was now after ten o'clock on a Sunday night. Oh drove toward Herscher via the main road since that's where the shooter's car had been parked. Jane found herself scanning the sides of the road, half believing that she would find her mother jogging along, pursuing whoever had shot Joe.

The other half-belief Jane was holding was, she knew, the more likely. Nellie was being held by someone who was willing to commit murder to keep them from hearing whatever Joe might have been able to tell them. And if Joe wasn't part of this Internet operation, what could he have said that made him a target? Was he sent to pick up that wooden slat in the shed and was it just a perk of his assignment that he'd be able to get a glimpse of the presale? It would be a day or two before they got any answers from Joe. And they needed to find Nellie tonight.

"By the way," asked Tim, "where are we going?"

"To inform Joe's closest relative," said Oh. "It's the right thing to do, don't you agree, Mrs. Wheel?"

Jane wondered if Oh had heard her telling the EMT that she was Joe's closest relative.

"It's pretty late for a pop-in," said Tim. "You two might be used to city hours, but in our little towns around here, especially on a Sunday night, ten o'clock would be the absolute cutoff for a visit."

Oh swung the car onto the main street and parked in front of Edna's Diner. The to-be-expected CLOSED sign hung on the door, and the bright neon window sign was off; however, there were interior lights on and a few customers remained at tables already cleared of dishes. The woman behind the counter was not the same waitress to whom Jane had leaked the news about Swanette's farm being a potential crime scene. This woman, slightly older, was glaring at the occupied tables, but was having no success at driving the lingering diners out. Jane was reminded of her first visit to Edna's when she spoke with the old-timer who first directed her to James Speller, to Cousin Ada's house. That waitress couldn't wait to get out the door and Jane imagined whoever pulled the Sunday-evening shift would be equally impatient to be off duty.

Something about the woman behind the counter reminded Jane of her mother. The way she held the rag with which she mopped the counter? Her flat-footed stance, one hand on her hip, when she cocked her head to listen to a request from someone at one of the tables? Jane was watching this through the lit storefront windows, an Edward Hopper painting brought to life, when she realized that the reminder of Nellie was all in the impatience of the woman. Jane watched her yell back at her customer, head shaking, her whole body shaped into a *no*.

"They're open later than I would have thought," said Tim.

"They closed a while ago, but she can't get rid of her customers," said Jane, translating what she read in the scene.

They had gotten out of the car, Tim hoping to run in and get some food, any food, to sustain them for whatever the rest of the night was going to hold. A couple walked out of the diner and Tim stopped them.

"You think they'll take a to-go order?"

"Are you kidding?" the man asked. "Edna used to stay open for Scary Night, but there's no way her daughter wants to miss her beauty sleep. She's booting everybody out."

"Yeah," his wife added, "Edna used to serve pie and coffee till midnight. Was the best Sunday night of the year for her, but this one thinks she's got better things to do. And they wonder why people end up going in to Kankakee or over to the Wendy's on the highway."

"Scary Night?" asked Oh.

The man waved as he climbed into a car parked down the street from the diner.

"Cover me," said Jane. "I'm going in."

Jane wanted to forestall any "we're closed" wrath, so she held up her hand as she entered Edna's.

"I know you're closed. I just had a question about the apartment upstairs. I heard it might be available," said Jane.

"Where'd you hear that?" the woman asked. How old was she? Jane had trouble distinguishing forty-something from fifty-something. The woman's hands argued for the older end of the range, but then again she was in the restaurant business which was also the dishwashing business. Everybody knew that was a hand killer.

"My brother was talking to Joe and since I just got a job at—"

"In case you or your brother haven't noticed, Joe is a few bricks shy of a load. He isn't even the tenant. Nobody'd let him sign his X on a lease, so whether he hitchhikes out of town or not doesn't mean anything about the apartment."

Jane was trying to think of another reason, any reason, to prolong this discussion when the woman added, "The other one up there might be available at the end of the month."

"Yeah?" asked Jane.

"I can't show it to you tonight. I have to wait until these losers leave, and I'm already late to meet my boyfriend. If you come back tomorrow, though, someone can take you up. Em's leaving before the end of the month."

"Moving out of town?" Jane asked, more and more aware of the inanity of this conversation. Oh had always told her that if she just listened for the right answers, it would be more important than asking the right questions.

"They got her into assisted living in Kankakee," she said, grabbing the check and a twenty-dollar bill from the last party to head for the door. "Need any change?"

They shook their heads and exited quickly.

"Better run, you losers. This bill's for nineteen twenty-five," she said, ringing up the sale and pocketing three quarters. "Big spenders wonder why they can't sit in here all night like I'm running a hippie coffeehouse."

"Em's going into assisted living?" Jane asked, stalling.

"How do you know her?" she asked, untying her plain white apron and locking the register.

One question too many. Jane shrugged and did her best I-don't-really-know-and-I-was-just-making-conversation kind of shrug.

"Are you a friend of one of her kids?"

Jane shook her head knowing she had a fifty-fifty chance of giving the right answer.

"Good. I'm already late and I don't want to get started. I could give you an earful of what I think of them."

"What's your name?" asked Jane. "In case I come back to look tomorrow . . . so I can tell them who told me about the apartment?"

"Mary Jane. Edna's daughter," she said. "Who are you?"

"Jane. Just plain Jane."

"I go by MJ around here, so if Lou or anyone's around, just tell them you're interested in Em's place. I'm hardly ever here. Just filling in tonight. Why anyone would choose to live in this town is beyond me, but—"

Tim tapped on the window, one hand clutched to his middle, hoping that he was miming hunger effectively.

"No way!" shouted MJ. Jane watched her bump open the kitchen door with her hip and rake her hand across the panel of switches that controlled the lights. Everything went off and only the glow from the street outside illuminated the diner.

Jane preceded her out the door. She thought about grabbing a few bags of chips off the rack and laying a five down on the counter, but didn't want to risk losing any goodwill she might have built up with MJ. She would remind Tim that they had to find Nellie, and as Nellie always said, hunger built character.

Jane rejoined Tim and Oh on the street in front of the car. MJ, who had said she was meeting her boyfriend, crossed the street. Jane assumed she was headed to her parked car, and was surprised to see her continue past the street toward Ada's side yard.

She was about to mention this when there was a loud noise from the rear of Ada Speller's house. It was an explosive and ominous chord of music, the beginning to a lugubrious-sounding organ piece that must have been carried over loudspeakers since it blasted through the whole main street. At the second note of the music, lights flared up from the backyard. They could see the light climb in the sky, over the front of the house, flickering and wavery.

"The house must be on fire," Jane screamed.

All three of them had their cell phones in their hands as they ran across the street, following the path of MJ who had walked around the side and disappeared into the backyard.

The tall wooden gated entrance to the backyard stood open. Posts were stuck into the ground on either side with grotesquely carved pumpkin heads spiked on top of them. Tim was the first to rush through the gate, stopping short so that Jane ran right into his back. Bruce Oh, at a more moderate pace behind them, simply stopped when he saw what lay before them.

Thirty to fifty people stood ringing the enormous yard, oohing and aahing as if they were watching Fourth of July fireworks. Instead of exploding chrysanthemums, wagon wheels, and waterfalls in the sky, however, there were rows and rows and rows of carved and lit pumpkins, staring out at them from the makeshift brick and board shelves that ringed the yard. Gigantic scarecrows had been stuffed with straw and were standing on poles and strung up in the trees, crouching over the spectacle.

"Scary night," said Oh.

"You can say that again," said Tim.

"That's what the guy at the diner called it," said Jane. "Scary Night. Ada talked about getting the pumpkins ready, talked about having parties and festivals."

A woman next to Tim turned to them with a smile.

"First time here?" When they nodded, she went on. "Scared me to death when I was a kid. I had nightmares for weeks. See how few little kids are here? It's all about the adults now who remember being scared. The teenagers in town think it's corny and the parents know better than to bring the little ones, so the crowd just isn't that big. Only those of us in between hoping we won't be scared out of our wits all over again."

"How does Ada manage to get all of this set up?" asked Jane.

"Who carves these things?" asked Tim.

"Who lights them?" asked Oh.

Jane realized that Oh had gotten to the heart of the matter. Ada drafted anyone and everyone into carving pumpkins during the week. Schoolkids probably came by . . . people who were in and out of Edna's all day. All of the ghosts who lived in her house were kept busy carving jack-o'-lanterns.

Who was responsible, though, for all of them coming to life, lighting up all at once to produce this spectacular show?

"Where is Ada?" asked Jane.

Before she even finished the question, Jane saw her. Cousin Ada wore a long black skirt and a cloak that had large pockets sewn into the outside. As she walked regally through the crowd, Jane saw some people dropping matchbooks into her pockets. A few folks next to the banks of shelves holding the lit pumpkins were slipping butane lighters back into pockets and purses. Jane could see that everyone who attended Scary Night was participating in the event. Scary Night regulars must have positioned themselves all over the yard and on some signal from Ada did their best to light the jack-o'-lanterns and back away so the blaze could be as coordinated as possible. Jane also noticed that one whole section of pumpkins was lit with strings of white Christmas lights inserted into the backs of the hollowed-out shells. Someone was in charge of plugging all those strings in to supplement the candlelight, and the effect, Jane had to admit, was spectacular.

Jane tried to follow the cord and find the outlet, wondering who might be the link to the house, since Ada's ghosts normally stayed behind the scenes.

A crouching figure behind one of the scarecrows slinked back toward the kitchen door. Since the only lights came from the jack-o'-lanterns, it was hard to make out whether the figure was male or female.

"Did you lock the car?" asked Jane. "Is Rita still in the backseat?"

Jane looked at Tim, who was still staring from pumpkin to pumpkin, openmouthed. She remembered Rita then because she noticed that Tim still carried the photo album under his arm, the one Rita had seemed so insistent upon Jane noticing.

Jane wrestled the book from Tim and told him that she was going to slip into the library and make sure the binding really was the same. She didn't know whether or not he heard her, but she couldn't hang around and make sure. She wanted to be right behind the person slipping into the kitchen. If ever there was an opportunity to catch a ghost, this was it. If she had the photo album with her, at least she could make an excuse that she had found it at the farm and was trying to return it.

It also made sense to Jane that one of these ghosts might lead her right to Nellie.

The last time Jane had been in Ada's kitchen, it had been filled with pumpkins in various stages of carving. Replacing all the jack-o'-lanterns were large bowls of candy. Homemade caramels were wrapped in waxed-paper twists, candy apples stood upright in rows on the counter. There were some bowls of purchased candy, too. Lollipops and small chocolate bars. Ada had made a few compromises, but Jane was pleased that she had been able to follow at least some of what she was learning were the family traditions.

Ada had a small lamp on the kitchen counter. Jane pulled the chain and set the album down, just to take a quick look at it before she began searching the house. For the first time she noticed that a matchbook was stuck between the pages.

Had Tim found one out in the yard and stuck it in there or has it been there all along?

"The EZ Way Inn?" said Jane aloud, reading the matchbook, noting its folds but recognizing the familiar script on the bar giveaway.

This matchbook had not changed color or typeface in twenty years, so despite the peculiar configuration of the matches, Jane recognized it right away.

Nellie had left her a clue.

"Okay," said Jane. "Nellie wanted her name to be prominent so we would know that she left this in the album. Why?"

Jane fingered the matchbook, then bent over the pages it had marked. A few photos were missing. The old paper corners remained and some writing in white ink.

The hay wagon . . . with neighbors.
Veronica, Nellie, and Ada. Sisters and cousins.

Those were the titles of the missing photos. There were three that remained. One of them was a copy of the same photo that Jane had seen at her mother's when they searched for a photo of Michael. Nellie's parents holding two babies. Jane had speculated that the two were Nellie and Veronica but Nellie had said no. It was too early. They would not have been born yet. Here, in Ada's album, or what was most likely Ada's parents' family album, this photo was captioned.

James and his new "twin" sister, Ada. With "Aunt Hettie."

The babies seemed to be the same age, maybe six to eight months. Ada, according to the caption, would be the one wearing the bonnet with ribbons. She was not a newborn, a new baby sister. So how could she be James's *new twin?* Who captions a photo like that?

Jane didn't really remember her grandma Hettie very well. Five years old when she died, Jane had feasted on the family stories of her legendary cooking, sewing ability, and violent mood swings. Nellie hated sewing—never even replaced a button or repaired a hem. She said it was because she didn't have the time, but Jane's Aunt Veronica had told Jane that their mother, Grandma Hettie, had been such a stern taskmaster that neither one of her daughters wanted to attempt needlework of any kind. Nellie had inherited the cooking gene—she couldn't stop herself on that—but she refused to keep needle and thread in the house.

Jane stared hard at this picture of her grandmother and grandfather holding the two babies who she now knew as James and Ada. James and his "new twin" with their "aunt and uncle." Hettie's legendary temper—the one that drove her to stab her own daughters with their embroidery needles if they made a mistake—was clearly not evident in this photo. Here, Grandma Hettie looked like a sad child, her eyes imploring the camera to look away, focus on the babies, on the tree behind her, on anything or anyone other than her. Jane had never seen a look like that. Pain, despair, terror, resignation—all there battling each other behind her eyes, all fighting to take over this woman, Jane's Grandma Hettie, standing up straight, wearing a plain black dress and cloche hat.

"Nellie saw something in this photo," whispered Jane. "That's why she marked it for us."

As soon as Jane spoke, she heard the creak of a door behind her. She ran her finger under the photo, freeing it from decades-old glue, and slipped it into her pocket. As soon as it was safe, she swung around, as prepared as anyone ever is to go eyeball to eyeball with a ghost.

Jane had to lower her stare to go eyeball to eyeball with the creature who had entered the kitchen through the swinging door that led to the dining room. Decidedly not a ghost, and very much of Jane's world . . . but how had she escaped and ended up in the house—through the front door, no less?

"Rita?" Jane asked. Her dog came over to her and licked her knee—the blue jeans that covered her knee anyway—sat down obediently next to her, and stared fixedly toward the opposite kitchen wall, where the open shelves and pantry were located.

"Who let you out of the car?"

"Who the hell you think?" answered a gravelly voice from inside the pantry.

Jane managed to keep her scream down in volume, but she couldn't stop it from escaping altogether.

The pantry door opened slowly.

Jane had been prepared for a ghost when she turned to find Rita, but nothing prepared her for what crept out from behind the pantry door.

Holding a very old—and, Jane knew, fragile—German papier-mâché devil mask worth at least five hundred dollars in front of her face, the spookiest figure from Jane's childhood scampered toward her.

"Scared you, didn't I?" asked Nellie.

21

Before Jane could even begin the litany of how-did-you-get-away-who-shot-Joe-what-the-hell-do-you-think-you're-doing-and-put-down-that-mask-before-you-tear-a-hole-in-it, Nellie tossed the mask onto the table and grabbed a chocolate bar from the bowl on the counter, unwrapped it, and bit into it.

"I'm starving," she said. "Ada usually has a pie around here somewhere, but I guess everything's out for Scary Night." Nellie peeked out into the backyard from the window over the sink and responded to her own question. "Yup, she's got about five or six pies out there and a ton of taffy apples. These just must be her spares."

Jane half listened to her mother while she contacted Michael. Tim and Nick had tutored her on the fine art of texting and although she was slow, and Nick laughed at what he referred to as "hovering thumb" syndrome, she had mastered the basics. Since she didn't trust her voice right now, Jane felt this was the safest way to let her brother and father know that Nellie was safe. Safe? Nellie was wolfing down her third Hershey dark chocolate bar and laughing over a private joke with Rita.

Mom wi me. not kidnapped. fine. will call soon. All okay.

Texting. Jane figured that someday she would be explaining the term *letter-writing* to her grandchild as something people used to do. *It was like texting with a pencil*, she'd explain. Then she'd have to answer her imaginary grandchild's next question: *What's a pencil?*

No time for domestic daydreaming. Nick was only a kid, not even in high school, and she and Charley were far from grandparents. Far, perhaps, from being a family at all. In the flicker of all the lights from the jack-o'-lanterns, in the middle of the creaks and groans of this haunted house, Jane allowed herself, for just a moment, to think that she might have imagined the whole conversation with Charley. Perhaps she just dreamed the whole thing. Jane looked down at her phone, allowed herself to push the button that revealed the received phone call history, and watched Charley's name appear on top of the list. Proof. No dream.

Jane shook herself and flipped the phone closed with a definite click and slipped it into her pocket.

Nellie stood up straight after whispering one more secret to Rita and looked up at her daughter who stood nearly a head taller than she.

"You look like hell," said Nellie. "What's the matter?"

Jane began to shake her head, to swallow back any words that might come out, unfiltered, scared or angry, then an internal switch flipped—on instead of off for a change—and she took a deep breath.

"You want to know what's the matter? I start out my weekend trying to get to the bottom of an Internet scam that may or may not involve Michael. Simple plan since whoever his twin is seems to be operating out of Herscher, a stone's throw away from you guys. Then I get pulled into Swanette's house sale and she gets attacked. I meet your cousin Ada, whom you've managed to hide from both

Michael and me all our lives, and she's living in a haunted house. Then when I have a pretty good plan for luring Swanette's attacker out, you call for lights, camera, and action a little too early. We get poor old Joe shot and you disappear. One of the police even tried to say you might have been the one to shoot him. I thought Dad was going . . ."

Although Jane had begun the speech full of anger and purpose, the more she unraveled the evening's events, the more ridiculous sounding and complicated and hilarious the whole thing seemed. When she pictured her dad ready to deck the officer who had tried to put Nellie in the shooter's position, all of the fight left her voice and she began to laugh.

Nellie grinned. "He was going to defend my honor, was he?"

"Oh yes," said Jane. "And you should have seen how scared the guy was when he saw Dad's face."

"Good." Nellie unwrapped a candy bar and shoved it at Jane. "Eat this. You look like hell."

"So you've said," said Jane, accepting the chocolate. There were a few oohs and aahs coming from the backyard. What was Ada up to now? Fireworks?

Nellie told Jane how she ended up in the backseat of whoever had shot Joe.

"I covered myself up. We only drove for a few minutes. I knew we hadn't gone farther than town. I stayed put after the car was parked and the driver got out. Then I counted to twenty-five, figured whoever it was was far enough away and I climbed out. The car's a little wagon-type thing that's parked out in back of Ada's garage with a bunch of others. It was dark, so I couldn't see the color and I don't know cars, so I just took out my house key and put a big scratch in the side so we'd know the right one later. Then with all the gawkers here for Scary Night, it was easy to mix in with the crowd."

"You keyed the car?"

"He shot that boy!"

"He? Who was the driver? Who shot Joe?" asked Jane, unwrapping another candy bar for herself.

"How the hell do I know? I kept my head down while we were driving, and when I get out, there's a hundred people out there with those damn pumpkins. Could be any one of them. Did you get the message I left behind?"

"Not right away. Rita kept pointing to the photo album, but we didn't pay any attention at first."

Nellie knelt down and draped her arm around the dog's neck.

"You're better than Lassie, you know that?"

"Why did I grow up thinking you hated pets?" asked Jane.

"Because I do. Most of them are dirty, smelly, and don't belong in a house with people. And that's because most people don't take care of them right or get bored with them or don't train them or pay attention to them after a while. I don't like most *pets* but that doesn't mean I don't like animals. It's not that different from people, Jane. I like some animals and I don't like others. This one, this Rita, I just really hit it off with," said Nellie, looking directly at the dog, who looked ready to lay down her life for Nellie.

"Well, that's quite different than with people," said Jane. "You hate most people."

Nellie laughed. "I don't hate them. I just don't have the patience for them. People can be such time wasters. Most of them anyway."

Jane was oddly pleased. This was an insightful conversation

she was having with her mother. Perhaps a shooting and a possible kidnapping was all they needed to give their relationship the little boost it needed. Fear and danger certainly seemed to help them communicate.

"So I think I interpreted the message you left behind," said Jane. "But I think you ought to tell me yourself what this photo means to you." She pulled it out of her pocket.

"Ada's mom, or whoever, wrote under one of them pictures that Ada was James's new twin sister and under that other one of me and Veronica and Ada, the photo said we were sisters and cousins," said Nellie.

"I got to thinking about my mother and dad. You know they were married eight years before they had me and then they had Veronica the next year. Ma always talked about how poor they had been and how sick she and Pa were when they were first married. Pa lost his job because of something and then was in bed for six months with some kind of fever. They really had hard times. Then she'd tell me about her brother and his wife and how they were so rich and important out in Herscher and how their farm never went under and how they always had plenty of everything and how they always got what they wanted. She'd talk about it and go on and on, then get all weepy, then get real mad and blame me and Veronica for something we never did and make us sew or scrub something that was already clean."

"You think Ada isn't your cousin after all?" Jane asked softly.

"Ada's my sister," said Nellie.

Jane tried to think of something to say. This was monumental, she knew, and she also knew that she would never be able to read what this meant to Nellie by staring into her poker face.

"That means she's your aunt," said Nellie.

"Wow," Jane said, nodding, and wishing her comment held slightly more weight.

"I'll say," said Nellie. "Now you got two old ladies to take care of and one is even more batshit crazy than the other one."

Jane began to laugh, really appreciating this new self-awareness that Nellie was demonstrating.

"We're going to have our hands full with her and Veronica who, you know, is a few bricks shy of a load," said Nellie.

So much for any self-awareness.

"A few bricks shy of a load?" said Jane. "I just heard that about someone else tonight . . . right. So, do you think you know who Joe is, too?" asked Jane.

"What the hell is going on out there?" said Nellie. The crowd noises had gotten louder and Jane followed her mother to the window over the sink. A huge pile of wood had been built up at the very end of the backyard that backed up into now plowed-under fields. Jane couldn't see Oh, but thought she made out Tim's profile in the crowd.

"Does Ada make a bonfire on Scary Night?" asked Jane.

"Fire department shut that down years ago. She got a ticket when James was still alive and he told her no more fires."

"But this year he told her to build one," said a voice behind them. "A little scary, isn't it? I'm afraid it might get out of control."

Jane and Nellie both turned to see a woman who had come in so quietly that neither had heard her. Just as Jane had described her to Ada . . . she moved quietly, like a cat. Neither noticed that she had taken Rita's leash from the floor and looped it over and tied it to an iron rail bolted into the frame of the dining room door until the woman pointed it out.

"That's convenient, isn't it?" she asked. "Ada uses that to anchor a loom she uses for weaving. Her brother, James, sunk it into a beam in the wall when they were just teenagers, so it'll never pull out."

Rita whimpered. She seemed to be agreeing that she might be stuck for good.

"I know you're not a ghost, now," said Jane. "You're the woman I met here the first time I came. You were in the study reading the mail that was on the desk, complaining about Honest Joe's Internet auctions. You said you dropped in to check on Ada."

"I lied. My brother and I actually live here most of the time. Ada doesn't know. There are rooms upstairs where Ada never goes. Brother James left her a note a few months back with the groceries and told her to stay out of the east wing of the house. Told her there were some bad ghosts there who wouldn't bother her if she didn't bother them. So I spend a lot of time here."

Jane and Nellie hadn't moved from the window. They had remained frozen there, instinctively perhaps, since Jane noticed now for the first time that the woman held a gun pointed at them.

"I've been listening to you talk. You're Ada's sister," she said, looking at Nellie. "That's terrible news."

"Why?" asked Jane, trying to spot the nearest weapon in the kitchen. She had been here twice in the last two days, and each time, the kitchen had been completely littered with carving knives of all shapes and sizes, and now she couldn't locate even one sharp object within reach.

"If that's true," she said, "that means you're Ada's closest relative."

"Yeah, so?" said Nellie.

"Closer than me," said the woman. "The way I put this together is that Ada owns all this and if she and James were just cousins and you are her sister ... Well, Cousin Nellie, that means you stand to inherit everything from Ada."

"You lost me," said Nellie. "Mind if I have some more chocolate? I haven't eaten dinner." Nellie reached for candy and began unwrapping Hersheys two at a time.

"You remember Brother James? My father?" the woman said, still sounding calm, but growing more agitated. Jane could see it in the way she gestured with the pointed gun.

"If Ada is my cousin and not my aunt, I don't have much of a claim to this estate, do I? Especially if she has a living sister. Not unless you two are out of the picture."

"I have a brother," said Jane. "And my mom has another sister. Getting rid of us doesn't get rid of the problem. We can work out some kind of division here. There's plenty of time to work out the details of a split ... Ada's healthy as a horse."

"Sounds to me like you're the only two that found the little family skeleton. And Ada might be healthy," said the woman, smiling for the first time. "But she's not fireproof."

That was when Jane noticed the boxes in the dining room. Their captor had left the door open and Rita's leash kept it open as the dog had put herself as far from the woman holding the gun as possible. Rita kept Nellie and Jane in her sight and Jane wondered what command Miles had taught the dog that would signal her ... enable her ... to break the leather braided leash and go for the gun-woman's throat. Jane feared that command might not exist.

Jane could see from across the room that the boxes were filled with the Halloween decorations taken down from the dining room. Ada would not have taken them down herself—Halloween was still a week away. She would certainly keep the house decorated for the trick-or-treaters.

"Why did you box up the . . . ?"

"The stuff's worth a lot of money. It would be a shame if it all burned. My brother's been taking out the books one by one . . . the ones that are worth the real money. He's such an idiot, he doesn't even know why I want them. He thinks I read them, then return them. What a sap . . ."

"You shot him for being a sap?" said Nellie. "Man, if I killed everybody I thought was an idiot, it'd be a lonely damn world."

"What do you mean, shot him? Joe's out at Swanette's snooping around for the sale. You're a tricky old woman, cousin, but I'm not my brother Joe. I don't fall for that stuff."

"Joe got shot tonight," said Jane. "If you didn't do it, then someone else—"

"Shut the hell up. How am I supposed to hear the signal?"

Nellie had picked up one of Ada's homemade taffy apples, studded with chopped walnuts, and raised it to her mouth. Jane knew that there was no way Nellie was going to bite into a sticky caramel apple. It wasn't that she didn't like them . . . caramel, along with chocolate and potato chips, was one of her main food groups. She just never ate messy, sticky things in public. As she told Jane many times, there was nothing like a set of dentures to make one into a sneaky private eater. At home, Nellie might cut that caramel apple into a dozen tiny pieces and enjoy it alone at the kitchen table, but here? There was only one reason to pick up something fairly heavy attached to a stick.

Just as Nellie flung the apple directly at the woman's head, Jane grabbed her mother and pulled her down, out of the line of fire. As much as Jane wanted to admire her mother's perfect form—Nellie looked like she had been flinging knives at a target every day of her life—Jane feared the gunwoman might have the time and presence of mind to fire off a shot. No need to worry. The sticky apple caught her in the eye, and Jane heard the gun clatter to the floor. Jane dashed around the wooden kitchen island, grabbing a cutting board. When she got to the woman, who had rubbed walnut pieces into both eyes and was screaming and swearing in pain, Jane hesitated for only a second before hitting her over the head with the heavy slab of maple.

As many times as Jane had seen someone knock another person out by hitting them over the head with a heavy object—in movies or on television—no one had ever mentioned how hard you were supposed to hit them. Jane didn't want to kill anyone . . . she just wanted to get her mother and her out of the kitchen, out of this house, as fast as possible. Jane picked up the gun and put it in the pocket of her sweater. That was another thing—no one told you how hard to hit someone and no one told you how heavy a gun actually was. Her cardigan pocket sagged down, opening slightly.

"You're going to stretch the hell out of that sweater and drop the gun to boot," said Nellie. "Give it here."

Nellie took the gun out of Jane's pocket and put it into her own jacket's flapped patch pocket. "Now that's a pocket that can hold a gun," said Nellie, patting it and smiling. She ran over and unhooked Rita, letting the leash dangle from the door frame.

"Do you want to take these boxes?" Nellie asked.

"Yes, but there's no time. I don't know if this house is going to blow or what the signal is supposed to be, but it's clear they want to burn the place down with Ada in it. It must be insured for—"

"A million," said Nellie. "James insured the place and all the antiques and stuff and had a policy on Ada's life, too. When he got sick, he took it out. I know, because when Dad and I took over some of the paperwork and stuff here, we were going to drop it, but James had paid it up for a few years in advance. Named his heirs as the beneficiaries, but of course, Dad and I didn't know his heirs and figured we'd just let the policy lapse when it lapsed. Never heard anything about where Martha went or whether she ever had the baby or not."

Jane looked down at the unconscious woman. "She had a baby all right. Two apparently. Her brother, Joe, and her. Now we've got to get Ada and get out of here. This one is obviously working with others, maybe somebody from the diner—someone was giving her a signal about the fire or—"

"Holy smoke," said Nellie.

Out the window, Jane saw what her mother had just reacted to and they both ran outside. Ada had been handed a lit torch, and she had touched it to the bottom of the pile of wood at the edge of the property. If the teenagers had actually thought the pumpkin lighting "too corny" as one of the townspeople had told Jane, they apparently thought bonfires were plenty cool. A large group of high schoolers were grabbing the jack-o'-lanterns and throwing them onto the fire, the candles inside the pumpkins adding flame, if not fuel, to the already enormous conflagration.

"Ada's cloak," Jane shouted to her mother. "She's too close. It's going to catch fire."

Nellie nodded and they both fought their way through the crowd, which had grown into something other than it was when Jane arrived. It was younger, tougher, uglier, more caught up in the pyrotechnics and a more menacing spirit of Scary Night. Jane saw two boys pulling down a hay-filled scarecrow, preparing to haul it down from the tree and throw it onto the fire.

Jane reached up and tugged on the arm of one of the boys.

"Don't do it. The fire's too hot and high now. That hay is going to burn like—"

"Wasn't our idea . . . she told us to," said the other boy, continuing to pull at the rope.

"Well, I'm telling you not to," said Nellie. "Don't make me take out my little friend," she added, patting her pocket.

"Mom!" shouted Jane. "Help me get Ada."

Jane had never been part of an angry mob, but she supposed that moving through one must be very similar to working through this crowd to get to the bonfire. What had seemed like a manageable group of neighbors oohing and aahing over the lighting of row upon row of carved pumpkins had morphed into a much larger crowd. Jane felt certain that if a Frankenstein monster were hiding on the outskirts of town, this was the very posse that would pick up lit torches and go chase it down.

"Dave!" Jane shouted. "How did you get here?"

The lighting technician was holding a bottle of beer in one hand and waving the other in the air, like he was at some rock concert. Jane half expected him to be holding a lit Bic and calling for an encore.

"I was drinking with a bunch of locals at that biker bar and somebody came in and said there was a bitching bonfire at Ada's, so I just followed the crowd. I just wish I had some cameramen here. This is like being in one of those B-movie fright-night sets. I would hardly add lights here, just film it in the available—wouldn't it be cool?"

Somebody had passed the word to a bunch of bored locals drinking away their Sunday night after the football games had ended for the day . . . that explained the sea change in the crowd. Ada didn't know that her friendly neighborhood haunted house had taken on a new dimension. Jane could see Cousin Ada, now Aunt Ada, standing much too near the fire and waving her arms, those billowing sleeves and the edge of her cape coming closer and closer to the flames.

"Dave? Remember my friends—Tim and Oh? Seen them?"

Dave shook his head.

"Look for them, okay? Tell them to call the fire department and the police if they haven't already. There's someone in the kitchen who needs to be arrested."

Dave was asking her something, but she had moved on. She could barely see Nellie to her left, also fighting her way through the crowd. Jane had to get to Ada and pull her away before Nellie got antsy and began firing shots in the air. Who knew how many others might have guns here? This could turn even uglier.

Jane elbowed a teenage boy hard in the side to get him out of his front-row spot. He pulled back an arm to strike, but then saw Jane with her best innocent I-could-be-your-own-mom face pasted on and his girlfriend pulled him back. Jane wasted no time grabbing Ada and shouting into her good ear.

"The fire's getting out of control. Come with me, Ada."

"Nellie's girl?"

"Yes, it's Jane. Nellie's here, too. We want you to come with us."

"I always tend the fire. James told me it would be the biggest ever this year."

"That wasn't James, Ada. Come with us."

"Where's Nellie?" asked Ada, looking around. Even though it was nearing midnight, the moon behind clouds and the sky completely starless, Ada still wore her dark-tinted glasses.

Jane could feel her lungs burning with every breath and the ash stinging her eyes.

"Come on," said Nellie, grabbing her from the other side. "We got to get you out of here."

Ada became more cooperative as soon as she felt Nellie tugging at her from the other side. Jane looked behind her and saw Tim struggling with a garden hose that lay tangled next to the house. Oh stood under the kitchen window and Jane could see that he was talking into his cell phone. She realized that her entire body had been a clenched fist the whole night, and when she saw her two partners in action, albeit too far away to actually communicate with, she felt herself relax.

"Do you need some help here?"

Jane turned at the sound of a friendly and competent voice. Linda, the nurse whom she had met earlier when she dropped by to perform her surreptitious health check on Ada, was at her side.

"We're trying to get Ada out of here," said Jane. "Can you help us?"

"Sure. Let's get her back by the garage. My car's parked around here somewhere and I've got some bottled water and some tissues. This ash is starting to spread—it's killing my eyes. If the wind picks up any more, that fire's going to spread to that shed."

Ada was quiet, almost docile, once they got out of the crowd and away from the smoke and ash.

"I feel like I've got splinters behind my contact lenses," Linda said, a tear streaming from her left eye.

"I have to pass out the food now," said Ada.

Jane wanted to get Ada safely away from the house. She had successfully completed her first knockout, but she had no idea how long the woman in the kitchen would remain unconscious. Jane had thought she heard her moaning slightly when they were running out of the kitchen door. That could have been wishful thinking. Jane was still afraid of how hard she had swung that breadboard. She decided allowing Oh and the police to deal with her would be a fine idea while she got Ada out of harm's way. She could ask Linda to take them back to Swanette's. There were enough police there to keep Ada under guard until everyone was rounded up.

"I need my handbag," said Ada. "It's got my important papers."

"You don't need anything," said Nellie. "We'll get it later."

Ada insisted that she never left her property without her handbag. It was a rule she lived by and she dug her heels in hard. "It's on the kitchen counter," said Ada. "Right by the flour canister."

"I'll get it," said Jane. It would be easier to get Ada into the car if they just went along with her, and Jane wanted her off the property. "You guys get in and I'll be right back."

Jane helped Ada into the passenger seat while Linda climbed in behind the wheel and Nellie got into the back. So many cars were parked on the grass that at first Jane wasn't sure Linda would be able to get out of the impromptu parking lot, but there was a narrow path straight ahead. Jane had to move sideways between Linda's car and the one snugged up next to it. As she held her breath and crab-walked, she looked down, into the backseat where her mother had picked up a raincoat off the floor and was feeling it as if to test the fabric.

Jane looked down at the car. She sucked in her breath as hard as she could so she could see the body of the vehicle, and in the light shining down from the corner of the garage, she saw the deep fresh scratch that could only have been made deliberately by someone holding a key and determinedly running it the length of the car from back door to taillight.

As soon as Jane realized this was the car belonging to the person who shot Joe, she knew something even scarier. Nellie would know she was in the same backseat and Nellie had a gun in her jacket pocket.

Jane danced around the car and yanked open the back door where Nellie was holding the coat she had used earlier to cover herself up on the floor of the backseat.

"Get out, Mom, you go get the purse," Jane said, yanking Nellie's arm to get her out of the car. "You know the house better than I do. You go."

Jane didn't take the time to sort out her motivations. She knew that if Linda had shot Joe, she had a gun. And she knew by the bulge in Nellie's front pocket that she hadn't gotten rid of hers. She didn't want Nellie to pull an Annie Oakley in the car as soon as she put two and two together.

Too late, of course. Nellie was good at math and holding on to the coat for dear life. Jane pulled her mother up by her elbow and literally lifted her out of the backseat and out of the car. If Nellie hadn't been so light on her feet, she would have lost her balance, but she danced a few steps backward like a punchy bantamweight, and righted herself as Jane climbed in, taking her mother's place.

"Go get the purse," said Jane, slamming the door shut and locking it.

Luckily Linda was busy fastening Ada's seat belt and having difficulty cinching the belt around the voluminous folds of her cape. Fussing with the belt, she hadn't seen Jane manhandle her mother or Nellie run off toward the house clutching the coat from the backseat.

"I can't stand this burning in my eyes," said Linda.

"Do you want me to drive?" asked Jane, not sure that she really wanted to be behind the wheel with someone who had already shot someone tonight sitting behind her.

"I've just got to get these contacts out," said Linda. She reached across Ada who had grown very quiet and opened the glove compartment to get her case and tissues. She turned on the interior lights and pulled down the visor. Staring into the mirror, she stretched her eyelid until she could pop out first one lens, then she did the same with her other eye. She used the tissue to wipe her eyes, then looked in the mirror at Jane in the backseat.

"Much better now," she said. Her bright green eyes had stopped tearing almost immediately. It wasn't the only change. One of those bright green eyes had ceased being bright green. Jane could see it was now brown. Heterochromia. Just like her brother Joe. It had skipped her sister who was unconscious—Jane hoped—in the kitchen, but Brother James had passed his eye abnormality on to two of his three children. Three. Jane hoped the number of offspring stopped at three.

Jane was successful at not allowing any recognition to register on her face. Linda turned her attention to Ada and asked if she was feeling comfortable.

"Seat belt's not too tight, is it?" she asked.

"My eyes," said Ada.

"It's the ash," said Linda, "from the fire. Don't rub them. Let them tear and you'll be fine."

"Our eyes," said Ada, taking off her dark glasses.

Linda handed her a tissue. She showed absolutely no reaction to Ada's face with her glasses removed, but Jane knew Linda was busy figuring something out.

"Ada, was your purse on this side of the sink or that side?"

asked Jane, hoping that her poorly formed question would make Ada turn around in her seat. Although the seat belt and her enormous cape held her mostly in place, she turned her head enough for Jane to look directly into her aunt Ada's eyes.

Two big brown eyes, identical to Jane's own, stared back at her.

"Our family eyes," said Ada. "Two different colors."

Jane saw in the way that Linda straightened her shoulders and took in a sharp breath that she knew she had been discovered. Always careful to wear her contacts, she had hidden the family resemblance that might make her known to Ada as someone other than the itinerant health professional she pretended to be.

Jane thought it might help if she played dumb and directed Ada away from the heterochromia. "Ada, you have beautiful brown eyes, perfectly matched!"

"But I'm supposed to have two colors. The family eyes. Mother said that even though I couldn't see well, I should wear the dark glasses so I could be like Brother James. So people would think we were the same. I could see Brother James's eyes. He was my twin. My mirror."

Linda started the car and slowly began to creep forward, threading her way between the rows of parked cars.

"Let's wait for my mother, okay? She went to get Ada's purse. Remember?" said Jane.

Linda looked straight ahead. The visor was replaced, the mirror folded, and Jane couldn't see the look on Linda's face. She wasn't sure she wanted to.

"How did you get my brother's eyes?" asked Ada.

Linda pulled out of the field, drove exactly four car lengths down the street, then turned into the parking lot next to Edna's Diner.

"I got them the usual way," said Linda, so softly that Jane leaned forward to hear her. "I got them the usual way, Aunt Ada."

Ada shook her head, confused.

"She's not your aunt, actually," said Jane. Linda parked the car.

"Tell me all about it inside, Jane," said Linda. "And let's not do anything that would startle Aunt Ada, okay?" Linda patted her pocket, and Jane noted that she was much more subtle about it than Nellie was when she wanted to demonstrate that she was packing heat.

Jane nodded while Linda leaned over to unfasten the seat belt. Jane was pleased to note that the car was parked under the light in Edna's parking lot, passenger side facing the street. Jane felt in her pocket for her car key, and when she let herself out of the car, she firmly drew two diagonals at about forty-five degrees from the end point of Nellie's original mark. Linda, luckily, was struggling with the seat belt and muttering about the fastener so did not notice any scratching sound. So far so good. Jane stood blocking her crude sign while Linda helped Ada out of the car. She gestured that Jane was supposed to precede them into the back door of Edna's which led to the upstairs apartments.

Jane led the way, making as much noise on the steps as possible, hoping that the old lady, Em, whom MJ had said lived in the other apartment over the diner was a light enough sleeper to wonder about all the noise. Maybe she was one of those nervous old ladies who would call the police when she heard people clomping up the stairs.

In contrast, Ada stepped lightly, not struggling at all while going up the steep flight. She hadn't said anything since Linda had parked the car. If Ada was confused, she saw no need to complain. Jane knew she didn't see that well, but instead of being agitated by being out of the comfort zone of her own home, she seemed only mildly curious about where she was and what might happen next.

Jane stopped at the top of the steps where there were two doors facing each other. Linda nodded at one and Jane turned the doorknob, letting them into the unlocked apartment.

The apartment was simple. There was no entry or foyer. Once in the door, you stood in the living room, and from that room, you could see a galley kitchen, a bathroom, and a short hall opposite which, Jane surmised, led to a bedroom. The floors were hardwood, but there were no rugs and the windows had blinds, but no curtains. It was not a well-lived-in home. A sofa bed was pulled out with a tangle of sheets and a thin wool blanket on top of it. Under the living room window, which faced the main street, meaning it had a direct view of Ada's house and yard, was a scuffed card table which held dirty coffee cups and a few priority mail cartons from the post office.

If Jane had wandered in alone, she would have said that it was an uninhabited apartment, abandoned by deadbeat tenants who shouldn't be holding their breath waiting for their cleaning deposit to be returned.

Linda quickly folded the bed up, dingy linens inside. She told Ada and Jane to sit, then took out her own cell phone.

Whoever she called did not answer. Linda crossed to the window and shook her head as if to clear it. When she turned back to Jane and Ada, she had made a decision.

"I have your family eyes because your brother James is my father," said Linda.

"No," said Ada.

"Yes. He married my mother and never told you. Then he threw her out when she got pregnant," said Linda.

So far, this was the same story Jane had heard from Don and Nellie.

Ada shook her head.

"Yes, your brother James, my father, wasn't such a nice man, Ada," said Linda. "He mellowed after a few years. Mother kept coming back to him, asking him to take her back, hoping for a handout, and every time she came crawling back, he got a little softer hearted. Finally, he told her she could stay around and he'd take care of her. Us. Because now there were two more kids."

"This is not my brother," said Ada, putting her own dark glasses back on.

"I think you better look at me when I'm talking to you, Ada," said Linda.

Jane stood up. She recognized the tremor in Linda's voice as someone who was coming unglued fast. Even a desperate woman like Linda wouldn't harm an old-timer like Ada, would she? Then again, Jane reminded herself, Linda had shot her own brother a few hours earlier.

"Linda, she's too old to harm you. Can't you leave it—" began Jane.

"You're a tough old bird, Ada, and you're not senile or crazy, either. I've been watching you for years. I think you knew all along that your brother had a family. You just kept him on a short leash with your crazy-and-blind-as-a-bat routine," said Linda, shoving Jane hard back down on the couch.

"You know, Jane, I'm a desperate woman, so don't test me right now. I've got some logistics to figure out."

Linda casually took out the gun from her jacket pocket and waved it at Jane. Jane took her aunt Ada's hand.

"Now, Ada, my father told my mother that there was money

in the house. Hidden away in books and secret compartments in the furniture your father built. Know anything about that?"

Ada sat still as a stone.

"I think he was lying, though. I think the money was safe in the bank and invested in the farmland, that's what I think. Joe and Cindy like playing treasure hunt, but I think Pops was just playing games. But Daddy took out an insurance policy on you and left papers filed with an attorney in Kankakee claiming me and Joe and Cindy as the heirs to the family estate. He got you to sign a lot of papers before he died, remember?

"I've been a patient woman. I worked my way through nursing school, I've taken care of my silly sister and half-wit brother. I've taken care of my mother even though she never could get out of her own way to take care of us. I figured I could be patient and wait for you to die. I keep an eye on you, Ada. And you," Linda said, pointing a finger at the woman, "you pay me back by staying healthy as a horse."

"It's not going to do you any good to harm her," said Jane. "She's not your aunt . . . she's—"

"I know," Linda screamed, turning to Jane. "She's *your* aunt. And I knew when you started snooping all around the old photo albums and papers that my stupid brother and sister had been stealing to sell on e-frigging-Bay or some other Internet auction that all of this was going to come out. Those stupid children. I told them to leave it all alone . . . all the stuff . . . so I could get rid of the . . . I told them we'd own everything if they'd just stop risking it all. But no, they had to be as stupid as my father—taking stuff from storage lockers and nickel-dime selling it off. Stealing from Swanette's mother-in-law. Lying about antiques and putting fakes up for auction—like nobody would come looking for them! You know what excites them? Selling some worthless thing for a hundred damn dollars on the Internet!

"I was willing to wait until you died, Ada, I really was. I knew Nellie was your sister—I found the papers in the old Bible that told the family story about you being given away to your aunt and uncle to be raised as their own. Boo-hoo. My father knew, too, so he got you to sign stuff over to him and his heirs . . . whenever they presented themselves. Said it couldn't be broken as long as Nellie didn't come snooping around."

"Nellie's girl," said Ada, turning to Jane.

"Nellie's girl," said Linda. "Turns out she's the biggest snoop of all. First out at Swanette's and then at your place, Ada. But if you and poor Nellie's girl both die in the fire, then I'm the only one left who knows the truth. The Bible I rescued from the library will name me and Cindy and Joe as the true heirs. I'll see to that. I can pick up the pieces of my confused family life and start over with the money from your estate, Ada."

"The fire's there," said Ada, looking out the window, where the light from the bonfire could still be seen behind her house.

"Yeah, it's going to turn out just a little differently than planned. Your house was going to burn down tonight, Ada, but as it turns out, I've gotten fond of that old place anyway. People would miss it. It's a landmark."

As Linda talked, she began picking up papers from the kitchen counter and cramming them into an old leather briefcase. An old family Bible was in the kitchen and Linda stuffed that into the case, too.

"Nobody'll really miss Edna's Diner, though. They'll love the new place she'll put up with the insurance money."

Jane knew that Nellie would have located Oh and Tim by

now—that they would find them any minute. Then again, what if Cindy, the little sister, woke up and stopped Nellie . . . if she really did run into the kitchen for the handbag? What could Jane do to stall so that Nellie could spot the car?

"You don't have to kill us, Linda. You're not desperate . . . you haven't done anything wrong, have you? Not yet. You weren't in on all that Internet scam stuff, were you? That was Cindy and Joe. Ada could still leave you everything . . . she could sign over property to you now while she's alive. . . ."

"Have you forgotten all about your little buddy, Swanette? I barely tapped her in that shed. I needed to get the Bible and the photos out of there. So stupid of Cindy to store so much out there. I didn't mean to kill Swanette . . . she turned and I—"

Jane realized she still held one ace.

"You didn't kill her."

Jane saw that Linda thought she was being played and stood up to head off another tirade.

"Swanette's fine. She's recovering. It was a bump on the head and I can get her not to press charges. She's still groggy, hasn't made a statement. She won't identify you. I can get her to say she tripped. We made up the rumor that she died. Oh and Tim and me . . . we spread it around town to draw out whoever would want to get their stuff off the property before we sold everything. We knew if whoever had hit her thought she was dead, thought it was murder, they'd have to come back there. We were there waiting. It was all about the Internet scam—Joe and Cindy. Not you—you're not even involved in that, right? The police knew we were going to do it . . . that's why they were there when we found Joe in the shed," said Jane.

"Swanette's dead?" asked Ada.

"No," said Jane. "Not dead." It had been a crazy idea, but Jane was so sure that someone would show up to get rid of that piece of two-by-four—but only if whoever had hit Swanette thought they had killed her. There were no official announcements yet, just Jane and Tim and Michael spreading the rumors all over town. The police wouldn't have gone for it at all except that Oh was able to persuade them that the plan couldn't harm anyone. Tell that promise to poor old Joe . . .

Linda began to smile, staring right at Jane with those disconcertingly different-colored eyes.

"Swanette's not dead?" she repeated. "You swear?"

"I swear."

"You stupid cow," said Linda, letting fly with the back of her hand and the grip of the gun. "You made me shoot my own brother? I thought I had to cover up a murder so I had to keep him quiet and you made me shoot my own stupid brother?"

Jane fell to the floor, her face stinging and her ear numb. Damn family loyalty. Apparently Linda could call her brother and sister idiots, but just let someone else set them up as targets and she went all "sisterly" ballistic. Jane decided not to mention that she had hit Cindy over the head with a maple cutting board.

"Family," said Ada. "Blood's thicker than water."

Linda was right about one thing. Ada wasn't as wacky as she appeared to be. She had followed this crazy scenario down to the letter. Jane hoped they got out of this mess—she'd like the opportunity to get to know her aunt Ada.

"Downstairs," said Linda.

She marched them out of the apartment. Jane realized they had only gone up there to get the papers she needed and the family Bible.

"Mother!" Linda pounded on the other apartment door.

Em! The waitress, MJ, had told Jane that Em's apartment would soon be vacant. Em wasn't short for Emma, it was M. Martha Speller.

A small old woman answered the door. She was dressed in a light blue knit traveling suit, vintage 1970s, and she carried a small suitcase. It wouldn't have been such an odd sight except for the fact that it was well after midnight.

"I'm ready to go to my new place, just like you told me to be," said Martha.

"We're all going downstairs together. Mother, you remember your sister-in-law, Ada?"

Martha Speller's face contorted with fear. Brother James must have told some wild tales. Martha turned away, fearing she was about to be cursed by a Gypsy or thrown down the stairs. Instead, Ada put out her hand.

"How do you do? I'm sorry James never introduced us."

The diner was dark although some light spilled in from the street and there was still a glow from Ada's backyard. Linda told her mother to go out and sit in the car.

She swore under her breath when she saw the broken hasp on the storage room door. Out of one small kitchen window, Jane could see a car exiting the field behind Ada's house. The bonfire must be finally dying down . . . or had been put out by Tim if he'd ever gotten the hose untangled. Jane thought about how much business Edna's could do if she was still open all night. All of those bikers from the bar and townspeople and teenagers, crazed from the bonfire and too much alcohol—wouldn't they be starving? Wouldn't they love breakfast at Edna's?

"It won't make sense, us in Edna's when it burns . . ." said Jane.

"Edna keeps the gas cans in back and the fire's going to start there," said Linda. "I guess if you two are locked in the kitchen, that's as good as the storeroom."

"The police will figure it out. Detective Oh, Tim, Nellie, they all know. . . ."

"They know that Joe and Cindy ran a scam. I'll get to Joe and he'll stay quiet. Cindy doesn't talk. . . ."

"But—"

"But Ada's crazy. She's wandered into Edna's before in the night. She pretends not to leave the house but she walks all over town, don't you, Ada?"

Ada shrugged. "I don't sleep much. I walk."

"And you, brave and helpful Jane, would follow your cousin and even try to save her if you saw a fire start—"

"Linda!" Martha's voice was thin and reedy, but loud and clearly frightened.

"Mother, I told you to go wait in the car."

"I'm afraid of dogs, you know that."

Linda moved to the doorway of the kitchen to see what her mother was talking about. Jane pushed Ada away in case Linda turned back and fired at them.

"Open for breakfast!" Jane said aloud, fingers crossed.

Jane used both hands to push every switch on the wall into the on position. Each fixture, sign, novelty light, and overhead bulb in the diner flashed on, including the window neon that announced that Edna's Diner was open for business. The cars exiting Ada's Scary Night bonfire all began turning into the parking lot, horns honking, people shouting out of their windows.

"Edna used to be open all night on Scary Night," said Jane to Ada. "Did a great business, I heard."

"That's why she always said I could come into the kitchen at night for food. Gave me my own key. She said having a scary lady in a haunted house was good for business," said Ada. "I'm a tourist attraction."

When Linda blinked in the sudden brightness, the first person she saw come through the door was not Martha Speller. Instead, Officer Cord, his gun drawn, had insisted that he precede Bruce Oh.

Jane met Oh, second through the door, who pointed out to the parking lot. Rita sat in front of Linda's car, her doggy head bobbing directly under the keyed-in arrow that Nellie had begun with her line and Jane had finished with the two diagonals. If there had been a spotlight trained on the tableau it would have, in effect, said, "THIS WAY," pointing into the diner.

As it was, people were swarming the parking lot and trying to jam their way into Edna's. Cord and two police officers took Linda into custody.

"We have her sister," said Oh. "You gave her quite a bump on the head."

"Yes," said Jane. "I have to talk to you about that. I think I need to take some classes or something. I'm not sure how hard I'm supposed to hit people."

"It looks like someone knew how hard to hit you, Mrs. Wheel," said Oh, barely brushing her cheek with his finger. "You will have a black eye, I'm afraid."

Jane nodded. She could feel it now, her cheek warm and throbbing. It seemed like a very small pain compared to the heartbreak she saw unfolding in front of her. Nellie approached Ada, who held out both hands to her. All those years they had missed being sisters. And Martha, dazed, watching her daughter being led out of the diner by the police. Family messes, lies, secrets. Skeletons in the closet. Scary stuff. Jane went over to Ada and Nellie and pointed to Martha, who stood paralyzed. Someone was going to have to take care of her. After a quick headshake at Jane's bruised eye, Nellie nodded and went over to Martha, leading her to a table and placing her sad little suitcase at her feet.

"I'm going to put on coffee," said Nellie. "Hell, Edna won't care. I'll ring it up for her."

"Just coffee?" asked Tim. "C'mon, Nellie, let's serve breakfast. Tell me what to do and I'll be your sous-chef."

"I don't know what a damn sous-chef is. You just come with me and do everything I tell you to do."

"Exactly," said Tim, giving Jane a squeeze as he followed Nellie behind the counter and into the kitchen.

Ada asked a few of the neighbors to go over to her kitchen and bring over the pies and homemade treats she hadn't gotten a chance to serve.

Jane grabbed a plain doughnut from under the glass dome on the counter and slipped out into the parking lot. Rita still sat at attention under the arrow.

"Here you go, pal," said Jane. "Thanks."

Rita looked at the pastry with a certain amount of canine skepticism. Jane didn't usually offer such bad-for-you human treats, unless of course she had forgotten to buy dog food.

"It's okay, girl. Nellie told me to give it to you," said Jane.

Jane sat next to Rita reviewing the evening, the day, the weekend, and thinking about how tired she should be and how awake she was. The crash would come soon enough, but now, the cool dark morning felt like a good time to be awake.

Detective Oh brought Jane a cup of Nellie's thick black coffee and sat down next to her on the pavement, their backs braced against Linda's vandalized station wagon. From inside the diner or Ada's house or someone's car, Oh had grabbed a wool stadium blanket and now placed it over Jane's knees.

"A full night," said Oh.

"What I don't understand," said Jane, "is how—" But she stopped herself. She had been going to say that she didn't understand how her grandmother could have given up her firstborn daughter and then lived her whole life with the secret . . . just down the road.

But it was too big to put it into words.

"Mrs. Wheel," said Oh, "I think when you have rested and we are back in Evanston, we need to have a little talk."

A little talk. That was never good. A little talk was what you had when your boss thought you were slacking or when your parents thought you were lying or when your teachers thought you were cheating. Or when your husband was leaving you.

"Oh?" said Jane.

"Yes," said Oh, with a rare smile.

"No, I mean, what do we have to talk about? Are you firing me?"

"I invited you to be my partner, so I hardly think I could fire you just like that. No, I want to talk to you about self-defense. I want to talk to you about some techniques for communicating with me. I want to talk to you about not getting into the car with someone who has a gun . . ." said Oh.

"Oh," said Jane.

"Yes," said Oh. "Your mother told me you threw her out of the car, then got in yourself. She came to find me, and we ran back to the car, but you were already gone."

"Linda already had Ada in the front seat. And she didn't know that I knew that she ... oh, you know."

"Yes, I do," said Oh. "But I never again want to find you with this. . . ." And for the second time in their relationship, friendship, partnership ... whatever it was between them ... Detective Oh touched Jane. He laid one finger on her cheek and outlined the bruise that was continuing to spread from cheekbone to eye. "This," he said, "has taken me aback."

"Janie!"

Jane was so taken aback herself, she hadn't noticed that the car that had just pulled into the diner was her father's Chrysler. Don and Michael got out of the front seat. Don opened the back door for Claire Oh, and the three of them walked over to Jane and Oh, still sitting on the ground. Jane still had one arm draped around Rita but she reached her other hand out to her brother who pulled her up into a standing position. Jane kept her head slightly turned away, wrapping the blanket capelike over her shoulders. It was dark enough for the three of them not to notice her black eye or the blush that had spread over both cheeks.

"Your mother called and said you saved the day," said Don.

Jane started to protest that she had fallen into saving a small part of the day, but Michael shushed her.

"Don't worry, she said she helped you and you couldn't have done it without her."

Tim opened the door and yelled for them all to come and eat breakfast.

Jane let everyone walk in ahead of her ... her dad and brother, Bruce Oh and his wife, Claire ... then Jane hung back, she told herself, for just a minute more with Rita. There was something about this air, this time of day, just before sunrise, that made her not want to miss anything. If she went inside now, if she turned her back for a minute, the sun would pop up, it would be Monday morning, and this magic hour would disappear.

"I could bring you some bacon and eggs, Rita," said Jane.

"Like hell you will," said Nellie, who had, as usual, sneaked up on Jane. "You don't feed a dog table food."

"Unless it's your pancakes, right?"

"I got an ice bag to put on your eye. Your dad didn't see you yet, did he? He's going to have a fit," said Nellie.

"I talked to Charley tonight, I mean last night . . . in the middle of all this," said Jane.

Nellie took the plastic bag full of ice and wrapped it in a small clean dishtowel and touched it gently to Jane's cheek.

"He's not coming home from South America. Nick's coming back next week, but Charley's going to take a job down there. That's what he said."

Jane wasn't sure why she wanted to tell her mother all of this right at this moment. Maybe it was because Charley's news was a part of this whole topsy-turvy weekend, so she was determined to get it out now, before the sun came up and it was just another Monday morning.

"And that's okay with you, huh?"

"Of course not," said Jane, "but he's entitled to make up his own mind, isn't he, I mean . . . what can I do if he—"

"Yeah, well, whatever. Tonight I found out I got a big sister. Crazy as a loon and blind as a bat, but she's my sister and I'm glad to finally have her. Better late than never. I suppose my ma had a good reason for letting her go like that, but I expect I'll never know exactly what it was. Or how she could live with it all her life. And I suppose I won't know why you're letting your husband go like that, without a fight, but if that's what you want to do, I'll go along with it. You're my daughter. I'll be on your side. I just don't want you to screw up that son of yours . . . he's a good boy."

Jane was confused. Nellie blamed her for everything . . . always. She pried and poked and judged and juried. And now . . . was she using reverse psychology? What was this new technique?

"Janie, you listen to me. You like this life, this solving problems and finding the bad guys. I can see why. It's exciting. It's satisfying. And if it's the life you choose, that's fine with me. Charley wants to have a satisfying life, too. And if you can't do it together, you'll do it apart. Just don't lie to your boy. He'll be all right. Just love him and put him first. Everything else will follow along."

Jane never wanted the sun to come up. Listening to Nellie in the dark like this, she felt as if she were in the magical childhood she imagined, but wasn't sure she ever experienced. Where did all this wisdom come from?

"That's what your dad and I did and look how good you and Michael turned out."

Jane took a deep breath. Okay, so today, at this moment, she wasn't doing so well as "wife," but her stock as a daughter had just risen. Nellie thought she'd turned out okay. And Nick came home next week, so she would have plenty of chances to be a good mother and she would do her best. Bruce Oh thought she was a worthy partner . . . he was actually taken aback by her, whatever that meant. And coming out the door of Edna's Diner was her best friend, Tim Lowry, with a plate of scrambled eggs and dark brown toast, almost burned, the way he knew she liked it.

Scary Night had been a scary night. Now, just a silver thread in the east, day was breaking. Jane looked at Nellie, who was whispering some secret of life in Rita's ear, then she turned back to the spreading light.

The sun was coming up. There was nothing she could do to stop it. So Jane Wheel ran her hands through her hair, straightened her shoulders, and decided to meet Monday morning...maybe even the rest of her life...head-on.